INFERENCE

INFERENCE

Joel Tagert

JJ Hall
Denver, CO

For Meg

INFERENCE

THE KID'S BODY was found stuffed into a plastic garbage bin in an alley in lower Queen Anne. The bin belonged to the pizzeria next door, but the corpse was discovered by a homeless man named Geoffrey McCulley around 8:30 a.m., which is when he usually went through the bins in the alley, looking for uneaten pizza or anything else that might be useful or enjoyable. The corpse was neither.

The 911 call, however, was made by the pizzeria manager, whom McCulley informed about his grisly discovery a few minutes later. The manager, not quite believing or understanding what McCulley was saying, came out to see for herself. It didn't take her a few minutes to react. She got on her phone in seconds, and placed the call at 8:41. She was relatively calm, all things considered, and proud that she had responded so quickly and appropriately to what was some seriously fucked up shit.

By 8:45 that call had been routed to Detective Tom Mueller. "Jackie, you hearing this?" he said.

She was already standing up from her desk, putting on her coat. "I got it. Looks like fun."

"Are you excited?"

"Thrilled."

"Bundle up. I have a feeling we may be spending some time outside." After a moment's thought he also grabbed a tie from his desk drawer and put in on. It was likely the morning would require a degree of solemnity.

A police auto was waiting at the door when they stepped out. "Hello, Detective Mueller," the auto said as they got in. "Hello, Detective Khleang."

"Hello yourself," Mueller said. The address was already cued onscreen and he tapped it forthwith. "Priority ride. Sirens on. Get us there fast, please."

"Yes, Detective."

The rush-hour traffic split before them like the Red Sea before the hand of God, the automated driving systems diverting cars smoothly into the right-hand lanes and returning just as smoothly when the police vehicle had passed, an ongoing wave. They averaged seventy-five kilometers an hour for the short ride from Capitol Hill and pulled up at their destination on Mercer in two minutes thirteen seconds. Two patrol cars were already there, the officers pulling tape across the alleyway's mouth like kidnappers silencing a scream. A few bystanders stood on the other side of the street gaping and holding up their handsets to record this possibly valuable view.

They got out of the auto. It was drizzling and cold, but that was to be expected in December. Mueller recognized the officer with the tape and nodded at him. "Chuck! What's happening?"

"You the happy couple taking over this shitshow?"

"I think so. Did you take a look?"

"No. Carter did, though." He nodded at an officer Mueller didn't know. "I don't need that kind of stuff haunting me at night. I leave that to you."

"We appreciate it. Forensics here yet?"

"Nah. Those guys, they figure by the time they get here it's all over, so why hurry?"

"You have an ID?"

Carter answered, "Can't get one too easily. You'll have to take a look."

"Okay. Let's do a scan first, though."

Khleang was already pulling the equipment out of the trunk.

"You want the floater?"

He looked over the alley. Mud, trash, boxes. A trio of crows hopping and cawing over an open box, fighting for a sodden remnant of someone's pepperoni slice. There could be tracks in the mud, cigarette butts. Evidence. "Let's start with the tripod outside the alley, then the floater."

She set it up at the mouth of the alley. "Which can is it?"

Carter pointed. "The black one with the writing."

"Got it." She pointed the scanner in its general direction and started it up. A horizontal fan of white light flashed out and ran up and down over the mud, illuminating it in searing detail, creating a three-D recording of the scene at resolutions greater than the human eye could perceive. Themis, the Justice Department AI, would take the data and use it for Inference, extrapolating from the tracks, the brands of cigarettes, fingerprints on the plastic bins. Hopefully the rain wouldn't interfere too much.

The bum who had found the body was being held over by the pizzeria entrance, beneath an awning. Mueller glanced at him and murmured, "Agatha, ID please."

Agatha was quiet compared to some other AI assistants – one of the reasons he liked her – and the data appeared in his reading field sans comment. Geoffrey McCulley, born 2018, parents' names, links to them, blah blah blah, joined the Army, fought in Syria, dishonorably discharged May 2042... expand this... statutory rape. Charges dropped by the parents, but picked up by the military for legal reasons. Some years in the courts, ending in mandatory probation of one year. But then a lot of other problems. Spotty employment, difficulty finding apartments due to his sex offender status, a charge for aggravated assault, social worker reports describing mental health problems, depression, incipient schizophrenia. In other words, all what you'd expect from a beat-up sixty-two-year-old vet sleeping under a theater marquis. Probably he'd had nothing to do with it, but it was more than enough to take him in.

Mueller waved away the mote and came over to the awning. "How's it going over here?"

"You're not gettin' anything out of me," McCulley mumbled. "I served in the Army, I know how shit works. I'm just doing my daily."

The officer raised an eyebrow. "Just having a chat with Mr. McCulley here."

"Yeah, I see. Hi, my name's Tom." He extended his hand.

"You're not getting anything out of me," the man repeated. But he shook Mueller's hand anyway. Big, grimy hand, dirt caked under the nails.

"Pretty nasty thing to find," Mueller said. "Bet you weren't expecting that this morning."

"No, I wasn't expecting it." Okay, so he could respond coherently. "I wasn't expecting anything. Terrible thing." The man's eyes were suddenly full of tears.

"It is. I'm sorry you had to be the one to find it."

McCulley sniffled. "It's okay. I got a kid too, you know. He's a lot older. But last time I saw him he wasn't that old. Just a kid."

Mueller kept him talking for a few minutes, asking about his son, where McCulley was sleeping. The guy seemed to relax a bit. Mueller was good at that. *Patience is bitter, but its fruit is sweet.* Then he wound his way back to the matter at hand.

"You have any idea who it is, over in the alley? You ever see them before?"

McCulley's eyes darkened. "What do you mean? I've never seen him. Never in my life."

"Did you see anyone else in the alley then, this morning? As you were doing your daily, like you said?"

"Nobody there but the girl from the pizza place, when I went and got her. I don't know, maybe a car came through. Cars come through sometimes."

Well, they could check that, and would. Mueller thanked McCulley for his time, nodded to the officer to walk with him a little ways.

"You think he's involved?" the officer said.

Mueller shook his head. "No. Basically no chance. But we're going to have to hold him for a little bit anyway, at least until we get an ID on the victim."

The officer looked McCulley up and down skeptically. "I don't think he's going to want to get into the auto."

"That's fine. Just stand with him here, then. Shouldn't be more than half an hour or so."

Forensics had arrived and Khleang had finished her sweep, the little scanning platform returning to her hand, its tiny rotors humming faintly. She clicked it off and returned it to the trunk. "You ready to take a look?" Mueller asked.

"Ask her." She nodded at the forensics tech, who was standing in place, flicking her field. Probably looking at the holo of the alley they'd just recorded.

Mueller introduced himself pleasantly. It always paid to make a connection, in his opinion. "Deena Harrod," the tech said, thrusting her hand forward, returning his smile. "Nice to meet you." She was in maybe her early thirties, long blond ponytail, tanned skin suggesting time in the sun.

"Is it okay if we take a look?" he asked. "We need to make an ID."

"Sure, of course. Just step as carefully as you can. You need some gloves?"

"We got 'em," he said, breaking out a pair from a plastic package. He stepped forward then, and paused, crossing his hands in front of him.

"You just going to stand there?" Khleang asked.

"Yeah. Just for a minute."

Khleang let him. They both stood there, taking it in. He let go of his thoughts and just stood there, looking at the alley, listening, breathing. In-breath and out-breath, calm, easy, relaxed. Just listen. Just see. Autos passing on the street. McCulley muttering, arguing. Airplane passing far overhead. The mud dark at Mueller's feet, congealed in a low spot in the asphalt. Ripples on a puddle from the drizzling rain. Cinderblock walls a sullied beige, the sky pearlescent gray, the garbage can black, the police tape bright yellow. A crow looked at them and cawed, a dark beautiful sound, flapping its wings. Mueller's face and ears were damp and cold from the rain. He just stood there.

"Okay. Let's take a look."

The body was pale, so pale, and naked. It had been dumped head first into the plastic bin and the limbs were tangled at awkward, uncomfortable angles, the legs folded on top, one hand jutting up like the kid wanted to ask a question. It was a boy, maybe twelve or thirteen, the genitals visible and obscenely shriveled. The face was shadowed, down at the bottom of the can, the back of the head pressed against black bags, a bit of blond hair. A terrible thing, McCulley had said. A terrible thing.

They got the ID from a fingerprint, Khleang pressing one digit of the boy's upraised hand against the glass of her handset. Gabriel Leberer. His birthday was 9/19/67, making him thirteen. He lived in upper Queen Anne with his parents. *Had lived.*

"He didn't get far," Khleang commented.

"No, he didn't." Depressing. "No missing-persons report, though."

"Maybe he hasn't been gone that long."

Mueller nodded at the forensics tech, Deena Harrod. "What do you think? Preliminary time of death? Or cause?"

Harrod looked up from whatever motes she was examining. "Uh, time of death, not long. Maybe six or seven hours ago, put it between three and four a.m., say."

"Got a fresh one," Khleang said.

"Cause of death, not so sure. No wounds visible from this angle, but that's not saying much. Have to get it back to the lab."

Mueller looked in at the body again. "How are you going to do that, anyway?"

She shrugged. "We could take him out here, but I'd rather not. There could be evidence in the garbage can itself. So I'm thinking we'll just wheel the whole thing over to the lab and do it there."

"How long?"

She sighed. "Half an hour? We can do it fast or we can do it right. You decide."

"It's fine." Mueller said. He turned to Khleang. "I'll try for the warrant now."

Khleang shivered. "Sure. Can we get back in the car, though? It's cold out here."

They cranked the heat up. Khleang was always complaining about the cold. Said it was her Cambodian blood, though Mueller knew she was born and raised in Seattle. Funny, because he'd grown up in Hawaii and didn't mind the cool weather at all.

He rang Justice and got the judge on duty online. "Begin recording," he said. "This is Detective Tom Mueller, requesting an Inference search in the death of Gabriel Leberer, case number –" He glanced at it. "– B03-GI2-V98. The time is 9:34 a.m. on December 19, 2080. All crime scene data has been uploaded to Themis."

The judge was gesturing, looking over the crime scene. One muscle in her cheek twitched as she saw something distasteful. The body, certainly. "This is Judge Sylvia Havermeyer. You don't actually have a cause of death yet. You don't even know if it's a homicide."

"With all respect, your honor, I don't think he crawled in there himself."

"You don't know that," she snapped. "And I'm not going to start issuing searches based on presumptions, or because you want to be done by lunchtime."

It was a bad idea to talk back to a judge, he knew, but still: "Search will show the probability of murder. And if it is a homicide, the killer could be on his way out of the country right now."

"Pure speculation," she bit off. "And I'm not in the business of fantasy, I'm in the business of protecting people's rights. Find the cause of death. If it's murder, call me back. If not, don't." She waved her hand and hung up.

"That was maybe dumb," Khleang said.

"Yeah. It's true, though. Whoever did it could be running right now."

"Right, but now it's going to be even harder to get a search."

"You win some, you lose some."

While Mueller had been speaking with the judge, Khleang had started a search on the alley, hands flicking rapidly. "Unfortunately not a very busy neighborhood that late at night," she commented. "Everyone pretty much clears out once the bars close. Thirty-six passes on Mercer between two and three, but it drops to just eight between three and four, and nine the hour after that."

"So was anyone in the alley?"

"Yes, but I haven't actually watched it yet."

"I'll bring the popcorn."

They reviewed the footage. As each auto passed on the street, it swept its surroundings with a array of sensors, much as their crime-scene scanners had. This was necessary for the onboard AI navigation system, but it also created a holographic record of its surroundings as it drove, which was stored for some time – generally seven days – and was searchable by law enforcement. Or the records from the Sound Transit autos were, anyway, but that was by far a majority of the vehicles in the city.

Jackie's AI had no problem identifying individuals in the

alley, but what it revealed didn't look promising. At 2:45 a.m. three people went into the alley, but a follow-up search showed them walking down Queen Anne Avenue two minutes later. "We need a more precise time of death," Jackie commented.

"We'll get it soon," he said absently. "What about this guy?" He tapped the air, highlighting the figure. It was a man in a black jacket, hood up against the rain, walking out of the alley. Medium height, brown skin, clean-shaven. He wore tight-fitting black pants and pointed leather shoes. *A shadowy figure in the night.* The time stamp was 3:48:18.

"I like him," Jackie concluded. "But if he's stuffing a body in a can, how did he get it there?"

"Maybe he didn't need to go far. Maybe he lives nearby."

"'He looks at me and he says maybe, maybe, maybe,'" Jackie sang, from a current song.

Mueller ran the recording backwards and forwards, examining the face from different angles. "He look happy to you?"

She shrugged. "It's an auto scan. At night, in the rain. Maybe he's got a stomach ache."

"No, look. Like he's been crying."

"Could be. The time frame's right, anyway. We'll look at him. No facial lock, though." Meaning their system hadn't returned an ID. Probably due to shadows, poor image quality. "We going to go see the parents now?"

Mueller sighed. "Yeah. All right."

"You want to let them know we're coming?"

"No. We'll just see who's home."

"Okie doke." Khleang tapped the destination onscreen and hit the go button. It was a short ride up the hill. As they climbed Mueller looked back and saw the city falling away behind them, gray and misty, the Space Needle with its green Christmas-tree topper.

The house was on 8th Avenue, a street bounded on its downhill side by a steep concrete retaining wall built by the Works Progress Administration in the previous century, which effectively prevented its impeccable views of the Sound from being obstructed, ever. On sunny days you would see wealthy joggers running along the sidewalk or in the street itself, not infrequently pushing one of those bicycle-wheeled baby carriages in front of them.

"How much you think one of these places goes for?" Mueller asked.

Khleang didn't look up, still flicking data, looking at auto scans from that night. "Hm?"

"How much do you think these houses cost?"

"How much you want to pay?"

"Five million? Ten?"

"I'm going with the higher numbers. I don't think you could buy a tool shed in this neighborhood for a million dollars."

The auto pulled to a stop in front of the address. It was a middling-to-large Arts and Crafts style home with a covered veranda running along its front, bay windows on the second floor, and a small deck above the bay windows, the better to enjoy the view. The lawn was large and professionally tended, the bushes shaped and trimmed, with a small Japanese maple still clinging to its last fiery leaves and what he thought was a tulip tree minus the tulips.

As they got out Mueller saw a small white face watching them from the front window, a young girl with auburn hair. He raised a hand, not quite smiling, mindful how that might seem given the news they brought. The face disappeared. "*Someone's* home."

"Oh, goodie," Jackie said.

"Your favorite part of the job, I'm sure."

She shook her head. "This is why I have you. I'd probably do it in a text."

They stepped onto the veranda, rubber-soled shoes knocking dully on the wood, but before they could ring the doorbell the front door swung open. The girl from the window stood behind it, giving them an impudent look. "What do you want?" she said in an impression of gruffness. Mueller put her age at ten or eleven. Old enough to be smart but not be a teenaged know-it-all.

"Hi!" Mueller said in his bright way, unable this time to stop himself from smiling. "Who are you?"

"I'm Elsie," she said. She didn't return the smile, though. "Are you police?"

Mueller nodded, more solemnly than before. "Yes, we are. I'm Detective Mueller, and this is my partner, Detective Khleang. Are your parents home, Elsie?"

"My mom is." She was a very beautiful child. Her teeth were straight and even, her eyes large and dark, skin unblemished with hints of rose. *Enjoy it while it lasts, kid.* She was wearing a long-sleeved shirt printed in pink and white stripes with a band of yellow undershirt showing beneath it over shapeless tan corduroys. She hung on the door handle, examining them. Then, unexpectedly, "It's about Gabriel, isn't it?"

Mueller restrained himself from glancing at his partner. "What makes you say that?"

The girl looked past him at some indefinable point in the distance, at the leaden waters of the Sound, perhaps. "He didn't come home last night."

Khleang said, "Do you know where he was last night, Elsie? It's important if you do."

Elsie gave her a quick look of assessment, then said, "I'll go get my mom," and turned away into the house, shutting the door on them. Mueller and Khleang exchanged a glance but said nothing. Mueller's mind was fixed on the next ten minutes. Someone's life was about to change. It was hard not to feel yourself, as such a time, as the agent of tragedy rather than its messenger.

The door opened. The woman who stood there was a trim fifty years old or so, an intelligently lined face with intent eyes and aquiline nose, her brown hair cut shoulder-length with subtle red highlights, certainly dyed. She wore a cashmere sweater in sea-foam green with white slacks, both looking more expensive than any clothing item Mueller had ever owned. When she asked if she could help them, Mueller detected only the impersonal readiness one might give a census taker or salesman. He felt the responsibility of it, the inappropriate sense of guilt, settle on him like a iron yoke. He understood why even as he tried to let it go. It was very much as if he were about to wallop her in the face.

It wasn't the first time Mueller had had to do this. It was the worst with parents, though. Maybe it would have been even worse to tell a child their parent had died, but when that happened it got handed off to a counselor.

What about telling a little girl her brother's corpse was found stuffed into a trash can? "It might be better if we talked to you alone," he suggested. "Maybe we could go into the living room?"

"I want to stay," Elsie declared quickly.

Mrs. Leberer glanced at her unsmilingly. "Elsie, they've asked to speak to me. Don't make a scene."

"I want to stay," the girl repeated.

"This really isn't the time –"

"I'm *staying*. Unless you tie me up and carry me out of here, I'm staying."

Her speech patterns were odd, Mueller thought. Maybe it was just that, not having children of his own, he didn't spend much time with them. Were ten-year-olds always this assertive?

Mrs. Leberer sighed and threw her hands up. "Fine."

The living room was tasteful and expensive. Persian rug, designer furniture, what looked like a small Dutch painting in an elaborate frame, a music stand and cello set up in one corner. The windows offered the promised view of the Sound and the lawn, emerald now with the winter rain.

"What can I do for you?" Mrs. Leberer began.

"Your son's name is Gabriel?" he asked.

"Yes. Why, is he in trouble?"

He shook his head and told her what they'd found this morning. She said, "Excuse me?" and he repeated himself, speaking very clearly. She just looked at him, as they often did, looking for some way out. He could almost hear the thoughts running through her head, could feel them like physical things: *It's got to be a mistake. Maybe it's not Gabriel. Could this be a joke?* And one by one each thought hit the brick wall of their presence here and fell away like broken birds.

"Are you sure?" she asked finally.

"We're sure, yes." He looked at Elsie. Her mouth was slightly open and her brow was furrowed as she looked off toward the hallway. The house was absolutely silent. He expected to hear the ticking of a clock, somehow, but there wasn't one.

"Mrs. Leberer," Khleang broke in, almost the first she had spoken. "Can I call you Sarah?" The mother nodded mutely. "Do you know where your son was last night?"

Tremors ran through Sarah's face, all the muscles pulling downward, beginning to shake, and she rubbed her forehead, half-covering her eyes. "He was with Manish." Pronounced *ma-neesh.*

"Who's Manish?"

"How did he die?" Sarah asked.

"We're not sure yet," said Mueller. "He's been taken to a hospital for the autopsy to discover the cause of death."

"Sarah," Khleang continued, "it's very important that we act quickly, right now. Who's Manish?"

Sarah was starting to cry, though she was obviously resisting it for their sake. "He's... Gabriel's mentor, sort of. His friend. They worked together on things. He met him through the Aspire

Project over at Seattle Center."

"What's his full name?"

"Manish Gill. He lives over in Fremont. I could get you the address."

"We can get it," Mueller said. He exchanged a glance with his partner and Khleang whispered the name into her collar. She flicked at the search results and he saw them offered in a mote in his lower left field. He ignored them for now, intent on observing Sarah and her daughter. "How old is Manish?"

"I'm not sure. Twenty-six? Twenty-seven?"

"He's twenty-six," put in Elsie. "His birthday's just one day before Gabriel's. September eighteenth."

Sarah lifted her hand from her teary eyes and looked at her daughter, some silent message or warning passing between them. He waited, but neither one spoke. "Why was Gabriel staying the night with Manish?" he asked.

Sarah shook her head. "He stays over there sometimes. They work on different projects, all programming stuff. That's how they met, the Aspire Project. Sort of a science fair for high achieving students. They would partner with graduate students at UW."

"They weren't just science fair buddies," said Elsie aggressively. Again that oddity in her speech, the rapidity of it, the phrasing out of sync with her age.

And again a warning from her mother, an edge in her voice: "Elsie, I'd like to have your father present –"

"You have to tell them."

"We will, I just think your father –"

"He was his lover," Elsie said. Her face was white.

"Elsie!"

"Manish was Gabe's lover, and his birthday was one day before Gabe's. They're the same age."

Mueller tilted his head curiously. "You mean they had the same birthday."

"No, I mean they're the same age. Gabriel was twenty-six."

Mueller exchanged a startled look with Khleang, then looked back at girl and mother. Khleang's fingers flicked rapidly as she gave up the pretense of being offline and started pulling up data. Mueller asked, "We are talking about the same person, right? Do you have a picture?"

"He looks young," said Elsie. "He looks like he's thirteen."

"I need to talk to my husband," her mother said. "Elsie, we need to talk as a family before we talk to anyone else. We need to *come together.*"

"His ID says he was born in twenty-sixty-seven," Khleang said. "September nineteenth."

"It was *changed,*" Elsie said. "To protect him. Just like me."

This was rapidly entering strange territory. "How old are you?" Mueller asked.

"Elsie, I don't want you–" her mother began.

"I turn twenty-four in March," said Elsie. Khleang stopped gesturing, in astonishment, looking at the child. Because she *was* clearly a child. The skin was the telltale. It couldn't be faked. If she had had some disorder that prevented her from growing, still it would have shown in her skin, but instead she had the close pores, the subtly radiant complexion only seen in children.

"I'm not sure –" he started, but at that point Sarah Leberer abruptly stood up.

"I need to speak with my husband," she said. "And my lawyer, I think."

"Of course," he said after a moment. He measured the situation, considering mother and daughter, and stood up himself.

Khleang, though, was not so easily put off. "Sarah, as I said, time does matter here. If this person, Manish, does have something to do with your son's death –"

"*I know!*" Sarah snapped, beginning to cry again. "*I know!* But right now *I need to call my husband!*"

"Of course," Mueller repeated, and ushered Khleang out of the room.

Outside the rain had started drizzling again, wetting their faces as they stepped to the car. "What the hell is going on?" Khleang said.

"You got me. But I'm sure it'll be easier with their cooperation than without it, so ride easy."

"The girl obviously wants to talk to us."

"Sure, but it's not even clear if she can, legally, without her parents' permission. And given how weird the two of them were, I can't wait until the dad gets involved."

They got back into the patrol car and both of them immediately started flicking motes. "Agatha, call forensics," Mueller said. "I don't remember her name, the tech we were talking to earlier today."

"Is it Deena Harrod?" Agatha asked.

"Yes."

"Calling."

Harrod picked up after a couple rings. "Deena, this is Tom Mueller. I was hoping you had a preliminary cause of death for me. And I've got some other questions, too."

She offered him a POV link and he accepted, sharing it with Khleang. The interior of the car appeared to dim as his specs adjusted for a better visual. After a second's disorientation, he saw a brightly lit morgue and the kid's body lying face-down on a stainless steel surgical table, head turned to one side, eyes still open. Harrod pointed out a small, deep wound on the boy's back, colored a deep viscous red. "Preliminary cause of death is a puncture wound. It entered between ribs five and six on the rear left side of the body and pierced the left ventricle of the heart. The weapon was about five inches long, thin, sharpened on one side. Here's a model." She tapped her own field and a gray 3D model jumped forward.

"It's a knife," Khleang observed.

"A kitchen knife, almost certainly," Harrod agreed. "There are some further scratches on his heels, probably from being dragged, but otherwise there are no injuries indicative of violent struggle. He was on drugs, though."

"What kind of drugs?" Mueller asked.

Harrod switched from POV to a collar camera, their view swinging around to her face. "The initial blood screen shows RDMA and triserotosinine. Both taken recently, in the last twenty-four hours."

"I know RDMA." Kids called it Rapture, took it at parties. "Trisero-whatever, that's an prescription med, right?"

"Sold as Serenex. It's a common psych med. Basically it's supposed to level out your moods, give you a feeling of normality." She grinned. "Maybe I should get some." These forensics people always weirded him out, how cheerful they could be standing over a kid's corpse.

A kid or not? "Got another question for you." He related what Elsie had told them about her brother's age. "Is that possible?"

Harrod looked at him and back at the body curiously. "I don't think there's any age *disorder* here, if that's what you mean. He looks like a normal kid. You know the birthdate's in the file?"

"I know. But is it possible?"

She considered. "Maybe. We haven't run any genetic tests yet. But we will, now."

"Do you have his medical records?"

"Not yet. We need the permission of the parents, remember. Or a warrant."

He nodded. "We'll get one. Run those tests, let me know."

"Will do. Give me twenty, thirty minutes."

He waved away the window and the interior of the car brightened. "Looking pretty bad for this guy Manish," Khleang said. "You want to call him?"

"I'm on it," Mueller said. In a moment he found Gill's number, no problem, along with his Facebook page, his Prosearch profile, and a bunch of other web hits. He browsed through them for a few minutes before calling. He liked to know who he was dealing with. Gill worked for a company called Insight Tech with offices in South Lake Union. His title was "Systems developer and metadata analyst," which could mean anything. Gill was published, too – articles in the *Journal of Information Science and Technology* and *Pacific Artificial Intelligence Quarterly.* He scanned the first few paragraphs of each article, but it was all gobbledegook to him. He passed them on to Khleang, who would probably spend tonight poring over them after two hours of jiujitsu and a meal out of proportion to her size. Meanwhile Mueller would maybe do some yoga and eat a salad.

Gill's number went straight to voicemail. Mueller left a message stating who he was and that he urgently needed to talk to Gill regarding Gabriel Leberer. Then he called Gill's company, Insight Technology, and got an AI secretary, detectable by the utter lack of emotion in the voice, the subtle spacing of the syllables, the carefully modulated newscaster accent. He asked for Gill. Again it sent him to voicemail and he left another message.

He called the company back. "Thank you for calling Insight Technology," the female voice declared in his earbuds. "How can I help you?"

"I need to speak to Manish Gill," he said again, this time adding, "It's an emergency. If Mr. Gill isn't available, I'd like to speak with his supervisor or someone in his department."

The AI responded immediately, marking it as a grade above most such systems. "Our director of human resources is Anna Pessolano. Would you like to speak with her?"

"Will she know how to reach Manish Gill?"

"I'm not sure," the AI said. Perhaps the three most common three words in the AI vocabulary. "Would you like me to contact her?"

"Yes. Go ahead. Video too, please."

Pessolano had a prominent bird's nose, sandy hair, a warm smile. There was a white wall behind her, presumably the back of her office or cubicle. "This is Anna," she said. "I understand you have some emergency?"

He introduced himself and said he needed to speak with Mr. Gill right away, but wasn't getting any response. She frowned. "I'm sorry, you're a police detective, is that right?"

He'd just said so. "That's correct. You can check with the Seattle Police Department if you like."

"May I ask exactly what it's about? Is Manish in trouble?"

"We'd like to ask him some questions." Which sounded better than *he's wanted for questioning*. "But it is quite urgent. Is he there in the office?"

She hesitated. "May I ask what the questions are regarding?"

He considered his wording. "They're regarding a young man named Gabriel Leberer. I believe Mr. Gill knew him."

"Is he being charged with a crime?"

He hesitated. "It's possible. For now let's just say we really need to talk to him."

She asked him to hold and her face vanished, replaced by Insight's logo, a sort of warp-drive-inside-an-eye thingie. Was she checking his credentials? Checking with her superior? Looking in Gill's office to see if he was there eating Cheetos and writing code?

A minute, two, three. Khleang's hands flicked beside him, signing with a rapidity he probably should have envied. Still no dad. Maybe he worked far away. But then, he didn't have police traffic priority like they did.

Pessolano's visage reappeared. "Mr. Mueller?"

"Still here."

"I'm sorry, but it looks like Manish isn't here today. I guess he called in sick."

"Okay. He's not telecommuting, though? He actually called in sick?"

"That's correct."

He asked if she knew any other way to reach him. She suggested his personal contact address. "Does he have an emergency contact on file with you?"

"Probably. One second." She fiddled with a mouse. A mote appeared in his field in front of her window and he accepted it with a tap. Nita Gill, listed as his mother. A Seattle address. "Is there anything else I can help you with?"

"I may need to talk with someone at your company later, if I can't get a hold of Mr. Gill. Would you be that person?"

"It depends. Is this part of an investigation of some kind?"

"A preliminary investigation, but yes."

"I'd have to consult with some other people, then." A company lawyer and her boss, for instance.

With the call ended, Khleang said, "You going to get a warrant now?"

"I could call his mother first. Or we could go to his apartment."

Khleang shook her head. "He's pulled a runner, I'm telling you."

He sighed. "Yeah, that's how it's looking. I'll get the warrant. Though I wonder if we should wait for Mr. Leberer here, see what he has to say."

"Why? I mean, yeah, we need to talk to him, but we've got enough for the warrant now. I say go for it."

She was right, but he didn't like to act blindly, and that's how he felt, like they were wandering in the woods in the dark. He had the curious feeling of being watched, but then he supposed that was endemic to urban life. He often wondered, too, about the extreme urgency of modern police work – if in the rush to apprehend all suspects, they didn't miss too much, rush to guilt, destroy lives like a runaway car tearing through a crowd.

20

But then, out-of-control cars were also a thing of the past. "You're right," he said. "I'll get the warrant."

Inference: the long-sought grail of law enforcement, situated at the crossroads of detective work and data analysis, enabled and executed by AI systems whose eyes and ears were every auto, every satellite photo, every phone, toilet and light bulb in the United States, a sea of data from which all human movement could be extrapolated like krill slipping through baleen. Or was it more like the scent of blood in the water, calling to sharks miles distant? Who knew how the machines thought?

This time there was no problem. Judge Havermeyer listened to his summary and just said snarkily, "See what another hour of work can do?"

He resisted rolling his eyes and smiled instead. Kill 'em with kindness. "Absolutely. Could we get a search warrant for Gill's apartment as well?"

"I suppose. Access Themis," said Havermeyer. For a second he thought she was giving him directions until he realized it was meant for her own system. "This is Judge Sylvia Havermeyer authorizing an Inference warrant for Manish Gill of –" She looked down at the address. "– 3601 Woodland Park Avenue North, Seattle, Washington, birthdate 9-18-2054, social security number 567-81-3882. Proceed."

"Inference warrant authorized," said the mysteriously androgynous voice of Themis, the Justice Department's AI. "Results are being compiled. This may take a moment."

The judge authorized a search warrant for the apartment, and it was done. "There you go, detective," she said. "Good luck."

"Muchas gracias, your honor." She hung up and vanished.

"We're on?" Khleang said.

"We're on."

"Here comes dad." She nodded at a black auto pulling into the drive. Privately owned, he noted. Mercedes. Smooth and shining as a black eel.

The man who got out had a white head of hair with faint traces of blond still running through it. Clearly where the boy got it from. He was wearing a suit and tie and rushed into the house with a look on his face midway between irritation and terror.

"Let's wait a minute," Mueller said. "He can hear the news from his wife and we'll look at the search results."

"Okay. Go."

"Open Themis," Mueller said clearly. "This is Detective Tom Mueller."

The AI's mote, a blindfolded marble head, appeared floating above the dash between them. It was just an icon, he knew, but it kind of gave him the creeps. He wished they had let it remain a still image instead of animating it when it spoke, which it did immediately, its voice sexless and emotionless yet still resonant. "Hello, Detective."

No password was necessary. Themis knew who he was by the sound of his voice in his collar mike, by the graphene circuits in his clothing measuring each stride, by the cameras in his specs and the auto, by a trail of data a mile long placing him here and only here, as the one and true Detective Thomas Hathaway Mueller.

"I have a few questions regarding Manish Gill, just identified by Judge Havermeyer. Please share with my partner here, also." When he saw Khleang had accepted the share, he went on. "First question: Did Manish Gill murder Gabriel Leberer?"

This time Themis responded visually rather than aurally, the words appearing in their reading fields.

Q: DID MANISH GILL MURDER GABRIEL LEBERER?
YES - 82.2% NO - 17.8%

"It's too vague," Khleang said. "Too much question of intent. Themis, did Manish Gill stab Gabriel Leberer?"

YES - 99.8% NO - 0.2%

"Did Manish Gill place Gabriel Leberer's body in the alley

on Mercer Avenue?"

YES - 99.9% NO - 0.1%

"Show me the top ten supporting items of evidence."

Ten motes appeared in two rows. The first was the video of a man walking out of the alley that they had seen earlier, his hood up, chin wet with rain. The second was a video they hadn't found yet, showing the same man in the driver's seat of a blue auto, pulling into a nearby parking lot. Other items included images of the auto from the day before, showing a blonde boy in the passenger seat: Gabriel.

"It's definitely him," Mueller said.

"It's definitely Gill at the scene, yeah. All right, Themis, here's the big one: Where is Manish Gill now?"

A map accompanied the address: 1551 19TH AVE S SEATTLE WA 98144. "Beacon Hill," Khleang observed. "Street viewpoint, please."

A medium-sized gray house with sky-blue trim. Separate garage. Scrubby-looking yard with a young cedar in front. "Supporting evidence."

Several motes popped up. One was from a public auto, which Gill had called in Queen Anne at 3:52 a.m. It recorded the entire ride to Beacon Hill. The interior view showed Gill sitting in the back seat with a black shoulder bag. His eyes were red and his hands flicked at the air. "Using his system," Khleang observed. "You think he knows the camera's there?"

"Everybody knows the camera's there."

Gill got out of the car half a block from the house on 19th Ave. The second item was a street cam on a light post on the corner. He walked over to the house, head down, looking surreptitious. When he reached the driveway, he looked around, then went to the gate to the backyard, fished around for the latch, and went in.

"He doesn't look like he knows the place," Mueller observed. "Like he's looking around for a way in."

"Yeah, maybe." A light on a motion detector clicked on, but no one came outside. "There could be a camera in the light," Khleang said.

"It's not showing in the search."

"Themis, does that light in the video have a camera, and can we get access to it?"

"One moment." They waited. "Affirmative. Downloading video now."

The video from the light was low-quality, grainy, the shadows stark. Gill looked around in the backyard. When he reached the back door to the garage he stopped, crouched before it, and withdrew something from his jacket pocket: not a key. It looked like a screwdriver or other device. In a moment he opened the door and went inside, stepping very quietly. Strangely he didn't shut the door behind him, leaving it open.

"And that's it? He's still there?" Khleang asked.

"There is no evidence of his departing this address," Themis replied.

"Did he at least close the door?"

"Negative. The door was closed at 7:05 a.m. by Michelle Gorman."

"Is there video?"

There was. In the early morning dimness a middle-aged black woman in gray sweatpants and a blue T-shirt opened the back door of the house and a little Welsh Corgi ran out. She stood on the back porch and lit a cigarette. After a minute she seemed to notice the open door to the garage, staring at it with a frown. "Goddamn it," she muttered, barely audible.

"She wasn't expecting it," Khleang observed.

Gorman walked to the garage, peered through the open door, and went inside. In a few minutes she came back out and closed the door behind her, the dog running up to her with his tongue out. "Come on," she said to him, and went back into the house. End of video.

"She didn't see him," Khleang said.

"We don't know that for sure," Mueller pointed out.

"That's how it looks. She sees the door open, assumes maybe someone's broken in. She goes inside, sees nothing's missing, figures maybe someone just forgot to lock it. Meanwhile the guy's in there the whole time, hiding in the rafters or something."

"Maybe." He ran it through in his mind. "But if she doesn't know him, why did he choose this house in particular?"

"Shit, it doesn't matter. He's still in there now, that's the point. Mercury, tactical support, please." Where Themis dealt with Inference, Mercury was SPD's generalized AI assistant. The officer on duty answered immediately.

"You don't want to talk to the dad first?" Mueller objected.

Khleang looked at him like he was crazy. "The perp's in Beacon Hill. You think the kid's dad will be happy if we're sitting around chatting while his son's killer is out there?"

"Tac squad 2," the officer repeated impatiently. "What's up?"

Khleang outlined the situation briefly, offering the details online. "Suspect may be armed and dangerous. Requesting tactical unit to support arrest at 1551 19th Ave South."

"Affirmative. Estimated arrival in three minutes."

"Great. We're a little further away than you, though. Can you wait before entering?"

"Will do. Slowing vehicle for your rendezvous."

"On our way." She tapped the address onscreen. "Priority ride. Sirens on." She hit the go button once more and the auto spun around in the street, accelerating rapidly. Mueller glanced at the house and saw Elsie's face at the window, watching them speed away.

Tactical had a secure workgroup going, labeled TAC2-19-12-80. Khleang requested access and after a second Mueller did too, their auto already whipping down Queen Anne Ave toward downtown. TAC2 was composed of six officers, headed by Otis Mirman. Mueller recalled seeing Otis around, a big muscular black man in his early forties with a saturnine demeanor. They had up a walk-through of the street in question, which was entirely residential, proximity to I-90 presenting a barrier to commercial development of the area. "Limited exits from the garage. Door in the yard, main garage doors facing the alley. Single window in the yard. Jackson and Deng, we'll drop you off here –" He dropped a pin at the entrance to the alley. "On my signal you run up that alley and stand by the garage door. Themis, do they actually use this garage for parking? Is there a car inside?"

Themis's icon winked on in miniature high in the visual field. "Negative, Officer Mirman. There is no indication of a vehicle entering or exiting the garage since 2068."

"Good. Does the door even open?"

A moment's pause. "I'm not sure."

"So probably not, but we'll have you two out there anyway. Me and Gorshy will enter with the ram via the door in the yard, Haley and Tafoya, stay in the yard and watch that window, move where you're needed. Detectives, you say the suspect may be armed?"

"It's possible," Khleang replied. "He's wanted in connection with a stabbing. The weapon hasn't been recovered yet."

"He also has no other history of violent behavior," Mueller put in, giving Khleang a look. "And right now there's no indication he's in possession of a weapon."

"Understood," Mirman affirmed. "Concussion charges, no live ammo. Set your pieces." They heard him call out each officer's name as he visually inspected their firearms to ensure they were on the correct setting. The last thing the department needed was a police shooting. They hadn't had one in three years, and the chief was intent on preserving that record. "Detectives, I'd appreciate if you'd stay behind until the area is secure and the suspect is in custody."

"Absolutely," Mueller said. The auto hit I-5 south and started really accelerating, now that they were off pedestrian streets. Nearby buildings passed in a blur, downtown sliding by on their right. He glanced at the speed readout and saw it reach 195 km/hour before the auto slowed slightly to merge onto I-90, pressing them into their seats like kids on an amusement park ride. "What's your fastest land speed?" Khleang asked. "Fastest you've ever gone?"

Mueller shook his head. "I don't know. Are you counting trains?"

"Psh. No. In an auto."

"I don't know. Two-twenty?"

"Three-forty," she grinned. "Police cruiser, this Drecksler 460 they'd seized, out in Wyoming. Buddy took me for a ride-along, did an override on the safeties. You hit a hill, you just go *flying*. But it has this flexible suspension to manage the landings. You got to try it."

"Yeah, I'll do that." She laughed at him, and at his tight grip on the door handle. They swung off suddenly, slowing as they hit Rainier Avenue. "ETA one minute," she said to the workgroup, unnecessarily.

"Affirmative, one minute."

"Thirty seconds."

"Jackson, Deng, are you in position?"

"Affirmative," Deng answered. "Awaiting your signal."

"Ten seconds." They had slowed to seventy on the residential streets. Primarily older houses here. Yards in various states of maintenance, green lawns. When they hit 19th Ave, two blocks away, Mirman said: "On one. Three. Two. One."

They saw the tac unit vehicle, an armored van with big smart-grip tires, turn the corner and race up to the house. Four officers in black assault gear spilled out the doors and ran toward the garage in pairs as the detectives pulled to a stop, their auto parked precisely two inches from the curb. Mirman reached the side door, stuck a small directed explosive near the knob, and lay flat against the wall as he hit the command. A muffled crack, like someone hitting a pair of two-by-fours together, and the door blew inward, followed on the instant by Mirman and Gorshkov, rifles leveled, yelling *"Police!"*

Mueller and Khleang got out, standing by the auto until the tac team was finished. But after an anxious two minutes the two officers came out empty-handed, looking toward the detectives. "He's not here," Mirman called toward them.

"You sure?" Khleang yelled back.

"See for yourselves."

The woman they had seen earlier in the surveillance video, Michelle Gorman, was opening the back door, dressed now in blue jeans and a loose green sweater. "Excuse me!" she called. "What's going on?"

"Ma'am, please go back inside," Mirman ordered with a pointed finger.

"That's my garage –"

"Ma'am, we'll speak with you in a minute, but right now we need you to go back inside your home and shut the door."

She looked like she wanted to argue the point, but she did as she was told, standing just inside the screen door looking out. Mueller and Khleang went into the garage and looked around. It was an old brick rectangle, dim, damp and cold. Mueller found a light switch and turned it on, the single fluorescent flickering and then holding steady. Obviously no one had parked a car here in a while, the garage now used exclusively for storage. Boxes piled near the side door. A couch in the back, a dresser, a china cabinet, a couple bicycles. Nothing big enough to hide in. Mueller circled around the couch, raised the cushions, opened the doors of the china cabinet. There were some boards laid across the rafters and Khleang found a short ladder and went up to look around, poking at boxes with the handle of a steel rake.

"Anything?"

"There's nobody here. Or if there is, he's a fucking master of disguise." She came down from the ladder. "If he was here it would show on infrared anyway."

Mueller switched to infrared himself and looked around. Cool blues and greens all around. He switched back. He circled the garage again, moving stuff around, looking for a trap door in the floor or some such. "He's not here," he said finally.

Khleang snorted. "Master detective here. They pay you for this?"

He chuckled. Said to his system, "Themis. Gill isn't at the address you provided. So where is he now?"

"There is no evidence of Manish Gill leaving 1551 19th Avenue South."

"You have access to our systems, you can see what we're seeing. Is there anywhere in this garage for him to hide?"

A brief pause. "Negative. Manish Gill is not inside this structure."

Khleang laughed. "Brilliant analysis, computer." If it were a person, it would feel hurt, but then, it wasn't. "So where is he?"

Another pause, then that too-common AI refrain: "I'm not sure."

Khleang snorted in disgust. "I ever tell you my favorite oxymoron?"

"What's that?"

"Computer intelligence."

"He was here," Mueller observed. The drizzle had stopped, but the grass was still wet and gleaming emerald. Drips off the fir tree by the fence. "Then he left. The door was still open. But the motion detector in the surveillance camera here didn't turn on." He nodded at the light above the back door.

Khleang stood hugging herself against the chill. "Well, obviously he left. But there are cameras in the street lights too.

Autos passing. If he went far, Themis would find him."

"So maybe he didn't go far." He nodded toward the back door, where Michelle Gorman was still standing, looking at them.

She noted their attention and called, "Can I come out now?"

Mirman glanced at her without interest, rifle cradled like a child in his arms. "You want us to stick around, or are we done here?"

Khleang tilted her head. "The warrant is for this address, right? Not just the garage?"

Mueller nodded. "Yeah."

"So we search the house."

He raised a hand to the owner and walked toward the door. "You can come out now," he said companionably.

"Great," she said, and stepped out onto the small back stoop. He went over to her, stood with his hand on the metal rail. He introduced himself and briefly explained the search. She nodded slowly, concern written on her face. "The garage door was open when I let the dog out this morning," she observed. "I thought maybe it was neighborhood kids, looking for something to steal. But there's nothing much worth anything in there."

Mueller realized he didn't have a printed image of the suspect, flicked at his system and had it display on the front of his specs. He took them off and held them out so she could see Gill's face better. "Have you ever seen this man before?"

She shook her head, lips turning down in judgment. "No. I don't know him."

He put the specs back on. "His name's Manish Gill. Does that sound familiar?" Again, no. He explained that Gill had broken into her garage and her eyes widened in alarm. "At this point he's no longer in the garage, but we believe he's still in the area. We'd like to search your house to make sure he's not inside."

She hesitated. "I'm not hiding him or anything. I don't

know the guy."

"We didn't say you were. He may be there without your knowledge."

She looked back at the house as though it had suddenly sprouted fur. "Okay, sure. You can search it. It's just me anyway."

Mueller nodded at the other officers and he, Khleang, Mirman and Gorshkov went in through the back door, the other four taking up positions around the house in case Gill was inside and decided to make a run for it. The house had three bedrooms, one and a half baths, and Gorman's breakfast dishes in the sink. He took note of the photos on the mantel, many showing Gorman with a bald white man and a girl, obviously their daughter, progressing from infancy to adulthood. They went through the house for twenty minutes, looking in every closet and corner and pulling down the ladder to the attic, but Gill wasn't there. Themis confirmed their conclusion and they went back outside. "He's not here," Mueller said to Gorman once they returned to the backyard. She exhaled audibly and her shoulders drooped in relief.

Khleang nodded toward Mirman and asked, "You guys have a drone pack?"

"Better believe it," said Mirman. "We gonna get to use it?"

"If he was here, and if Themis hasn't picked him up somewhere else, there's a good chance he's still in the area. How far can the drones go?"

"Depends how thorough of a scan you want. Low resolution, they can do a ten-kilometer radius. High res, maybe two."

They split the difference and decided on four kilometers. Tafoya went into the van and brought out a big silver box of brushed steel. She set it on the concrete of the driveway, turned it so the broad side was facing the sky, and fiddled with the setup on her system. "Ready?" she asked.

"Do it," Mirman said. She tapped an unseen button and the

box unfolded like origami in reverse, the top and sides retracting to reveal the drone array within, the hummingbird-sized robots held in three tiers that expanded upward to provide more space for takeoff. A low hum rose in pitch as the drones powered up, and suddenly they burst out of their container like flung darts, graphene wings opening and catching them in midair two feet out, still in precise geometric array. They hovered for a second around the unit while it checked their status, and the tac team grinned in enthusiasm. White light flashed from the drones' sensors, and they began flying in an outward-moving spiral, building a high-resolution three-dimensional model of the area, seeing every blade of grass, every old shovel leaning against a fence, every barking dog. Like the God of the gospel, Themis would see each fallen sparrow.

"How long?" Khleang asked.

"Twenty-two minutes," Tafoya answered.

"Are these guys armed, out of curiosity?"

"Minimally. They've each got a little taser dart in them, if someone's running and you want to stop them quick. Might not sound like much, but when you consider there's thirty-six drones in the swarm, it's nothing to fuck with."

Of course, the drones would only scan exterior properties, not the insides of buildings, so if Gill was hiding inside, he'd remain undiscovered. On the other hand, the increased detail in the scan could help Themis with Inference, revealing traces of Gill's passage.

While they waited for the drones to finish, Mueller and Khleang went back inside to talk with Gorman in her kitchen. "Does anyone else live here with you?" Mueller asked.

Gorman shook her head. "No. It's just me. Should I be concerned?"

"I only asked because of the pictures on the mantel. Seemed like maybe you lived here with your husband."

"I did." A flicker of pain across her brow. "He died recently."

"I'm sorry to hear that." Khleang murmured her sympathies beside him. "And your daughter lives elsewhere as well?"

"She's in Denver. She moved out ages ago. It's just me."

He kept her talking for a little while, asking what she did for a living. She was a schoolteacher; taught fourth grade at Beacon Hill Elementary. Normally she'd be in class by now, but school was out for the holidays already. "Is there any reason you can think of why someone would come here? Anything in your garage they might want to steal?"

"I don't know, a bicycle? Some hedge trimmers? You saw the garage. There's nothing much in it."

She was right, but Gill had come here for a reason. "Is it possible he knew your husband or daughter?"

She shrugged. "Of course it's *possible.* I could call my daughter and ask her, if you want."

No reason not to. "Would you, please?" She got her daughter on her home line, on a screen in the kitchen, but after explaining what had happened and showing her the picture, the girl just shook her head and said she'd never seen him. That left the husband, if indeed there was any connection at all. But there had to be *some* connection.

"What was your husband's name?"

"Richard Gorman."

"What did he do for a living, if you don't mind me asking?"

"Actually he worked for the Justice Department," Gorman said. "The computer crimes section. They have offices downtown."

That was interesting. Khleang had already found Richard Gorman on the DoJ system and was requesting files, seeking a connection, but many of the files required special permissions. "And he passed on this last year?"

"This last July." She looked off toward the distance, hugging herself, and Mueller saw the gray sky reflected in her eyes like two wet pearls. "I've thought about moving, getting an apartment. Maybe I will. I don't know."

Khleang let her hands drop, refocusing on the woman in front of her. "I wouldn't worry about this," she said. "The guy who broke in, he's not ... it's just a random event. Probably he was confused about who lived here and left when he realized he was in the wrong place."

"Oh, I know," Gorman said. "That's not the reason. Are we done here?"

When they came back outside the drones were returning, one by one, to their case. "Themis, let's see what you got," Khleang said. The AI's mote appeared attentively before her. "Where is Manish Gill now? Or failing that, where did he go last night?"

"Manish Gill's current location remains unknown," Themis declared dispassionately. They sighed. "His known movements last night are indicated on the map."

They spent some time looking at the map and the evidence for Themis's conclusions. Patterns in the grass indicated that Gill had indeed come back out of the garage; footprints in the mud in the alley showed him walking down Terrance Street. He had continued through the woods bounding I-90, at which time his trail abruptly disappeared.

"He caught a ride," Mueller said. "Crossed over the barrier and got picked up."

"It's not possible," Khleang protested. "Look, he can hide in the woods, for a little while, because surveillance there is light, it's blocked by the trees. But on the freeway? Even in the middle of the night, there's a constant stream of traffic. There's more surveillance there than anywhere in the city. Every minute there's a scan. And to get a ride at all, a vehicle would at least have to slow down."

They went and had a look, following a series of footsteps Themis highlighted for them in glowing yellow, like a path marked for kids in an elementary school. They parked at the edge of the woods and followed a trail down a ravine and then up again through the underbrush to the highway, getting rather damp in the process. At the concrete barrier the trail ended, cars rushing north in an unending stream, their navigation systems spacing them at precise intervals. They refrained from actually stepping over the barrier, since that would set off all kinds of alarms unless they initiated a police detour. The shoulder was surprisingly clean, but then again public autos would issue you a ticket if you threw anything out the window.

They walked along the barrier for twenty yards in either direction, but came up with nothing more interesting than the gray and moldering remnants of what may have been a raccoon. "Even just *standing* here Themis should have found him. How is that possible? Themis, can we see video from the time in question? Video from passing vehicles?"

They could, of course. According to Themis he had reached the barrier at 4:26 a.m. They started five minutes before, paying particular attention to those videos between 4:26 and 4:31. Two vehicles had passed between 4:26 and 4:27, and they slowed the videos down and watched intently. It was still dark, the road lit by the autos' headlights and the amber street lights, but the area where they were standing was entirely dark, and the lidar had picked up nothing. "He could just be crouched down behind the barrier," Mueller said. "Could have stayed like that for who knows how long."

"And then what? Traffic would only have gotten thicker the later it got in the day."

They checked to see if any vehicles had slowed down in that stretch of highway; they had not. "Maybe he flew away," Mueller said.

"Is that a joke?"

He shrugged, offering a wry half-smile. "Maybe, maybe not. He was here. Then he wasn't. Ever see one of those backpack helicopters?"

"I've *flown* one. I also know they're pretty big, actually. Like a big camping pack. He didn't have anything like that with him in the auto."

"Not in the auto. But what about in the garage?"

She frowned and nodded. "I guess it's possible. Maybe the trees would screen him from the lidar until he had enough altitude that the auto scans wouldn't see him. They're noisy, though."

"No one really around here."

"Rebecca Gorman didn't mention anything like that."

"Maybe she didn't know her husband had one. Maybe she thought it was an ordinary backpack."

"Man..." She shook her head. "Those things don't *look* like ordinary backpacks. They look like some crazy robotic shit. They're expensive, too. Anyway, we're way off in speculation here. You might as well say, maybe he was picked up by a transporter beam from outer space."

She was right, of course, and how often had he told himself to refrain from speculation? Even so, Gill had gone *some*where. "Do you get the feeling we're being led around by the nose?"

Her eyes narrowed. "What do you mean?"

"Gill's a techie. He specifically was an AI researcher, cognition systems, the very kind of stuff Themis is built on. He must have known what we would do. He must have known we would run Inference on him."

"You think he found a way to avoid Inference?"

"The proof is in the pudding." He gestured at the highway, the patch of salal where Gill's last footsteps still glowed. "He's not here."

Three options presented themselves once they were back in the auto, running the heat vents at full in a probably futile attempt to dry off their pants legs. They could return to the

Leberer's house in Queen Anne to continue interviewing Gabriel's family; they could go to Gill's apartment in Ballard; or they could go to lunch.

"Lunch sounds good," Khleang said. "But we should secure the apartment. For all we know the guy's there now, laughing at us."

"Themis says not."

"Themis says he's still standing by the highway back there. Themis is full of shit."

"Hm." He frowned. "When was the last time you heard of Themis being wrong about a location?"

"I've heard of it."

"When?"

"I don't know. We could look it up."

"Okay. Let's look it up." He sighed. "And let's go to the apartment."

"Okey doke." The auto departed at a far more sedate pace than the journey here and Khleang worked her magic on her system. In thirty seconds she said, "There's quite a few instances of unknown locations, even in the last ten years. Or vague locations, broad areas like a park, where there isn't a lot of surveillance. Also cases of suspects fleeing the U.S. altogether, escaping to the Free States or wherever."

"Fine. But what about an actual *mistake*? Claiming someone's in one location when they're not?"

"One second." She kept flicking. "Okay. Uh, 2070. Themis claimed Michael Barbas, guy who beat his wife to death, was at a 7-11. Turns out it was someone else with a freakishly close facial match. Barbas was actually hiding out in Tukwilla."

"Ten years ago."

"It's not infallible," she pointed out. "Really, it was bound to happen sometime. It's just a computer system. Anyway, maybe he hasn't gone far. He could be in someone else's backyard right now, hiding under someone's old canoe or something."

"In which case he'll turn up soon."

"He'll turn up soon one way or the other. That's the thing about Themis. You can hide for a while, but sooner or later it'll find you. You know one of the most common ways it tracks people? The toilet. Every time you flush, the city water system takes note of the amount of waste passing through the pipes and correlates it to your location. It's not all satellite surveillance."

"What if he's pooping under the canoe?"

"Then he really is up shit creek." She grinned.

Gill's apartment in Fremont was in a newish building, stylish and efficient, with a big overhanging solar roof. The downstairs was occupied by a Cafe Campari, a Greek bistro, and a bicycle shop. The apartment had a view of Lake Union, but the walls were remarkably bare, the furniture good quality but generic, the sort of modern stuff you'd find at hip designer stores named after tertiary colors, like Sienna or Verdigris. Maybe it had come pre-furnished.

They let the techs do their scan before entering. "Detectives," one of them called from the entrance to the bedroom. "You'll want to see this."

They crowded behind him and looked over his shoulders, their eyes falling like magnets to the bed. The white-and-brown comforter was in a rough pile on the floor, but the top sheet, if there had ever been one, was missing. In the center of the mattress, like a present laid upon the baby blue sheets, accented by smears and dots of blood, was a fine wood-handled fileting knife. The tech's little drone flashed its white light over the room and themselves, recording their somber expressions for posterity.

"That pretty much erases any lingering questions of guilt," Khleang said. Analysis from the holoscan revealed Gill's fingerprints on the knife handle. After Khleang conferred with the tech for a few minutes, it also found the RDMA, on an amber plastic pill bottle in the bedside trash.

Mueller nodded at the clothes thrown on the floor. "You

think those are the kid's?"

"Good question," Khleang said. The drone returned to the tech's hand and he moved away from the door. "Go ahead," he said.

Khleang snapped on a pair of latex gloves and they went in. She knelt and gently checked the tags on the jeans. "26-26. They're his." She lifted the shirt, turned it over. "No damage to the shirt."

Nor were there any other signs of struggle. The blood was on the bed only. The lampshades were upright and undisturbed. There was a glass of water on the table, still mostly full.

"Killed in his sleep," Khleang concluded. Mueller nodded, envisioning it. "They take the Rapture, they go to bed. They fall asleep. Gill gets up, goes to the kitchen, comes back with the knife. He sits on the bed, right over the kid, who still doesn't wake up. Then... hck." She makes a downward stabbing gesture. "Or maybe even positions it over the kid. Right over the heart. Boom. Hammers down on it." She shook her head. "It's cold."

"It is," he agreed. He kept staring at the bed. "Does that seem like enough blood to you?"

She cocked her head. "No. You're right. He's stabbed near the heart, he should bleed like a motherfucker, right? You remember the Delillo thing?"

"I'm not going to forget it anytime soon." Emily Delillo had stabbed her husband in his sleep, over and over. The bedroom had looked like an abattoir. Blood on the walls, splatters on the ceiling, blood pooled and puddled on the floor. "Of course, she stabbed him a lot more than once."

"Even so. Maybe he tried to bandage the wound? Stop the bleeding? Maybe the kid was actually stabbed somewhere else, then moved here?"

"I think then there'd be a blood trail leading here. No, he was killed here in bed. And if Gill tried to stop the bleeding, obviously he failed. And where are the bandages?"

They checked the kitchen. The knife was one of a set, its slot alone empty. They spent some time going through Gill's personal effects, but they were few. Plenty of clothes in the closets, though of course they wouldn't notice what was missing if he had packed anything. Almost no paper documents in the place. No printed photos on the shelves, no snapshots of family on the mantel.

"You know why that is, though," said Khleang. "These kind of guys, they live their whole lives online. They go to work, they sit in front of a screen or in their fields. Anything they write, it's online. Anytime they talk to their friends, listen to music, play a game, it's all Eyenet for them. They see a blank wall, they just change the scenery in their field."

Mueller had already come to much the same conclusion. "We need access to his accounts."

She nodded. "Next best thing to the man himself."

"Can Themis get that stuff?"

"Depends. We can try it."

She ran the query through Themis. It offered them any number of accounts associated with Manish Gill, and for a while they sat at Gill's dining-room table browsing through them. These included an account for Lore, a popular video game, and Gill's work address at Insight Technology. When they tried to access the two accounts, however, Themis twice told them ACCESS NOT AVAILABLE.

"Why aren't they available?" Mueller asked.

"They're blocked," Khleang replied.

"We have a warrant. Can't Themis just, you know, reach in and get it?"

Khleang chuckled. "No. They have their own AIs."

By the time they finished at the apartment it was one-twenty. "I'm about ready to gnaw off my leg," Khleang declared. "Where you want to go for lunch?"

They decided on Pho Le's, back in Queen Anne. As they

crossed the bridge from Fremont Mueller mused, "Why did he move the body so far? I mean, if he was going to just dump it in an alley, why go to another neighborhood to do it?"

"Maybe he thought it would remove suspicion from him? It the kid's found on his block, everyone'll know he did it."

"And then he leaves the murder weapon on his bed, covered in blood? Doesn't make sense."

"Maybe the kid wasn't dead yet. Maybe Gill was going for help, trying to get him to a hospital. Then he realizes Gabriel's dead, panics, gets rid of the body and takes off."

It made some sense, he saw, although when he looked on a map, the closest hospital was in Ballard. Still, maybe Gill hadn't realized that and was heading for one of several in Capitol Hill. "Speaking of the auto," Khleang continued, "Themis, where's the vehicle Manish Gill used to move Gabriel Leberer from Fremont to Queen Anne? Where is it currently?"

Themis displayed its location on a map and read the address, currently parked in the University district. The auto had been flagged, they noted, for uncleanliness. Khleang had Mercury lock it down and send it to the station in Cap Hill, where forensics would look at it.

Pho Le's was on the avenue's downward slope, in one of the innumerable mixed-used buildings erected earlier in the century, retail on the first floor, apartments above. It was a hideous building, its red and gray panels bespeaking solely a developer's desire for the largest possible profit margin, but the broth had a touch of pineapple sweetness, and the extreme slope of the avenue meant the shop had retained a view of the city from its few window seats. Most prominent was the new Space Needle, precisely twice the size of the old one at twelve hundred and ten feet tall, wearing its Christmas-tree topper, which Mueller's (non-police) partner, Chris, always said looked like a pointy gnome hat. Behind the Needle were the hundreds of towers of downtown, and the thousands and thousands of mixed-use buildings, much like this one, that accommodated the metro area's six million citizens.

Even as the south reeled from the slow, inexorable disaster of global warming – the growing deserts, persistent droughts, hurricanes, floods like Biblical judgments – the north had prospered, people flocking to its cooler climes and still-vigorous economy. Where one tech titan perished, two sprang up in its place, sleeker, slimmer, smarter. Microsoft was gone, Boeing reduced to a shadow, but the skyscrapers filled again with programmers for Cognition, Flick, Oculus, INFIX, a hundred thousand workers building the AIs and Eyenet line by line, frame by frame, like the subcellular organelles of a great unseen body.

The food came and they focused on adding condiments, sipping broth, and slurping up noodles. Mueller had gotten a large veggie, heaped with bright green broccoli, carrots, bok choy, and fried tofu, while Khleang got the mixed meats, a disturbing pinkish-gray pile of shaved beef and pork with a few small shrimp on top. She saw him eyeing it uneasily. "Don't say anything."

"I wasn't going to."

"You were thinking it. I know how it looks."

"Nope. Looks great."

"It's delicious, actually."

"I'm sure."

"Whatever."

"I'll be right over here eating these veggies if you need me."

"Well, I won't."

Twenty minutes later Mueller sat back, wiping broth from his mouth and sipping on ice water. Khleang had gotten a Thai iced tea and was sucking on the sweetened condensed milk through a straw. Her bangs were cut brutally short, the rest of her dark hair cinched back in a tight ponytail. She was petite, just five-two, athletic, her shoulders a bit broad beneath the jacket and blouse she wore. They made an odd couple, he knew, he being a full foot taller, sandy blond and gawky. But he liked that, how they balanced each other. "How's Drake?"

Drake was her three-year-old. "He's great. We've started taking him to daycare for a few hours a day. At first he really wasn't sure about it, but now he loves it."

"Hm." The sun had finally come out, reflecting brightly off the millions of windows downtown and enlivening the greenery that gave the Emerald City its moniker. "What do you think it'd be like, to have the mind of a twenty-year-old in a ten-year-old's body?"

"Isolating," she said after a moment's consideration. "I mean, if everyone was that way it wouldn't be, but if it was just you and a few others, I think you'd feel very alone."

"Yeah. But would you think more like a twenty-year-old, or more like a kid?"

"Probably mentally, intellectually, more like an adult. With the skills and knowledge of an adult. But socially, I have to imagine more like a child. So much of being an adult is wrapped up in relationships, and sexuality, career, all that. That's what it means. If we see someone in their twenties, and they've never experienced those things, we say that they're immature."

He nodded. "Makes sense."

His earbuds rang with the sound of a hooting owl and he looked down to see who was calling. *Who, who.* Khleang apparently was receiving the same call, her lips twisting in distaste. "It's Willie White."

"You don't want to talk to our beloved lieutenant?"

"The guy's a toad. But I guess we're obligated."

When Mueller answered, Willard White ghosted in next to Khleang, Mueller's system placing him in an empty seat. Khleang was right, there was something batrachian in the lieutenant's drooping flesh and buggy eyes, an impression that his full mustache failed to amend. "Lieutenant, how are you?" Mueller began, swallowing a bit of broccoli.

"You're at lunch?" White said, gesturing at the table and sounding more or less outraged. "I just wasn't aware you were enjoying such a relaxing afternoon. I assumed maybe you'd be busy trying to find this kid's killer."

"We have been, Willie," Khleang said. "Which I would think you would know."

"Yeah, and your perp's still not in custody."

Khleang looked around as if in surprise. "He's not? Crap! Thanks for letting us know, boss. We'll get right on that. Do you think he's here in the restaurant?"

"I didn't call to get sassed, *detective.* I want to know what happened."

"Themis fucked up, Willie. That's what happened. What do you want from us?"

"I want to know *why* Themis made an error. Then I want to know where the guy *actually* is, and I want you to put him in handcuffs. Soon."

"Well, that's what we're *doing.* You can literally see everything we've done this morning and everywhere we've been. So what's the problem?"

"The problem is that you're sitting on your asses while this guy's out doing–"

"We're not fucking *robots*, we have to eat –"

"– God knows what, in who fucking knows where –"

"Lieutenant!" Mueller said loudly. This was heading nowhere good. He wasn't sure what White's intentions were, but once Khleang's combative instincts were aroused, they were hard to turn off. "As I'm sure you're aware, we have a right to an hour-long lunch, as negotiated by the union, barring emergencies, which this is not. If you have a problem with that, I can put you in touch with a union representative and you can discuss it with them."

White made a *pah* of irritation and leaned back in his chair, waving his hand. "Look, I just need to impress upon you the urgency here. I just got off the phone with Barrett." Lonnie Barrett was the current chief of police. "And *he* just got off the phone with the mayor, who apparently expressed a clear desire for this case to be solved quickly and neatly. In other words, for your perp to be found and put in jail, there to rot until the public sees fit to do otherwise."

Khleang started to exclaim, but Mueller raised a calming hand. "Probably the error with Themis is just temporary, and as soon as Gill goes out on the street, or buys some food, or whatever, Themis will know. But until that time, we'll have to use traditional investigative methods, which means there's no guarantee of a fast resolution."

"Find him," White enunciated. "Fast." With that he waved his hand and vanished from the table.

Khleang shook her head, mouth in a tight line. "How is that asshole our supervisor? Explain that to me."

Mueller shrugged sympathetically. "There's no justice in the world, less we give birth to it."

"Very poetic."

"I try." He moved his water glass around the table, arranging it in a more pleasing pattern. "Question is, if the chief called Willie, and the mayor called the chief, who called the mayor?"

She thought about it. "The dad," she said finally.

"Yeah, probably. Let's go back up the hill."

Daniel Leberer had a wild look about him and the air of a man used to giving directions. When they knocked he waved them in with a tight-lipped "Come on," and then sat on the couch as though striking it. "Did you find him?" he demanded.

It was characteristic of Mueller that the more emotional a situation became, the calmer he himself felt. "We did, yes."

"And is he in custody?"

Mueller looked around the room. Elsie was looking at him attentively, curled up in a corner of the couch. Her mother,

Sarah, was next to her, arms protectively around her daughter. "I'm sorry, who are we discussing?" Mueller asked.

"Manish!" the father yelled, pink face reddening. He bounced off the cushions, stalked two paces, turned. "Manish fucking Gill, that slippery shit! The motherfucker who killed my son! That's who! Do you have him in custody?"

Mueller said clearly, "No. We don't."

Daniel Leberer gazed about the room with an air of outraged incredulity, spreading wide his arms for the gods to witness this transgression. "Well, *why... fucking... not?*"

Khleang spoke up. "Mr. Leberer, Manish Gill is certainly under investigation. But this investigation is absolutely in its preliminary phases. With all respect, it's only been about five hours since your son's body was discovered. We're still gathering the most basic sorts of physical evidence."

"He was *with* fucking Manish! I'm telling you that's who he was *with!* You need to go arrest him and put him in handcuffs so I can go spit in his face and kick him in the fucking *balls!*" This last in a roar. His face was vivid, almost fluorescent pink. Khleang's expression, meanwhile, was turning stonier and stonier, as if she were staring down a basilisk.

"Daniel," his wife said, "you need to sit down. And calm down."

"Where is he?"

"We are looking for him," Mueller said. "And as soon as –"

"What does that mean, 'We're looking for him?' I thought these days you guys just entered a name and your system told you the guy's sitting on a toilet at Second and Mercer. What about those amazing Justice Department AIs we keep hearing about? Catch a guy in ten minutes, autos to his door, drones with tranquilizer darts, all that stuff? Why isn't he in custody already?"

"We are looking for him," Khleang said. "And we will find him. But in the –"

"What does that *mean?*" Daniel yelled. "Do I need to do this myself?"

"Daniel!" his wife snapped. "Sit down." But he hardly glanced at her, caught in some loop of rage and grief, like an animal twisting in a trap.

It was Elsie who finally knocked him out of it. "Daddy," she said. When he didn't stop his tirade, she yelled in her high voice: "Daddy!"

He looked at her, virtually quivering with emotion. "You're being an asshole," she said.

His eyes fixed on her and then closed. His breath caught. Then he sat down on the couch and sobbed.

It took a little while, but finally he got up and went into the bathroom. "I'm sorry," Sarah said.

"It's understandable," Mueller said. "It's going to be hard for a long time. We can put you in touch with a grief counselor who will help you through this."

Daniel returned. It was obvious he had splashed cold water on his face, though his eyes were red-rimmed and his light hair was mussed. He was otherwise, Mueller thought, a handsome man, though with his age an inevitable heaviness had settled on his medium frame. Mueller had looked at the wedding picture on the mantel, earlier, seen the very blond and bearded younger man, a great carefree smile on his face; but somewhere along the way the corners of his mouth had turned down and creases had carved themselves into his brow.

"We need to talk about Gabriel and Manish," Mueller said. Daniel looked at the floor, shielding his eyes with his hand. The girl and her mother looked at them but didn't volunteer anything. "Elsie said a little while ago that they were lovers. Is that true?"

Daniel shook his head and gave a little groaning exhalation. Finally Elsie said, "It's true."

"We don't really know..." her father muttered.

"*I* know," she said. "You didn't want to know."

"When you say 'lovers,'" Khleang said, "you mean..."

"That they were having sex." She rolled her eyes. "Obviously."

Khleang looked toward Sarah. "Did *you* know?"

Sarah looked out the window. "I knew. He told me a few months ago."

"But *you* didn't know." To Daniel.

He sighed and spoke into his hands. "He tried to tell me. I told him I didn't want to know about it. I tried to stop him from seeing him."

"But you weren't able to."

"What was I supposed to do, chain him to a radiator? He probably would have picked the lock anyway."

There was too much they didn't know. "Before we go any further," Mueller said, "what did you mean about your ages? How old are you, Elsie? And how old was Gabriel?"

There was another silent family conference of gazes, eyes flicking around the room like the lasers of a complex security system. Then Daniel sat back and sighed. "Have you ever heard of Dr. Samuel Liebskind?"

Something glimmered in Mueller's memory, but he couldn't bring it fully to light. "It sounds familiar..."

But Khleang's eyes had widened in sudden comprehension. "You're wunderkind."

Elsie smiled slightly. "Wunderkinder, technically."

Back in the late fifties it had been the story of the decade, a media firestorm erupting around the kinetic, burly Dr. Liebskind and the twenty-three children who were his intellectual if not physical offspring. Liebskind, a research geneticist and man of many talents supported at the time by the University of Washington, was the shining light of his field, winning a Nobel Prize (since revoked) in 2050 for certain extremely abstruse insights into embryonic nerve development that subsequently produced a cure for multiple sclerosis. These insights themselves were the product, in part, of an ongoing revolution in genetics research enabled by AI analysis of the still-mystifying human genome.

Having reached such heights at midlife, however, Liebskind sought to ascend to the heavens by tinkering more substantially with the stuff of life. The MS cure depended on the screening of prospective parents, and the wealthy of Seattle partook in the program early on, donating their hair follicles as part of a generalized screening that would warn them of incipient genetic risks, thereby ensuring their spawn the greatest possible health and themselves the greatest possible happiness. Of the thousands screened, seventeen sets of parents were told that alas, they possessed the very malignant genes the test was designed to catch.

In his way, Liebskind was perfectly conscientious. He had told no lies to these would-be procreators; their children would indeed have developed MS without his cure. Instead they reaped a crop of healthy, beautiful baby boys and girls, and all were glad.

For a while.

Within a year or two it became obvious something was wrong. The children were small, at the tail end of the scale for weight and height. Liebskind reassured each couple for as long as he could, noting that despite their diminutiveness, the children were in excellent health, indeed, were happy, smiling babies. But by age four, seeing their beloved son lagging behind his peers in most measures of motor function, seeing him still a foot shorter than the other kids in his playgroups and preschools, one pair of parents, Richard and Maria Selva of Green Lake, finally broke free of Dr. Liebskind's fierce medical embrace and took young Patricio for a battery of exams at the Boston Children's Hospital.

And the initial tests confirmed Liebskind's own calm if occasionally domineering assertions: Patricio was a normal little boy, albeit very small, slow to walk and slow to talk. He was alert, his heartbeat, organs, and brain function were all normal. Barring a few colds, he had had no serious illnesses and seemed unlikely to develop any.

When a bit of blood was run through a gene sampler, however, the doctors sat up straight. They ran more tests. They exclaimed in amazement. They consulted their own medical AIs. They ran predictive models, and brought in their own genetic wizards.

Yes, Liebskind had cured Patricio's incipient MS *ab ovo,* replacing this allele here, that acid there, to make the child's nervous system a thing of unblemished beauty and functionality. He had also, however, effected a massive series of changes involving thousands of genes, mostly related to the endocrine system.

They worked backwards from Liebskind's work, and in a couple of days – because such things are *very* computationally intensive – their AI finished its simulation of Patricio's growth from birth to death, which mirrored the reality so far. Their consternation turned to amazement, then to outrage.

The fact was, Liebskind had achieved something incredible. According to the model, Patricio would grow and age in a completely normal way – but at half the normal rate.

Right now, that meant he appeared a little slow and a little small, the development of his musculature and nervous system lagging behind his peers'. But when he looked to be ten years old, his peers would be full-grown adults. When he looked old enough to drink, his peers would be developing wrinkles and gray hairs. And when he looked sixty, the oldest, longest-lived members of his generation would be in their graves.

Because Liebskind had achieved – or so the AIs claimed – what no doctor in the history of humankind had achieved: a significant increase in not only the *average* age of a human, but in the *maximum* age. Barring accidents or life-ending disease, little Patricio could reasonably expect to reach one hundred and sixty to two hundred years of age.

Which may or may not have been fine for Patricio and his parents (time would tell if the simulation was correct, or if Mother Nature was more fickle and more subtle than expected). But it *was* certain that Liebskind had broken half a dozen laws regarding experimentation on humans, parental consent, and conspiracy, as well as bypassing the involved protocols required by his hospital, the government, and the medical community regarding the genetic alteration of human patients generally. He had, indeed, veered deep into Dr. Moreau territory, a region that had long haunted those already on the forefront (or edges, depending on how you looked at it) of scientific research.

The doctors talked to the lawyers. The lawyers talked to the police. The police talked to their nascent AI, Themis, which told them that Liebskind had left for Singapore three days earlier.

No fool, Liebskind had run his own entirely internal predictive analysis and concluded that if he stayed in the U.S. he would end up in a jail cell, possibly for a very long time. On the other hand, he could go to Singapore, which continued to have significant disagreements with the United Nations regarding genetic engineering, and whose companies were perfectly eager to press him to their bosom and shower him with money. With considerable foresight he had transferred most of his assets to a Singaporean bank and leased a comfortable apartment with a pleasant view of Pasir Ris Town Park and the waters of the Jahir Strait. He wasn't much for tropical climates, sweating readily, but both apartment and hospital had excellent AC, and he took to wearing loose linen shirts outside of work.

The children, meanwhile, were closely watched, both by medical experts and the American public, who saw little Patricio being held by his parents on *60 Minutes* and the round of talk shows all through that summer of '59. The Selvas wanted Liebskind extradited, somewhat understandably, although several hosts pointed out that Patricio didn't exactly seem to be suffering from the doctor's tampering, and if the predictions ran true, might we not be looking, in this restless toddler, at the future of the human race itself?

That was a big *if*, the parents rejoined, and they would have preferred for Liebskind not to roll the dice with their child. Liebskind, meanwhile, had no fear of defending himself and his work publicly, appearing on many of the same programs to hail his work as revolutionary and himself as a visionary.

The other thirty-two parents, noticing the paparazzi around the Selva's home, by and large decided to stay quiet and protect their families from the uproar. The hospital administrators involved were commendably eager to protect said families (and, incidentally, their own careers), and closed ranks to prevent their names from being leaked to the press.

Years passed. Now and then there was a follow-up story. The Selvas achieved a minor celebrity to which perhaps they had never been averse. The number of stories dwindled. Liebskind stayed in Singapore and jogged in the park each morning, the sweat spreading in great dark pools on his T-shirts' underarms and backs. The children stayed children.

There were a number of nagging problems, however, not easily resolved. The first of these was schooling. While it was true that the wunderkind (as they were quickly dubbed) were slow to walk and talk, this had only to do with muscle control and development. At five they were as smart as any other kindergartener, but unfortunately they were half the size. At ten this was even more true, and any normal ten-year-olds they might have associated with were entirely unable to relate, treating them as unbearably know-it-all little kids.

Some of the parents advocated the creation of a special school, and the hospital administration supported the idea. A child psychiatrist named Arquette Kelly was designated the hospital's point person for the wunderkind (she having fought for the position, envisioning the flood of papers that would flow from her hand). For a while the school functioned as imagined, until some less scrupulous reporters finally got wind of it and managed to trace eight more of the children to their homes, demanding interviews with the parents. This mostly convinced these parents that maybe home schooling was best. In any case, in the American tradition of constant peripatetic migration, one family after another moved away, burying themselves in new communities in Pennsylvania and Kentucky and northern California, or to more private environs in what remained of the wilds of Idaho and Wyoming.

More substantial issues yet arose when the children neared the age of majority. At sixteen driving was out of the question – their feet wouldn't reach the pedals – but self-driving autos prevented this from being a real issue. But it was clear long beforehand that the rights usually accorded at eighteen posed difficult questions for the wunderkind, their parents, and the justice system. Were these individuals – none of whom had yet reached five feet in height, or grown a smidgen of pubic hair – to be allowed to join the military? To drink alcohol? To buy rifles (handguns being long outlawed outside the Free States)? To – and this was especially troubling – have sex?

To answer these questions, a district judge, working together with Dr. Kelly and representatives from the relevant government agencies, hammered out an agreement to protect all involved, and allow the children to pass, in an age of ubiquitous and instantaneous personal identification, as normal. Every other year their birthdates would be pushed up one year, thereby reflecting, more or less, their physical age.

Interpersonally, the wunderkind encountered still greater challenges. "Gabriel was troubled," as Sarah Leberer put it. "Maybe very troubled."

"He was in a unique position," Daniel muttered.

"He was manic-depressive," Elsie said flatly. "Maybe psychotic."

"Elsie –" Sarah began.

"It's true. It's going to come out anyway, so we might as well say it up front."

Mother and father both sighed deeply. In it you could hear years of sadness and difficulty, like a ghost wafting through the room.

"You have to understand the kind of frustration he felt," Sarah said, taking it upon herself to explain. "It's endemic among the wunderkind. In the first place, even when they're very young, they go through a prolonged period where they know consciously what they want, but they can't physically form the words. They want to walk, but their legs aren't strong enough. Then they see other kids doing these things faster than them, and it can create long-lasting insecurities. Anxieties. There are all kinds of ways to help ease this, like teaching the kids to sign, and limiting their exposure to fast-aging children, but in Gabe's case ... I don't know, maybe it was already too late by the time he went to the Wunderschool. That was the special school UW set up for them, you know. It only lasted five years."

"Did you go to the school?" Khleang asked Elsie.

Elsie nodded and signed something rapidly. Khleang smiled and signed back. "It must be nice when you're online," Khleang said aloud, referring to the sign language.

Elsie shrugged. "I'm pretty fast."

"Did you like the school?" Mueller asked. "Do you miss it?"

"It was okay," Elsie said, somewhat guardedly. "I'm glad they taught me to sign. I don't really miss it. Some of the kids there weren't well-adjusted."

And Gabriel, apparently, was one of those. Over the next couple of hours a picture formed of the boy, or man-child, or whatever you wanted to call him. The wunderkind.

Whatever developmental difficulties Gabriel had had in his

early life, it was soon clear that he was very, very bright, and his wealthy parents made sure he received the best education available. His interests lay in computer systems, electronic music, keyboards, science fiction, and Japanese. "He was good at all of it," Sarah said. "You should have heard him play his keyboards."

"He was incredibly talented," Daniel said. "He could have done anything."

Gabriel graduated high school early, when he looked to be about seven. Along with his piano teacher, his parents found him private tutors for general studies, mathematics, and Japanese. Computer programming he learned on his own, obsessing over it, occasionally staying up all night to work on some project or another. His father encouraged him, critiqued his work, pointed him in new directions, tried to connect him with computer professionals.

It may have been, even before he met Manish, that Gabriel had had some kind of relationship with his piano tutor, one Ken Schiller. The parents had trusted Schiller, it seemed, and thought him a good, steadying influence on a boy given to deep depressions and manic streaks. Soon, though, they began to be uncomfortable with the physical affection that Gabe showed with Schiller, sometimes standing too close, pinching Schiller's stomach, hugging him, though Schiller was also obviously uncomfortable with these displays. The parents talked between themselves, and asked Schiller to move on. They would find another tutor.

"Do you think they were actually having sex?" Khleang asked bluntly.

"We weren't sure," Sarah said. "But we suspected."

But Elsie said, "They were."

"Are you sure?"

"Gabe told me. He told me lots of things. " She nodded in her parents' direction. "They didn't want to hear it."

"That's not true," her father said.

"Of course it's true," she snapped. "You've had blinders on like a couple of horses drawing a cart. Hear no evil, see no evil."

When Gabriel learned that they had fired Schiller, he was furious. He tried to contact his tutor, but Schiller blocked his calls. The boy suspected that his parents had threatened Schiller with legal action, and it seemed Schiller was hardly as attached to Gabriel as Gabriel was to him. It was the first definitive break between child and parents, a spike driven into a glacier that soon began to fracture, a crevasse opening up between them.

"We'd had problems before," Sarah said. "Lots of them. It seemed like we were always squabbling about something. Gabriel wanted more independence, and who could blame him? But we always thought he would fare worse on his own than with us."

"Well, we were right, weren't we?" Daniel said bitterly.

Gabriel began going out at night, at first clandestinely, then openly. He refused to say where he was going, or with whom. Sometimes they smelled alcohol on his breath or on his clothes. He became obstreperous, saturnine, loudly proclaiming that by all logic he was an adult, he had a bachelor's degree, he ought to be allowed to get his own place and begin working a real job. This from a boy who looked all of twelve. They suspected he was meeting men he had met online, and were desperate to stop him.

It was an old story with new proportions, Gabriel coming both late and early to adolescent rebellion, even as his body was finally reaching a puberty of unknown dimensions and possible risks. One night, in a rage at his parents' intransigence, he smashed most of the downstairs windows in the house with one of his father's guitars. The police were called. The neighbors were scandalized. The parents said something needed to change, and for once, surrounded by shattered glass, Gabriel listened.

Years before he had stopped going to his therapist (Dr. Kelly, of the school) at his own insistence, but now he was persuaded to see her again. She talked to him for a couple of hours and prescribed triserotosinine, known more commonly by its commercial name, Serenex.

"He seemed better," Sarah said. "The Serenex worked. He was calmer, more enjoyable to be around. He seemed to settle down."

"It was like the good old days," Daniel said. "It was like getting our son back. He hadn't been doing much studying or work, you know, for a little while. Mostly he would just sit around and play Lore online, and then disappear until four in the morning, and throw a fit if we said anything to him about it. But now he was back to doing stuff, playing keyboards again, working on his software projects."

They were thrilled. They relented on certain issues, relaxing his curfew and encouraging him to enter the professional world, if such was possible. Through the Aspire Project, Gabriel met some graduate computer science students at UW. One of them was Manish Gill.

It seemed both son and parents had learned something from Gabriel's first relationship. This time they were all more circumspect, more careful not to disturb each other's peace. Gabriel worked with Manish online, along with several others, and occasionally met him real-world, at UW or for coffee. "I'm not sure exactly when they even met each other," Sarah said. "I think probably they'd been hanging out for a long time before we ever met Manish. He'd go to UW, and we thought that was a safe environment."

"He was working on stuff," said Daniel. "He showed me some of it. It was all AI-related, real cognitive analysis. We encouraged him. I thought maybe it had been a mistake to try to prevent him from getting a job. It was groundbreaking development. And you know, these days it's not that important what you look like as long as you have the skills. So he got this internship at Insight. I think they were wowed by him. I would have been. He was a star."

Pessolano didn't mention the internship when we called, Mueller noted. Just natural caution?

For a long while, a year, things stayed in a holding pattern in the Leberer household. Gabriel went to Insight's offices a few days a week. His parents met Manish, but also met any number of other people who worked for the company, and they kept their suspicions in check.

But it couldn't last. The more independence Gabriel had, the more he wanted. One day he said he wanted his own apartment, and he wouldn't be turned aside. He was actually being paid for his work now, he pointed out; Insight had taken him on as an independent contractor. But his parents refused.

"Why not just let him have it?" Khleang asked. "I mean, technically he was what, twenty-five already, right?"

Daniel's face darkened. "Technically. And maybe, had he been different, more stable, we'd have let him. If Elsie wanted a place, we might let *her*. But he *was* unstable. And age isn't everything. I mean, you mark the years on the calendar, but how much of maturity is also physical? Sure, he's twenty-five, but he was also going through puberty. Do you think *you* should have been given your own place and your own bank account, all those freedoms, when your hormones were raging like that?"

The parents clung to their boundaries, and the son pushed back in a rage. He began ignoring his curfew altogether, set up a Payway account as a means of circumventing his parent's control of his finances, and came home smelling of alcohol or pot.

"Was he getting it from Manish?" Khleang asked.

"We weren't sure," Sarah said. "Maybe."

"Who else?"

"Some boys. Kids his own age, or Ben Coutts. Or Elizabeth Moy."

"Who are they?"

"Wunderkind," Elsie said. "We knew them from the school."

"Do you still hang out with them?"

Elsie's eyes flashed. "*I* don't hang out with them. *Gabe* hung out with them."

"You don't like them much?" Mueller asked.

She looked away. "No. Not really."

Sarah reached over and rubbed her daughter's arm. "Elsie never got along with Benjamin. They got into some fights at school when they were little. Now, ten years later ..."

"He's a fucking asshole," Elsie said. "Always was, always will be."

Finally Gabriel told them about his relationship with Manish. He said they were in love. One night he didn't come home at all, and when they called it was obvious he was at Manish's apartment.

They fought about it. They threatened, they cajoled. When that didn't work, they called Manish and threatened and cajoled him. Manish, though, was an altogether different breed than his predecessor in Gabriel's affections. He said that if the Leberers reported him to the police, he would challenge any arrest, pointing out that the ruling on the wunderkind's age of majority had never been tested at a higher level than a circuit court. He had spoken with some lawyers who were certain that it would be struck down. By law, he said, Gabriel was an adult, even if his body lagged behind his brain. Meanwhile, the media would descend, and the minutiae of their lives would be cast about the internet for the masses to cluck at.

On the other hand, they could let go of Gabriel a little, and trust Manish a little, and accept that Gabe simply was not and never would be an entirely ordinary boy.

Mueller and Khleang had many questions, and the answers were often long. Sometimes the parents would begin talking about Gabriel and become caught up in their stories and talk on until they began to cry, Daniel especially. Sarah cried too, but Elsie never did, and said comparatively little. Was that normal?

Was she always so reserved? Mueller found her unreadable, her reactions a mystery. What was the child, what the twenty-four-year-old within?

At five-thirty Mueller and Khleang received a call from Deena Harrod. They didn't answer, but Khleang flicked him a private message: *We should wrap this up*. He signaled his agreement with a glance and a tiny nod and at the next pause apologized and said they needed to go.

"So obviously Manish hasn't turned up while we've been sitting here?" said Daniel.

Mueller shook his head. "No."

"We will find him," Khleang said. "It's only a matter of time."

The father started to voice some objection, but was cut off by his daughter: "Finding Manish won't bring Gabriel back, Dad." He looked and her and his head dropped, his eyes again filling with tears. Time to go.

They drove just around the corner while they contacted Harrod, mostly so the Leberers wouldn't see them sitting in their auto while they talked and think they were doing nothing.

"I don't think the kid was killed by the puncture wound," Harrod said without preamble. "It's not one hundred percent, but it looks like he may have been stabbed post mortem." She reviewed the details, citing the minimal blood loss that they had noted at the scene. On the other hand, the wound had been incurred very soon after death, within half an hour.

"So what *did* kill him?" asked Mueller.

"That's not as clear, but it's probably drug-related."

"You ran a tox screen earlier," Khleang said. "Didn't it show then?"

The answer was yes and no. The initial tox screen had shown RDMA and Serenex, but neither of those, or both together, was likely to have caused a fatal reaction. But a third chemical, called deletrium, had combined with the other two to act as a powerful depressant, shutting down the boy's central nervous system. First he had fallen asleep, then he stopped breathing. The deletrium was present only in trace amounts, but it had been enough.

"It's like a key fitting into a lock," Khleang said, looking at the models.

"I know, right?" Harrod said, with a touch of enthusiasm. "What are the odds?"

"You tell me," Mueller said. "What are the odds?"

Harrod shrugged. "Tiny. But then again, people have fatal drug interactions all the time. It could just be bad luck."

"All of which begs the question, what is it? Where'd it come from? Who gave it to him?"

Harrod shook her head. "I doubt anyone gave it to him. We're talking parts per million here. There's a good chance it's an accidental exposure. As for what it is, from what I can tell it's some kind of aerosol used in manufacturing. Beyond that, you tell me. You're the detectives."

They ended the call and talked it over, sitting in the auto. The rain had started again, the sky darkening toward night, the fine mist speckling the windows. Khleang turned on the heat. "You realize this could mess with our warrant," she said.

"Because the death may have been accidental."

"And more to the point, wasn't caused by a stabbing."

"It's still attempted murder. And about three other charges. We could get a warrant on that basis alone."

A boy takes an ecstatic drug with his older partner. Afterward the boy falls asleep, moving deeper and deeper into the land of night until he passes a final boundary and cannot return. His partner, meanwhile, awakens, or rises from a feigned sleep; he stalks into the kitchen, mind ablaze with what fury, what betrayal? He selects a blade, thin and cruel, glittering silver in the low light, and returns to the bed, where the boy lies face down, unmoving. He positions the knife over the ribs, grimacing, and with a grunt or a cry thrusts it into the boy's heart. But the boy issues no scream of pain, his body fails to jerk with violent death. He just lies there, until the man withdraws the knife, and at the sight of blood comes to his senses, the drugged fog clearing, the realization of what he's done pounding across his brain. He drags the boy down the freight elevator to the garage, calls a car and heads toward the hospital he himself attends, in Capitol Hill. Halfway there, two fingers at the boy's pulse, he sees it is useless; the boy is dead; his only hope for freedom is flight. He never suspects that his murderous rage has been only an afterthought, a footnote to an accident.

Careful, Mueller thought. Imagined scenarios were the enemy of reality. Better to wait and see; better to clear your mind and be fully receptive to what is.

Better to know your suspect so well that you would naturally anticipate where they would go and what they would do when faced with extreme situations. In this, they'd only just begun. Really, it was just as Mueller had long suspected: AI assistance had bred reliance upon those systems. Deprived of it, they faced an unhealthy, rapidly mounting frustration. In an age when cases were usually resolved in minutes or hours, arrests a matter of running a search and tapping a destination on a map, the idea that a crime might require weeks or months of assiduous work to understand became unacceptable in the minds of those involved.

Careful again. If they were unlucky or careless, that frustration could be directed at the investigators, and not at the crime.

"I'm going to have to roll home pretty soon," Khleang said. "You know, say hi to my family and all that. How about you?"

He considered. "We should at least check out the vehicle. Or I should. You can look at the recording whenever."

"You're going to make me look bad, if you put in overtime and I don't."

"Not at all. We're a team. What one knows, all know."

The municipal auto Gill had taken the previous night was being held in a secure underground garage, one of five, in the main station in Cap Hill. The tech who met him there turned out to be one of the guys from the apartment, name of Robbie Oda, who called over some mobile spotlights before doing his scan of the interior. In any case there was nothing much to see inside. The flagging for cleanliness Mueller had noted earlier ended up being for some fast food trash someone had left on the floor of the auto. "Any blood?" Mueller asked.

"Not inside the cab," Oda replied. "Got some fingerprints on the doors, that's about it."

The trunk was a different story. When they saw the baby-blue top sheet inside it they stood back like mourners before an open casket. Oda lifted his scanner and UV light shone out of it, flicking up and down rapidly. "That's blood," he said, nodding at the dark stains spotting the sheet.

"He put him in the trunk," Mueller murmured.

"He did indeed. Is that significant?"

"Yes." Because it implied that Gill knew Gabriel was dead before he ever got into the car. Had the boy been alive, Gill would have pulled him into the cab with him. He had never intended to go to a hospital. "Be sure to check the DNA on the straw on the soda cup, will you?" Because the only thing colder than stabbing someone and dumping their body in an alley is stopping by a Taco Bell afterward for nachos and a root beer.

When Mueller entered the apartment he heard Christian moving around in the living room, but there was no word of greeting from his mate. "Hello!" he called.

"*Valkyria!*" was the urgent response. "*Cura res!*"

"*Valkyria* to you too." He took off his shoes, threw his handset and specs in the charger bowl on the hall table, and turned the corner to see his beloved jumping around the living room, weaving and dodging and flicking arcane signs with his fingers. His contacts had gone the true black of full immersion, giving him an eerie vampiric visage. Chris was wearing navy blue athletic pants with white stripes down the side and a gray cotton T-shirt with a griffin printed on it in dark red ink. Mueller took a moment to admire Chris's long, lean figure, the play of his forearm muscles as he gestured, the deep tan of his skin (artificially acquired – Chris had a streak of frank vanity that Mueller didn't exactly encourage but didn't protest either). When Chris finally paused in his movements, Mueller said, "Hey!"

Chris jumped and made the time-out sign. "Pause," he said, redundantly. Another flick, and his contacts cleared, showing brown eyes that immediately focused on Mueller. "Hey! Didn't hear you come in."

"I know. You were –" Mueller chopped the air with both hands, jokingly. "Doing your moves."

Chris grinned. "Duelist. I was whipping this guy."

"I bet." Mueller leaned in, gave him a kiss. Damp sweat on Chris's arm where Mueller touched it. "You've been playing a while."

"Yeah, a bit. You want to play? We could do doubles."

"No, that's okay. Give me a minute to chill out. Then I'll probably make dinner." Too late for yoga.

"Sure, sounds good." Chris stood there uncertainly.

Mueller waved. "Go ahead, finish your game."

Chris grinned again. "Okay. If I wait too long I have to forfeit, you know." He flicked his hand and his contacts darkened again, sealing him off from the room he was in and plunging him into one of Duelist's environments. The game was decades old by now, but constantly updated, altered and elaborated upon, with a vast host of characters, races and classes you could customize to no end. The concept was simple. Basically you stood across from an opponent and cast spells via a combination of gestures and voice commands. They would do likewise, and a storm of arcane energies would fly between the two players until one or the other was blasted into the void. The dividing line between the two players prevented a break in the illusion, since no haptic contact was needed, and the game would scan the room you were in and alter the environment accordingly to prevent you from smashing into something you couldn't even see.

Maybe later Mueller would join him for a game, but probably not. Chris had partners online he could team with if he wanted to, players more at his skill level. Mueller would just slow him down. Anyway, while he thought he understood his partner's love of games, it was something he preferred to limit for himself.

Mueller fixed two simple salads for himself and Chris, mixed greens, avocado, feta, chickpeas, goddess dressing. A thick slice of boule on the side for filler. When Chris came out they sat at the small kitchen table and ate. "You play Lore, don't you?" Mueller asked.

"*Mostly* I play Lore," Chris said. "I just play Duelist when I want a little more physicality. When you play Duelist, you've got to stand up, move fast, which keeps you fit. Whereas most people play Lore sitting on their couch, which has the opposite effect."

"So I have this case..." Mueller explained, in minimal detail, about Gill and Gabriel playing Lore together. "But we don't have full access to their accounts. Is there any way to get it?"

Chris's eyebrows shot up. "You mean like, hack into Evreware's servers? Can't you just request the data?"

"Maybe, maybe not. I was just wondering."

A shake of the head. "If you don't already have access, you're not going to get it without a warrant. Evreware's pretty serious about privacy. I mean, people live their lives in Naxos. Social connections, financial transactions, bank accounts... if someone's really into the game, Evreware knows everything about them. They know your eye color and the shape of your dick, literally.

And their AIs are huge. Probably better than the military's. There's no way you're getting in without their knowledge."

"All right. I was just curious."

"Of course... if you just want some basic info, there are more traditional avenues of investigation."

"What do you mean?"

He shrugged. "You know these guys' usernames?"

"Sure. One second." Mueller flicked, realized his specs were in the charging dish, leaned over to a wall screen and sorted through windows until he found it. "Here. Olsol of Hangrin. Gabriel's avatar."

"Got it." In a moment Chris had found Gabriel's character profile and put it onscreen. The animation showed a elven figure in heavy armor of steel and gold with highlights of pale glowing blue, its architecture and joints suggesting something nearly robotic. He was seated upon an eight-legged horse, itself similarly armored, and in his right hand he swung a enormous hammer whose head was a black cylinder of rough-hewn rock. The face of this warrior, however, was recognizably Gabriel's, and his golden hair was held back by a golden circlet in the form of a serpent eating its tail.

"Nice mount," Chris said admiringly. "Some kind of enhanced Thydril. Nice armor, too. You know, this guy's playing at a very high level. World-class."

"Cool," Mueller said drily. "How about Gill? Name's Anaxarchos of Milasa."

Anaxarchos was a lich warlock, blue eyes burning from beneath an ornate black cowl filigreed with silvery circuit patterns, transparent ghost hands holding the reins of a giant snake made of smoke and flames.

"Also powerful. Not remotely the number of followers Olsol has, but that mount makes my dick hard. Better than the Thydril, you ask me. Naga like that can tunnel through space, let you teleport, basically." He flicked through the profile some more. "This might be something. He's a member of Inversus."

"Who?"

"Inversus. They're a guild."

"Ah. For the game."

"Well, yeah. But a guild isn't just for gaming. The best guilds are whole social networks, like real-life fraternities. There's an application process, entry requirements, ongoing membership requirements, dues. They tend to specialize. Like there'll be a guild for plumbers, say, or gay strippers, or people who love Siamese cats, whatever. These guys..." He pointed at the lich. "They're hackers. White hats."

Mueller looked appraisingly at the figure. "His hat's black." Chris rolled his eyes. "Who says they're white hats, though?"

"They do."

"How do you know they're not ripping people off on the side?"

"I don't. Hell, they probably are."

"So why do you say they're white hats?"

Chris laughed. "Maybe these guys are ripping off this company or that, or killing their AIs or whatever. But the black hats are murdering people for money in the third world. It's all relative."

Mueller rose the next morning at five-thirty, as was his habit on workdays. Friday today. As he washed his face he wondered what the weekend would bring.

He went into the study in his sweats, arranged his meditation mat and sitting cushion, and lit a stick of incense at the little altar. The porcelain Kannon looked serenely down at him from her shelf. Still dark outside, the occasional wet susurrus of a car passing on the street as the city roused itself from slumber. A lot of stuff to do today. They'd have to prioritize. He started mentally making a list, let it go, redirecting his attention to his slow and steady breath, the sound of a door opening and closing in the hallway. Tried to keep his eyes open, let that go too, sat with them closed until the bell sounded from the wall speakers at the end of forty minutes.

Chris still hadn't gotten up by the time Mueller walked out the door at seven-thirty. Chris had never been an early riser. They'd been together five years now, but sometimes Mueller still wondered how long it would last. He had long felt that while he understood Chris well enough, Chris had never entirely understood *him*. They had some shared interests – travel, exercise – and similar tastes in movies and music. They were both atheist, both vegetarian. And certainly Mueller continued to be attracted to him, to the point where he wondered if that physical desire was really at the core of their relationship. Was that enough? Maybe it was, if you treated each other well.

But part of him kept half-expecting Chris to just... get bored. To wake up one morning, realize he wasn't interested in this old guy anymore, pack his stuff and move on. But maybe that was just Mueller's own insecurity talking.

He walked to work, as was his habit. Hobos, anarchist kids, still camped out under the trees at Cal Anderson. If the weather turned any colder they'd have to find warmer lodgings. A cyclist passing him, armored in a tight-fitting cap and fluorescent gloves, rolling through the crosswalk. Time was there'd been a traffic light there. It had been removed a few years ago; the autos were programmed to slow down at that point, stopping only if needed.

Khleang was ten minutes late. "Sorry, Drake's sick. Threw up all over the couch. Felt bad leaving Jaret with it."

"Is he okay?"

"He's fine, probably the flu or something. Jaret's handling it. Let's talk about what we're doing today. I'm feeling a little anxious about it."

Gill had not surfaced overnight, furthering the likelihood that he had found a way out of the state, and more remarkably, out of Themis's gaze. This left them to work the case in the old way, following up on questions, interviewing person after person, trying to understand what had happened and why, and determine where he had gone from traces too subtle for even the bloodhound net of the AIs to sniff, from the aether of motive and capability.

First priority was interviewing Gill's mother, Nita Gill, who lived up in Shoreline. As they were getting their things together to leave, however, they were accosted by Willie White, his torso bulging from the cheap suit he wore like the bow of a barge. "Leaving so soon? You just got here."

"Well, the case is out *there*," Khleang said snarkily. "You know, witnesses, evidence, that kind of stuff? Maybe you've heard of it?"

"Maybe. So where's Gill?"

Khleang rolled her eyes. "He's not *here*, that's for sure."

"I *know* he's not here. I saw the scene by the highway. I want theories. Ideas. Where'd he go? How'd he do it? Why can't Themis find him?"

Khleang pursed her lips, obviously preparing a further retort, and Mueller diplomatically stepped into the gap. "Will, it would be premature at this point to say. If we voice a theory, we risk committing further resources to it. The theory starts directing the investigation instead of the other way around."

"I need *something*," White said. "Got another call from the chief this morning, checking up, and I had no idea what to tell him. It looks like we're sitting on our hands."

Mueller sighed. "Give us til the end of today. Could be he'll pop up. If not, fine. We'll have a *theory*."

White gave him a hard look with his frog eyes. "Four o'clock. Then we talk." He stumped off down the hall.

"Guy's a poet and he don't even know it," Khleang said.

Nita Gill lived in a nice enough townhouse, her husband long since deceased. But she seemed to know nothing, and by all appearances Manish had made no attempt to contact her since Gabriel's death. "I don't know," she said over and over, sitting primly upright, eyes wide. "Manish is a good boy. He would never hurt anybody."

"Think she knows anything she's not saying?" Mueller asked his partner afterward.

"Nah. Nothing. Worth keeping on eye on her, though. He might try to make contact eventually."

Item number two was the deletrium, which after all had actually killed Gabriel Leberer. The bottle on which it had been dusted was an ordinary amber prescription bottle with the label torn off. There were several fingerprints on the plastic. Most were Gabriel's, which meant they may have been wrong in their assumption that Gill had purchased the drugs. The other print was a partial; while too incomplete for a perfect match, Themis identified it as most likely belonging to Ben Coutts. The ID that came up showed a pimply red-headed kid of twelve.

"Great, another wunderkind," Khleang said. "Can't wait to see what he's like. No doubt a perfectly well-adjusted young man."

"Doesn't look like it. Multiple charges for vandalism, petty theft, breaking and entering... he's been a bad widdle boy." And now, it seemed, he had moved on to drug dealing.

The Coutts kid lived way south, down by SeaTac at 179th. Dilapidated ranch house in awkward aqua, chain-link fence around an untended yard that was nevertheless green from the winter rain. Camper shell squatting outside the fence, for a truck that had probably been scrapped twenty years ago. A blank-eyed owl cut from rusting iron greeted them at the fence gate.

The door was answered first by a barking German shepherd and then by a tired-looking woman wearing blue jeans and a shapeless gray sweatshirt from a charity run five years past. Her red hair marked her as, in all likelihood, the kid's mother. "Good morning," Mueller began. "Are you Rebecca Coutts?"

She raised a plucked eyebrow, lips pursing in irritation. "Let me guess. Seattle PD. You're here for Ben."

"We need to talk to him," Mueller agreed. "Is he here?"

"What'd he do this time?"

"He's not being charged with anything. We just need to talk to him."

She stood aside and waved them into the house, sighing long-sufferingly. "He's downstairs. Playing video games. That's really all he does. All he cares about. We try to get him to go outside, go to school, get him interested in anything, but all he wants to do is sit in a dark basement with his contacts blacked out and his earbuds on high. If we want to talk to him we have to send him a message. Which he'll ignore. Then at nine he'll disappear, come back whenever he feels like it." She shook her head.

"Kids can be difficult," Mueller ventured.

"You have no idea." She opened the basement door for them and gestured them down.

True to her description, the lights downstairs weren't on and the basement was dark, the only illumination coming from a couple of small window wells on the west and east sides of the basement. Ben Coutts was sitting on the couch in the darker of the two rooms, hands flicking rapidly, his subvocalized commands a stream of low muttering.

"Ben!" his mother called. When he didn't respond, she reached out and pinched his shoulder. He emitted a little curse in surprise, said "Pause," and his contacts cleared. "Jesus Christ, Mom, don't *do* that, you have no idea what I'm..." His rebuke cut off abruptly when his eyes finally focused on the two officers standing behind her. "Who are they?"

"They're the *police*, and they want to talk to you. What did you do this time?"

His eyes darted between the detectives and his mother. "I'm not talking with her in the room."

71

She made a *psh* of irritation, throwing her hands in the air. "You see how he is? It's always like this. Every time you try to talk to him –"

"That's because *you treat me like a child!*" the boy yelled. He jabbed a finger at the dog, lying near the stairs. "You treat *Lacy* with more respect than me. Now get out! Go!"

"Good luck," Rebecca Coutts said bitterly, and went upstairs.

Ben sagged back into the cushions, right hand rising to flick signals at his system. His red hair was much longer than in his photo, tied in a greasy ponytail that fell down his back. His jaw was triangular, cheeks freckled, ears big, arms thin and wiry. He looked like a boy, but the sense of weariness and the redness of his eyes said otherwise. "Sorry," he said curtly. "Dumb bitch. Also, I'm kind of busy right now, so can we make this quick?"

"She's your mother," Khleang said, arms crossed. "You don't think she deserves a minimal amount of respect?"

"What, like I chose her from the mom catalogue? Sorry, I'm not going to congratulate her for just reproducing. Having a kid isn't an accomplishment. It's not like writing a book or climbing a mountain. It's just biology. Pigs do it, rats do it, insects and reptiles and fucking flamingos do it. Some guy stuck his dick in you. Awesome. Good job."

"You live in her house."

"I pay rent," he snapped. "I'd get my own place if it weren't for some serious inconsistencies in our legal system."

This was going nowhere, Mueller thought. "We're here to talk to you about Gabriel Leberer."

"I figured." Still he flicked, hands in constant motion, eyes fixed on his system.

"Are you aware that he died the night before last?" Khleang said.

"Sure. That's what I meant when I said I figured."

"How did you hear about it?"

He rolled his eyes. "Little thing called the internet? Heard of it?"

"Specifically how did you hear about it?"

He shrugged. "Playing Lore. Guy named Krakn told me."

"When did he tell you?"

"I don't know, yesterday morning? What does it matter?"

"We haven't made any public statements. How did he know Gabriel was dead?"

He snorted. "What year are you living in? Someone dumps a body in an alley, people talk. They take videos. They track your auto back to the Leberer's house. Someone in the family calls a relative or a friend to let them know, and that person talks. Or maybe it was one of you, someone in the police department. It doesn't matter. The whole world knew Gabe was dead by like, ten a.m. yesterday."

Move on. Mueller asked, "When was the last time you saw him?"

"I don't know. Last week?"

"Where did you see him?"

"Right here."

"Did you sell him some drugs?"

A little smirk appeared on Coutts' face. "Do I look like a drug dealer to you?"

"Your fingerprints were on the bottle. A little prescription bottle that the drugs were in."

The smirk turned to a scowl. "Doesn't mean anything. Gabe probably swiped it when he came over."

Khleang gave him a hard stare. "This'll go a lot better for you if you cooperate. If you don't, we'll get a warrant and search this place, see what we come up with. Maybe confiscate your computer, see what's on that."

Coutts looked at her, saw she wasn't joking, shook his head in irritation. "Look, can we go somewhere else? This place –" He shook his head at the basement. "It's just depressing. Also, like I said, I'm in the middle of something."

"Where do you want to go?"

He flicked a hand and an invite appeared in their fields. The two officers exchanged a glance and Mueller shrugged. If it made the kid more comfortable, he couldn't see any harm in it. He accepted the invite and the room darkened to black.

When it brightened again they were in a tower. The room was roughly the same size as the basement they'd been in, but the ceilings were much higher, and arched windows open to the air ran all along the west wall. Through them he could see a vista of plains and distant mountains, with a broad river flowing nearby. He stepped over to a window and looked down. There seemed to be a sizable army encamped around the tower, assembled in units of cavalry, pikemen, archers, and vees of flying cavalry circling in the sky. The sun was a hand's width over the mountains and sparkled on the river.

The room itself was richly appointed in baroque style, some kind of pointy crest inscribed on the marble floor, Coutts slouching on a golden throne before them. He was dressed in semitranslucent green armor that appeared cut from dark emeralds, and a black cloak was draped over his shoulders. His gloved hands shimmered with orange fire, echoing his hair, which here flickered and flared in a spiky upright style like something alive. He was also taller, broad-shouldered, muscular, an older, idealized version of his young self. Mueller looked down, saw to his amusement that his own slacks and overcoat had been transformed into medieval finery, doublet and hose. Khleang was similarly attired.

"This is Lore, right?" Mueller asked.

Coutts grinned. In making the transition here his demeanor had instantly changed from boyish sulk to easy arrogance. "Welcome to Naxos. I take it you don't play."

"My boyfriend does. I've watched a few times."

"What's his username? I'll send him a present." He snapped

his fingers twice and a sword appeared floating in the air before him.

"Better not," Mueller replied. "There are police regulations about receiving gifts." Although Chris would probably enjoy it. "Is this your place?"

"It's the Tower of Amanthus. And yes, I control it."

"Is that like, a big deal?" Khleang asked.

"Yes," Coutts said. He nodded toward the window. "You see that army out there?"

She stepped a couple paces and looked over the edge. "What about it?"

"It's mine. We're about to invade Daggoran."

She raised an eyebrow. "So?"

"So I'm the fucking *general* here. And right now there's about twenty people all trying to talk to me while I'm piddling around here with *you*. And another twenty thousand or so down there waiting for us to give the word and move out."

She squinted again at the crowd below. "You mean those are all real people?"

"Yes! So whatever you're going to ask, can you make it snappy, please? Otherwise I could be deposed."

She snorted and sat down on a gilded chair, which not coincidentally was a real chair in the basement, and crossed her arms. "Your friend's dead, and all you want is to get back to your video game?" He started to say something and she talked right over him. "We'll take as long as we need. And if we have to go down to the station to do it, we will. We've got interview rooms there that work as Faraday cages, did you know that? No more internets."

He rolled his eyes. "It's fine, whatever. What did you want to ask me?"

"Did you sell RDMA to Gabriel?"

"If I say yes, are you going to arrest me?" His hand reached out and flicked at something. Messages, probably.

Mueller and Khleang exchanged a glance. "No," Mueller answered. "Not if you cooperate."

"Then yes. Last week. Next question."

"Where'd you get it?"

"From a guy. And I'm not telling you who it is. He'd be seriously pissed if you go knocking down his door." His hands flicked again, eyes focused on unseen motes.

Mueller shrugged. It probably didn't matter that much, and if necessary they could run Inference on it. "Where'd you get the bottle it was in?"

Coutts frowned. "What?"

"The bottle," Khleang said. "A little prescription bottle. Like this." A mote of the bottle appeared in her hand and she tossed it to him. He caught it, looked at it and shrugged.

"It's my dad's. I don't know, one of his prescriptions. I peeled off the label. I needed something to put the pills in, and it seemed better than a plastic baggie."

"Did you know what was in it?"

"I don't know, I think his ulcer medication?"

"Do you know what deletrium is?"

Mueller watched the boy's expression closely, but saw only puzzlement and irritation. "Never heard of it. Why?"

"The bottle was coated with it," Khleang said. "Gabriel died of it."

Coutts' hands fell to his sides as he looked at her in surprise. "What? You don't think..."

"You handled the bottle last. And you knew what else you were giving him. Did you know Gabriel was also taking Serenex?"

"Sure I knew. But I thought he was stabbed. Everyone says it was his boyfriend."

"How do you know that?" Mueller asked, genuinely curious.

Coutts shook his head in dismissal. "Like I said, it's all over the internet. Ask anyone. But I don't know anything about something being on the bottle. It was just a pill bottle." He rapidly drew a sigil in the air, smokeless lines of fire following his burning forefinger. This was accompanied by a rapid tapping motion with his left, and a transparent shield with hexagonal facets appeared at his side.

"Maybe we should go to the station," Khleang said, obviously annoyed that they didn't have the kid's full attention. "I'm not sure you're appreciating the seriousness of the situation."

"No, I get it!" Coutts protested, but without stopping his activity. Items and icons were appearing all around him, buffs and enchantments, a crown of green fire on his brow, a screaming wyvern suddenly landing on a perch outside. "I know it's some serious shit, and I'm sorry Gabe is dead, but I can't just stop what I'm doing. I've been working on this for months. Come back tomorrow."

A volley of coronets sounded outside, and they heard the clangor of weapons being struck against shields. Khleang looked at Mueller. "What do you think?"

Her subtext, of course, being: Do we cut short his online party and bring him in? "You said it's your dad's prescription?"

"That's what I said."

"Where is he now?"

"He's at work, like always."

"Where's that?"

"Anodynamics. Out by Boeing." The noise outside had coalesced into a chant, a single word or name repeated: *cogent,* maybe, or *Kojin.* With a flourish and a sudden downward sweep of his arms, Coutts' avatar struck the ground with his fists and a wave of green energy bounded outward, igniting the emerald of his breastplate so his whole figure was a rippling incandescent green against the darkness of his cloak. "I've got to go. Good luck and all that." With that he ran and leapt out of the open window onto the wyvern's back. It reared once, shrieked like a raptor, and with a great flap of its wings launched into the air over the waiting horde.

Immediately Khleang cut the connection and disappeared from the room. Mueller followed suit, finding Coutts still seated on the couch, raising an unseen sword with his spindly arm and yelling some battle cry *sotto voce.*

"Looks like fun."

Khleang shook her head. "Kid's a total snot."

He shrugged. "He's a kid."

Anodynamics manufactured waldoes, mechanical hands and arms used in factories around the world. On the way over Mueller wondered idly why then the waldoes didn't assemble themselves in the factory; the answer, it turned out, was that they did. The assembly process was almost entirely automated, they were told by a man whose title may have been shop steward or robotics engineer (it wasn't clear where he stood in the company hierarchy). Parts were delivered by self-driving trucks, unloaded by self-driving forklifts, and assembled by self-directed robots to form more robots. If the raw materials hadn't been extracted from a hundred different sites around the globe, they could very nearly have made a self-replicating factory, like the one on its way to Mars.

"Sort of the thing about waldoes," the steward said as they wound their way through the enormous hangar-sized factory, machines whirring, buzzing, cutting and drilling all around them. Safe pathways for humans were marked in green footprints, like in the halls of an elementary school. "They can do most anything a human can. More, really."

This raised the further question of what function a human served in this land of machines. At first, seeing Lionel Coutts lying awkwardly on his side on the floor, crowded by bulky, unmoving machines, reaching with some device into a recess of concrete and steel, Mueller thought he might be performing repairs. Then he realized the device was in fact a small vacuum cleaner. Ben Coutts's father was, in effect, a janitor.

"Couldn't you just have a robot do that, too?" Mueller asked the steward, his voice relayed over the sound-canceling protective headphones they wore.

The man, whose name was Richard Bai, looked embarrassed. "Sometimes it's hard to reach into the corners. Or it needs degreaser or whatever. I guess someone upstairs did the math, decided it was cheaper just to pay somebody." He raised his voice. "Lionel. Some people here to see you."

Lionel turned his head at an angle, frowned at them, and began inchworming his way out from the machines. He was a small man with deeply receding brown hair and a heavily lined forehead, thin lips, hints of the son in the protuberant narrow chin. He wore a one-piece gray coverall now smudged brown with dust along the right side.

As he was brushing this off half-heartedly, he asked with a suspicious look what was going on. When Mueller and Khleang introduced themselves, he said, "Is it about Ben?"

"Sort of," Mueller admitted. "But only indirectly." He explained about the bottle Ben had given Gabriel and the traces of deletrium found on it.

"Yeah, it's my ulcer medication," Lionel said. "I don't know about the other stuff, though. I keep the bottle in my pocket." He reached into a cargo pocket and showed them a small bottle, identical to the one they'd found. "You can see, it's sealed. I don't know how anything could get into it."

"Anyway deletrium's not dangerous in small amounts," Bai objected. "It's not like it's good for you, but you'd have to consume a lot for it to kill you."

"It acted in combination with other drugs," Khleang explained. This seemed to shut him up, or maybe ease his fears about company liability. Mueller expected Lionel to ask which drugs they meant, but he just frowned and kept quiet, maybe because he didn't want his superior hearing about his son's habits. "You use deletrium here in the factory, then?"

"We do," Bai confirmed. "It gets sprayed on some of the joints before they receive their final low-friction polymer. Two-part process. It's standard in the industry."

"Can we see?" Khleang asked.

Reluctantly he led them along another green-footprint pathway. They stopped before a rapidly moving assembly line, largely enclosed in plexiglass. A small metal door rose and fell with a rapid regular rhythm, like a busy little guillotine. The pieces being worked on looked like partially assembled arms, complex knobby structures jutting from a white cylinder like the carpals of a severed wrist. As each waldo entered the chamber, the door shut and the carpals received a silvery spray of aerodized deletrium. It moved on, was heated briefly to fix the spray to the part, and exited the box two yards down to receive more attention from a pair of whirling waldoes.

"You can see, it's totally contained. The whole factory's in compliance with OSHA standards. I don't see how it even could have gotten on a bottle, unless he dropped it on the line."

"Have you done any work over here at all recently?" Khleang asked. "Like in the past few months?"

"Sure," Lionel answered. "I sweep through here at least once a week."

"Any time you can recall working by this machine specifically?"

He exhaled noisily. "Maybe a month, six weeks ago, I don't know, one of the loads on the carts wasn't secured properly, and it overturned. Sent these little thingamajigs rolling all over the floor. Spent a couple hours crawling around trying to vacuum them all up. There's probably still a few in the corners."

"Any chance you dropped your prescription on the line?"

He shook his head vigorously. "No. No way."

"It's almost the only way it could have happened," Khleang

said apologetically.

"I didn't drop it," Lionel insisted. "I'd have had to drop it on the line, have it go all the way through, and pick it up there." He pointed at the rapidly moving waldoes at the end of the line. "*That* I would remember. It never left my pocket."

"Did you maybe just *take* one while you were working?" Mueller asked. "Maybe your stomach was hurting, so you stopped vacuuming for a second?"

A scowl. "I usually only take one with lunch."

"Ever skip lunch?"

"I guess."

"Think it's possible you took one over by here?"

He shook his head again. "No. I really don't think so." But a touch of doubt had crept into his voice.

They inquired about surveillance in the factory, and while it seemed there were numerous cameras – most of the waldoes themselves had small lenses – the data was saved for no more than a day, it being useful only for tracking errors in production. There were security cameras at the few entrances to the factory, but they showed only that Lionel had shown up as usual; he hadn't missed a day in a year, he said.

Mueller nodded at the small metal door of the machine. "If this door was stuck, even for a second, would the spray reach over here? Even a little bit?"

"It might," Bai conceded. "There's a suction fan inside the machine that eliminates it in the second before the door opens. But you can see, it's working fine. There's no problem with it."

Certainly it had to be an enormously unfortunate coincidence, one way or the other. Either Lionel had indeed dropped the open bottle and retrieved it a moment later, and was lying about it (Khleang's opinion), or the protective enclosure and fan had failed at precisely the moment when Lionel was getting out a pill.

There was a third possibility, that Lionel had sprayed the

bottle's interior intentionally; that he had then passed it on to his son; that Ben had known what medications Gabriel was taking and had researched the fatal drug interaction; that father and son had colluded in murder. But Mueller couldn't see it. For Ben to kill his friend (who knows why?) wasn't beyond the realm of possibility; but for his father to partake in the crime, the absurdly complex scheme, was far-fetched. "It was an accident," Mueller said as they exited the building. "Just one of those things that happen. You know, a guy gets off work, he meets a friend at random in the street, talks to him for twenty minutes, then walks around the corner just as a brick falls from a building and cracks him on the head. You can say if his friend hadn't been there, he wouldn't have gotten hit on the head, but it's not the friend's fault. It's just how it happened."

"Unless someone kicked the brick loose," Khleang riposted.

Insight Tech: floors forty and forty-one of a new building in South Lake Union, fully modern, endless panes of solar glass enclosing a curving three-sided structure like a pyramid seen in a funhouse mirror. Behind the front desk was a wall of water that somehow stood upright of its own volition, faintly rippling, with the ripples in its center flowing to form the Insight logo, the warp-drive-inside-an-eye design. Probably not water at all, Mueller reflected: some gelatinous compound electrified in novel ways. They were greeted there by an actual human receptionist, a beautiful young woman who promptly contacted Anna Pessolano, the HR rep they'd spoken with the previous day.

Pessolano ghosted into the reception area wearing a very smart off-white pant suit with a coral scarf. Of course, she could dress her ghost however she liked; for all they knew she was standing in her kitchen in her underwear.

"Is it possible for us to see you in the flesh?" Mueller asked. "I know everyone ghosts it these days, but I still like the human touch."

Pessolano laughed pleasantly. "It's *possible,* sure. But it would involve you flying to New York. I'm at our other office there right now."

"Ah." You could always tell a ghost by the lighting, he reflected. The cameras in his specs did their best to detect the light sources around him and shade the figure to match, but they never looked quite right when projected into a real background. "Well, here's the thing. We badly need to speak with Manish Gill, and so far we're not having any luck finding him. We were hoping you could help us."

She nodded sympathetically. "I did speak with a number of people in the company, and of course we'd like to do anything we can to aid your investigation. Can you tell us exactly what you're looking for? How we can help you, that is?"

"Do you know where he is?" Khleang asked.

"No, we don't. We did try contacting him, repeatedly."

"Is there any indication of where he might have gone? Any indication in his emails, for instance?"

"There's nothing clearly indicated, no. We did check."

"Can we see his email?"

Pessolano's look of friendly concern was unwavering. "We can show you those communications not related to his current projects."

Mueller asked, "How many people work for Insight?"

"One second." She consulted with her system. "Forty-two."

"Does that include Gabriel Leberer?"

She shook her head in a semblance of unhappiness. "No. It's as of today."

"When we spoke previously, you didn't mention Gabriel at all. Which is to say, you didn't mention that he worked for your company."

She raised an eyebrow inquisitively. "Is that a question?"

"Why didn't you mention it?"

"You didn't ask." She wore an innocent look. "And with all

respect, it would be inappropriate for me to volunteer information about our employees. Understand that in my position I do sometimes field inquiries, and I have to be careful what I say. You might think that you as police are the only people seeking information, but we have cutting-edge projects here, scientists and programmers at the top of their fields. We also have competitors that will go to great lengths to steal or disrupt whatever we're working on. Even telling you the nature of our projects can affect the direction of research in other companies."

"Were Gabriel and Manish working on a sensitive project like that?"

She shrugged. "They wouldn't be working here if they weren't."

"But it had something to do with AIs," Khleang said.

A tight-lipped smile. "Manish's CV could tell you that."

Khleang was looking seriously irritated. "Maybe you don't quite understand why we need to know." She called up some photos, stills of the kid's body. Crumpled in the garbage bin, blue-lipped on the exam table, a close-up of the knife wound in his back. "Gabriel Leberer. Age twenty-six, though he looked twelve or thirteen. Your employee. Stabbed in the back by Manish Gill, also your employee. Now. Do you have any idea why Gill would do something like that? Any insights at all?"

"No, I'm sorry. I wasn't close to either one, you know."

Mueller asked, "Who was? To Manish, first? Did he have friends among the staff?"

"I couldn't say."

"Were there others on their team?"

She considered the question, calling up a window. Finally she relented, giving them two names: Young-Soo Eum and Gillian Garcy. Eum was in the building; Garcy was at home but reachable by internet. Pessolano showed them to Eum's office and before she rang off asked them to keep her informed as to the progress of the investigation. "We're naturally very concerned."

Young-Soo was of an indefinite age, dressed in that careful corporate semi-casual style of slacks and button-up shirt, standing in an uncluttered, nearly bare office dominated by a treadmill workstation with multiple video screens positioned around it on adjustable arms, like the splayed forearms of a spider about to seize its victim in a flickering embrace. Floor-to-ceiling windows on the far wall with views of downtown. He was trim and neat, dark hair cut with what may well have been machine precision.

He stood facing them with arms crossed, his manner apprehensive. "I don't know where Manish is," he said with a faint Korean accent. "I have no idea." He further had no idea why Manish would ever want to hurt Gabriel; they were very good friends, he said. Best friends. He himself rarely saw either one outside of work. Had no idea about the details of their relationship, no knowledge of drug use.

"Did you ever hang out with either one online?" Mueller asked. "Socially, I mean, not for work?"

"No..." Eum said hesitantly. "Sometimes I saw them playing Lore. Maybe I join their raiding party, or they ask for my help crafting an item. Or they help me find resources or design a spell."

Interesting. This, it turned out, was a fairly common occurrence, with Eum joining them in Naxos once or twice a week. "But," he said, "everyone in tech plays Lore."

"And Gill has a pretty powerful character, I hear," said Mueller.

"Yeah, lich warlock. Some very cool spells. But Gabe is even stronger."

"He was?"

Eum nodded, a touch of gamer enthusiasm blooming in his voice. "Oh yeah. Super powerful. Olsol of Hangrin. Lord Invictus. His war hammer, called Omphalos, absolutely unstoppable. His mount, too, big Thydril, immune to magic attacks. He was on a big campaign to conquer Telladia. Maybe five hundred K followers."

"Followers being... actual people."

He laughed. "Yeah. Real people. Gabriel was top player on all West Coast. Now..." He shrugged. "It gets divided up. New factions, new leaders."

Gillian Garcy had even less to say. She ghosted into her office wearing a skirt and blouse, lounging on a chair, and this time Mueller would have bet she actually was in her sweats at home. Face and body rounded but not unpleasant, what one could call buxom, but then that too could be an artifact of her system, slimming her down or pumping her up. Red lipstick, hair likewise dark red, obviously dyed, deep eyeshadow. This was what he hated about ghosting: difficult to form a real impression of a person when their system masked their appearance. "I can't tell you much," she said immediately. "Though I think it's a fucking shame what happened to Gabe."

She too rarely hung out with the pair, admitting that most often she stayed at her home in Tacoma. Too long of a commute, and the work was all programming anyway. "Gabe was brilliant, though. Really a prodigy. It's terrible."

"What about Manish?" Mueller asked. "What'd you think of him?"

She shrugged. "I don't know. Not much. Super smart, of course. I mean, a real programming wizard, total tech head. One of those guys that starts programming when he's five and never stops. Kind of a creepster."

"Can you think of any reason why someone would want to hurt Gabriel?" Khleang asked. "Maybe in regards to work?"

"Maybe," Garcy mused. "You never know. You always hear about corporate sabotage and stuff, but Insight keeps us pretty well protected. You think that's what this is?" The prospect seemed to excite her, but when pressed she had no specific idea of threats. "All the big companies have teams working on similar stuff, and lots of smaller ones too. Intel, Samsung, Cognition, they all have an interest. They'd all steal us away if they could."

"And what exactly is your role on the team?"

She smiled condescendingly. "I've already been briefed by corporate. I can talk to you about any personal relationship with Gabe or Manish, but not about our work. Sorry."

Mueller and Khleang exchanged a glance. "You've been very helpful," Mueller said.

"Totally," said Khleang, rolling her eyes.

"One last thing before we go," Mueller said. "Do you play Lore?"

Garcy shook her head. "No. You ask because all these guys are obsessed with it, right?"

"Something like that."

When Garcy's ghost vanished, Khleang turned to her partner. "You actually think there's some connection with the game?"

He shrugged, frowning. "I don't know. Could be. Could be just coincidence. People in social circles tend to have similar hobbies, play the same games. Makes me wonder..." He flipped through his recent contacts and called Michelle Gorman. After some pleasantries he asked his question: Had her husband played a game called Lore, by chance?

"He did, sure," she replied. "It was kind of funny, actually. He picked it up just a couple of months before he drowned. I know he used to play games when he was younger, but it was the first time I'd ever seen him play as an adult. I guess he got an urge."

"Did he play it a lot?"

She sighed. "Well, it seemed like a lot to me. Most nights he'd play for at least a few hours."

He thanked her and rang off, turning to Khleang. "Think there might be a connection now?"

"Maybe. Or it's just a really popular game."

"Or it was related to his work somehow."

"We don't even know what he was working on."

"Exactly."

They didn't bother to move the auto, letting it sit parked outside Insight's offices in South Lake Union. Upon the city the clouds hung like a lead apron. The auto was more their office than the cubicles assigned to them at the station, the empty coffee cups from the morning (Mueller, tall soy latte, Khleang, grande quad-shot mocha) and their bags in the back seat making it feel lived in and homey. Within it they crisscrossed the city, virtually and physically, expanding the investigation's scope with each new call and conversation, like ripples spreading outward from pebbles thrown one after the other. If they were lucky, those circles would soon begin to contract toward a new center. If they were unlucky, they would move out and out until finally all movement died away.

Now they threw another stone toward the Computer Crimes Division of the DoJ, for which Richard Gorman had worked. Gorman's investigation had apparently been rated highly sensitive, and to gain access to his files required coordinating requests between SPD, a federal judge, and at least three officials of the CCD.

The regional director of the CCD, Jay Downing, was recalcitrant. "Leaking these files could ruin this investigation. Which is ongoing. Nothing you've described, nothing you've told me, indicates a clear link between it and your case."

When it became clear Downing wasn't going to relent, Mueller thanked him for his time and rang off. "No luck?" Khleang said.

"I'm not done yet."

"How do you figure?"

"Sometimes you appeal to reason, sometimes you appeal to

rank."

She looked at him curiously as he made another call. He was put on hold a couple of minutes, but finally got through. "Micky! It's Tom. I have a favor to ask." The conversation ran on pleasantly and agreeably, the favor granted.

"Who was that?" Khleang asked after.

"Michelle Isley. Hawaii senator."

Her eyebrows rose. "You called a senator?"

"We grew up together."

"And she can get us access to the CCD's files?"

"No. But she'll call the assistant attorney general, and he or she will call this guy Downing, and *then,* if all goes well, we'll have access."

She chuckled appreciatively. "You never mentioned you knew a senator."

"You never asked. Besides, if I called her all the time asking for favors, she'd stop listening."

It was twenty minutes before Downing called back. "You've got highly placed friends," he said. To his credit he seemed more amused than anything.

"You could be one of them," Mueller joked, and Downing chuckled.

"Fine. You can look at the files. But seriously, if these get out through you, there'll be hell to pay. That means no hard copies, secure locations, secure lines. Got it?"

They got it. The folder was titled Virgil and it contained twenty-two folders inside. Each of these, in turn, contained dozens of files: text, audio and video. "This is big," Khleang observed. After some initial searches they found a summary of about twenty pages. They read it in silence for some time, absorbing its contents.

Virgil was, in brief, an arms-dealing investigation. It detailed inquiries into numerous pieces of illegal weaponry that had found their way into the States, military-grade weaponry of remarkable variety and sophistication, ranging from simple automatic weapons to depleted-uranium ammunition to exotic biological poisons. After many months, one individual in particular was identified as the source of some of these weapons. He was known only as Agnos: the name of a character in Lore.

"I knew it," Mueller said.

"You win."

It had taken a good deal of effort, it seemed, both to find Agnos in the first place, and then to construct a believable identity for a buyer, suborning a minor-league con named Robert Mikal. Through Mikal they arranged a series of exchanges. It was nearly impossible to contact Agnos directly for a purchase; to gain his trust, they first posed as sellers themselves, offering various seized weapons and selling only to their target. The ethics were questionable, but the items were carefully selected to limit blowback – no high explosives or such, mostly specialized drones and military armor.

In return they obtained high-grade firearms, low-grade explosives, and Agnos's trust. Through Mikal they let it be suggested that they were a sort of wealthy hobbyist, some paranoid billionaire with money to spend on deadly toys. With each exchange Gorman sought more information about the seller, finally succeeding in contacting Agnos directly, in Lore. Another exchange was arranged.

On offer, on Agnos's side, was twenty pounds of strontium-90, not much, really, but useful for construction of a dirty bomb, and absolutely illegal. What was offered by the department was nowhere recorded.

"Covering their asses," Khleang commented. "You don't write it down, you can't be blamed for what happens with it."

The exchange was planned for July 5, but it never took place. Because on July 3, Gorman drowned in a lake.

As was often the case with drownings, his death came as a

shock and surprise. He'd had no serious illnesses, no heart problems to indicate a risk. He'd just gone out swimming with his wife and some friends on a bright summer day at Green Lake. Hundreds of people had been at the lake that day, picnicking and jogging, pedaling rented paddleboats around the small body of water. Gorman had swum out past the crowd, probably wanting a little exercise. Had he struggled, had he yelled, he might still be alive. But instead he just slipped down into the water and disappeared.

It wasn't long before his wife, Michelle, began wondering where he'd gone, but at first she assumed he'd probably wandered off without telling her, to get an ice cream or a hot dog, or to use the portable toilets. When he didn't return after forty minutes, she got up and started looking. Mueller imagined the successive explanations presenting themselves to her mind: He ran into someone he knew. He didn't want to wait for the toilets here, so he went somewhere else. He's back at the car.

As each explanation failed, and minutes passed, the concern grew. The last time she had seen him had been in the water. After two hours her whole party was searching. It was one of them, a work friend of Michelle's, who talked to a lifeguard. At four-thirty a scuba diver hopped in off the pier. It wasn't a deep lake. Five anxious minutes later he rose, pulled out the mouthpiece, and spoke into his collar mike. The lifeguards starting yelling for everyone to leave the water, and Michelle Gorman starting crying.

The official cause of death was drowning, naturally, though the causation wasn't exactly clear. Most likely, the coroner said, Gorman had suffered a heart attack while swimming. Unable to cry out, clutching his chest, he had sunk beneath the water and never recovered. This diagnosis was complicated by the fact that cardiac arrest was part of the process of drowning. Alternative explanations included a brain aneurysm, stroke, or seizure of unknown cause, all dangerous on land and deadly in the water.

The CCD followed the police investigation closely, but in the end had nothing to add. Gorman's death was mysterious, but not altogether unusual. People just drowned sometimes. It was cosmically bad luck, and that was all. In any case, it was hard to see what anyone stood to gain by it. They had a well-attended memorial service, and the investigation into Agnos continued without him.

Continued fruitlessly, however. With Gorman's death Agnos shut down, the Lore character deleted. They had already tried working with Evreware to discover any information about that account's owner, but it was routed through several anonymous foreign servers uninterested in cooperating with them, a predictable dead end. That character had been the single point of contact with the weapons dealer.

It was all very suspicious, but if Agnos had something to do with Gorman's death, he had succeeded in evading any justice or trail. There was simply no detectable mechanism for the death, and Agnos had vanished from whence he came. There the investigation ended, to the extreme frustration of all involved.

Mueller called Michelle Gorman, marking the call as urgent, got her after a minute standing in a hallway at the school where she worked. "I'm in class," she said. "Can this wait?"

"One quick question," Mueller said. "Do you know your husband's username, offhand? In Lore?"

She said no, but she would try to get it for them. "Is this important somehow?"

"It might be. Anyway, it's helpful."

After the call Khleang said, "*Do* you think it's important?"

"I wasn't sure before. But now, yeah."

She smiled knowingly. "You want to play some video games?"

"It's not that we *want* to, Jackie. We *have* to."

Neither of them, however, had played Lore, notwithstanding

their brief exposure as guests in Ben Coutts's tower. Fortunately Mueller knew someone who did, and after lunch they headed to Mueller's apartment.

Chris was delighted. "You need to play Lore *for an investigation?*"

"Actually, we mostly need *you* to play Lore. And to tell us about it."

He laughed. "Done and done. What do you want to know?"

"How does it work? How's it organized, what's the goal?"

"Well, there's not just one goal... here, follow me and I'll explain as we go."

Lore was one of the largest and most popular games in the world. In size and scope, in fact, it very nearly mirrored the world, Naxos comprising a planet about a quarter the size of Earth (the oceans were much reduced). Players chose from six starting classes, each greatly customizable over the course of play, and twenty or so starting races, which affected also where your character would spawn on Naxos. There were no separate "realms" or servers; all the players in Naxos existed in a single multiplayer realm, with millions of individuals interacting at any given moment.

Naxos had a complex economy, social structures, three-dimensional physical geography, biology, botany, astronomy. The game's designers had moved beyond the usual game dynamics and begun from first principles: an alternative physics that players could research and build upon. In fact, Christian explained, Naxos had begun as a Stone Age society, with players literally having to create their own weapons from rocks, sticks, animal bones, and simple spells, exploring what worked and building upon it. "It's a whole other level of complexity," he enthused. "If you get a microscope in Naxos and look at something, you'll see the grain of the wood, tiny insects, microorganisms in your blood. It's all there."

Over the course of years, the level of technology (or magic) steadily improved, until it had reached the current medieval state. Eventually it would achieve some science-fiction-fantasy pinnacle, at which time, players speculated, Evreware would either introduce additional planets to explore, or destroy Naxos in an end-times cataclysm and alter the baseline physics once more, forcing players to develop new items and new societies in the ruins of the old.

In the meantime, there were the usual sort of wars, for the usual sorts of reasons: competition over resources, money, land, opportunistic thieving, and more general threats to the populace like world-consuming demons, dragons, undead armies and the like.

"Ever hear of a player called Kojin, or maybe Cogent?" Mueller asked. "Seems like he was heading up a pretty good-sized army?"

Chris's eyes bugged. "*Kojin Tachimaru?* Lord Kleptor of Amanthus?"

"Sure... I seem to remember a tower called that."

"He's probably one of the top ten players in the world. And he just conquered Daggoran, which puts him in a good position to attack Nelmithea, although I bet Brynn Halsea will try to form some kind of alliance with the Jeth..."

"But these are real people?" Mueller interrupted. "These armies?"

"Oh, yeah. Every soldier, every cook, every smith. All real."

"Millions of them?"

"Millions."

Khleang said incredulously, "Every *cook?*"

"Yep."

"Why would you be a *cook* in a game?"

"Same reason you'd be a cook in real life. You've got the skills, and you need to earn a little money. Anyway once the battle actually begins, most everyone will fight. But there's a lot of preparation that goes into it, including food preparation."

"So you cook to earn money in the game..."

"Well, it's real money too." They looked at him blankly, and he laughed and shook his head. "You know this is part of what I do for a living, right? The Naxian economy interacts with the real-world economy in all kinds of ways. There's a direct exchange rate of Naxian gold for U.S. dollars. Anytime you want, you can cash out your earnings, and Evreware will deposit a check to your account."

"But... then how do they make money?"

He shrugged. "You have to pay to play in the first place. And of course you can move money in the other direction, buy Naxian gold with real money."

"Why would you do that?"

"To buy items you want, or real estate or whatever. Like I said, you can earn money in-game via your craft skills, but those take time and effort to develop, and most players would rather spend their time fighting, competing for prizes, trying to work their way up in the arena system or whatever. For every player getting paid to play, there's ten that blow fifty bucks a month on armor or spells."

"What do the top players earn?" Mueller asked, curious.

Chris ran a quick search and showed them the results. Their mouths gaped. Last year's top earner, Guan Yu, had taken home nine million U.S. dollars. The average in the top ten was more than three million. "Holy shit," Khleang said, exchanging a significant glance with Mueller.

"What do you think a player like Kojin Tachimaru is worth, then?"

Chris shrugged. "Hard to say. The thing is, it costs a lot to run a war, too. The trick is to conquer a lot of territory and then hold it and collect taxes for as long as you can. A lot of players bankrupt themselves – in real life, too, not just in-game – trying to conquer a territory, and ending up losing it too quickly to turn a profit. I don't know his finances. On the other hand, just that

Aurora breastplate he's got has to be worth a few hundred thousand or so."

"*Dollars?*" Khleang spat, incredulous.

"Dollars." A little defensively, he added, "It's a unique artifact. He made it himself. No one even knows how it works."

"But it's not real! It's just... pixels!"

"It's real in the game. Real enough that people would pay a lot of money for it."

Her astonishment turned to sharp suspicion in an instant. "Real enough that someone would kill for it?"

Chris laughed. "People try all the time, in Naxos."

While they were talking Michelle Gorman called them with her husband's username: Dublainn of Acragh. Unfortunately this didn't give her or them access to the account, but her position as primary beneficiary of Richard's property meant she could likely get it, and Mueller made her promise to attempt it ASAP.

"We could probably access Gabriel's account the same way," Khleang pointed out. She was right, of course. Something they'd have to pursue.

"What about this guild Manish was a part of?" Mueller asked Christian. "Inversus? Do you think you could get access to it?"

He shook his head doubtfully. "It's pretty exclusive, from what I hear. I could apply, but they don't know me outside the game. Guilds like that are all insider clubs. You get in because you know someone, and that's about the only way."

"Could you try?"

He groaned. "You know I already have a guild, right? I'd have to leave it, and there's no guarantee Inversus would take me. And even if they did, I'd be at the bottom of the totem pole again. Running bitch errands for the higher-ups, for months."

"It could be important," Mueller implored. "Besides, they're a good guild, right? Powerful characters and all that? Pretty armor, giant flaming swords?"

Chris snorted. "They're an awesome guild. I just don't think I can get in."

"Will you try?" Mueller said, faux-sweetly. "For me, baby?"

"Fine. But if I have to crawl back to my old guild two weeks from now, I'm blaming you."

Willie White had promised they'd meet at four, but in the end he didn't wait that long, ghosting into Mueller's apartment, where he found them at three. "I'm closing the case," he announced. "And reducing the charges against Manish Gill."

"He hasn't been formally charged yet anyway," Khleang pointed out.

"A technicality. When he's found, it'll be abuse of a human body, improper disposal of said body, obstruction of justice, and fleeing a warrant."

"The warrant wasn't even issued..."

"It's been issued now, and he's failed to respond to our summons. Doesn't matter. Let them argue it in court, I don't give a shit. Point is, you're going to file an official report on your findings, to the effect that the kid's death was an accidental poisoning, thereby providing closure for the parents, and for any other interested parties."

"You don't think that's a little premature?" Mueller inquired. "There's still a lot we don't know..."

"You mean, like, why do men have nipples? Why's the sky blue, and why are people such fucking idiots? You're right, I've got tons of questions. But this one was answered this morning, when you went to Anodynamics and found the source of the toxin that killed Gabriel Leberer. Case closed. Done. Finito. Let's move on."

Obviously he'd watched the holo recorded by their systems. "There's some indication that all the relevant parties –"

"There's no indication of anything. There's an *indication* that you're at home, *playing fucking video games,* and if you think I want to explain that to the chief, and the mayor, and the kid's grief-stricken parents, you're fucking insane. You have any idea what would happen if the press got a hold of this? 'Detectives Playing Games While Parents Mourn,' how's that for a headline?" His face had turned pink. "In ten minutes I want you physically present in the station, writing your report. That's an order."

When White vanished, Chris said, "I guess I get to stay in my guild, then." Mueller gave him a pleading look, which Chris frowned at. "You heard him. The case is over." Mueller thrust out his lower lip. "Oh, come on! Not the lost puppy dog! It's my guild." Khleang made the same face at him, lips quivering. "Fine!" he relented. "Even though your own boss says not to."

Mueller said, "A case being officially closed doesn't mean it's resolved. It just... shifts into a lower gear." He stood up and put on his jacket.

"But you can't, like, get any more warrants, right? Or spend your work hours on it. You can't question anybody..."

"No. But a lot of times investigations follow a certain curve. You ask a lot of questions, and for a while the answers keep coming regardless of your own activity."

Khleang chuckled. "He's trying to say that we've kicked a lot of shit downhill. Now we'll wait and see where it lands."

Mueller intended to spend Christmas Day at home, and very nearly succeeded. In the morning he fixed a proper breakfast of eggs and pancakes, served with coffee and Bailey's. He and Chris did the crossword and talked about last Christmas, which they'd spent with Chris's family in Portland. In the afternoon they walked to get Chinese at Bamboo Garden in Queen Anne, strangely close to the site of Gabriel's final resting place, but then after so many years as a detective, Mueller knew the ghosts lingering in every neighborhood. (There was an app, actually, that put a pin on a map every time there was a homicide, so that as you were sitting at your coffee shop, say, you could see that someone had had their throat cut on the corner back in 2036 or whatever. Gruesome, and naturally quite popular.)

On the way home it started snowing. They both looked about in surprise, this being the first and, for all they knew, the only snow of the season. "Good job, Seattle," Chris remarked. "Snow on Christmas. I didn't know you had it in you."

In the evening they watched an old movie on the wall screen in the living room, sitting together beneath a big blue blanket, drinking hot toddy in drowsy comfort. This was all anyone wanted, Mueller reflected. Warmth, physical and emotional. A sweet drink, a bit of entertainment, your beloved beside you. And for lack of it people schemed and fought and died.

They almost made it through a perfect day, a perfect Christmas. But at ten-thirty, as they were flossing and brushing in preparation for sleep, the house speakers chimed with a call for Mueller. From the sound (a quietish siren he'd selected) he knew it was his workplace with an urgent call. He sighed, spat into the sink. "Agatha, put it on speakers, please. Hello, this is Tom."

"Hi, Tom," came Willie White's voice. "Merry fucking Christmas, and sorry to disturb you, but people don't stop dying just 'cause it's a holiday. We got something you're going to need to come look at."

"Right now?" Mueller said. "I was getting ready for bed."

"You remember that kid you interviewed last week? Benjamin Coutts?"

"Sure. Why?" He set the toothbrush in its cup, stared at the striped shower curtain, well suspecting what White was about to say.

"He's deeeaaad," White sang. "Someone found him at the Ballard Locks. Turns out a body can't make it through the fish ladder. Who knew?"

"Drowned?"

"Yep. No other injuries. Probably upstream somewhere."

"You think it's a homicide, though?"

"I have no idea," White said. "I'm sitting at home in front of my fireplace watching the fire go out and drinking rye. That's what I have you for. The body's still there at the Locks, and it's going to stay there until you give the word. So hurry up about it. There's people want to go home and go to sleep."

When Mueller went outside he noticed again the strange quiet of the city on Christmas, the streets nearly devoid of cars and their ever-present hum. The snow fell in silence, leaving the asphalt wet and black, but sticking now a little to the grass. The police auto he summoned glided almost without pause along Eliot Avenue and Interbay and there was something dreamlike in the unstoppered movement through the still city. Or maybe it was just the traces of alcohol still in his veins.

When he got to the Locks, though, the feeling only deepened. He parked as close as he could and approached on foot, gazing at the white water churning from from the lower locks. Amber lights lined the concrete waterways, the city a black and irregular outline beyond them, the sky a close cap of glowing gray. He looked up, saw someone's silhouette wave to him from the top of the Locks, raised a tentative hand in reply.

On a concrete viewing platform, close to where a whimsical stainless-steel statue curled up from the concrete like a mechanical fiddlehead fern, the police had used orange pylons and yellow tape to form a little bedroom-sized rectangle around the body. It was necessary, perhaps, because of the small crowd of officers and witnesses around it, but Mueller could see at a glance that it was pointless, that obviously someone had pulled the body from the water, and where it lay now was irrelevant. Ben Coutts lay on his back with blue eyes open and unblinking in the falling snow, jaw likewise slack, red hair dark with water. He might have been doing sivasana, palms up, legs straight, just as he would soon look on the coroner's steel table. His expression, as was so often true of those who died unexpectedly, was of dismayed surprise.

Mueller greeted the other officers politely, even as he ducked under the police line to crouch beside the body. Coutts was wearing blue jeans and a puffy orange jacket with a black hoodie beneath it. Red Converse shoes, still laced up, ruby slippers on the unfortunate witch. Dressed for outside. All his clothes were soaking wet and if Coutts had been alive he'd have been freezing to death, but of course with the life gone from it the body was without a shudder. Deena Harrod, the forensics tech from a week earlier, was there too, running a handheld scanner up and down the corpse.

Mueller remembered her, from last week, being cheerful and energetic, but her "Evening, detective," tonight sounded tired and sad. "Nice to see you again."

"You too," he replied, feeling a kind of solemn hush about the scene, something almost ceremonial about the dead child in the pool of spotlights, the many adults standing around him talking quietly, the snowflakes sparking in the lights, the steady sound of the water nearby. Still speaking quietly, he asked, "What do you think?"

She sighed, placed a hand on her forehead, shielding her eyes. "I think he's dead." There was a waver in her voice and she wiped at her eyes. "I'm sorry. I don't know why this one is hitting me so hard. I deal with dead bodies every day, you'd think I'd be used to it."

"It's okay," he said patiently.

"I guess it's just that it's Christmas. I had such a nice day, and..."

"You need anything? Cup of coffee?"

She fluttered a dismissive hand and took a short breath, visibly donning her professional character. "I'm fine. I am." She waved the scanner at the body. "By all indications he drowned. Might have suffered hypothermia first. Hard to say. No other trauma apparent. Initial blood tests do indicate the presence of THC."

"How long ago did he die?"

"Not long at all. An hour, maybe. Not more than two."

"Any idea where it might have happened?"

"Somewhere upstream. Probably not far. Might have just sunk to the bottom except for this jacket he's wearing. It's slightly buoyant."

"Have you searched him?"

She shook her head. "Not yet. Be my guest."

He took a package of latex gloves from his pocket, tore it open and put them on. Patted the boy's pockets gently, feeling the cold water through the gloves. Found what he was looking for immediately, in the right front pocket of Coutts's jeans: a black Samsung Electron handset, top of the line.

He pressed the single button on its face to turn it on. It was unharmed by its immersion but confronted him with a screen demanding he enter his security icon, which of course he didn't know and wouldn't have been able to fake. It'd have to wait until later.

He heard Khleang's voice greeting one of the officers, looked up and made eye contact. She came over and stood looking down at the body. "Another one, huh?"

She was right, of course: the second wunderkind dead in a week. Unlikely coincidence. She asked about injuries and they said there were none. "Could be suicide," she mused flatly. She nodded her chin upstream. "If he threw himself off the Aurora Bridge, there's a good chance he'd end up here."

"Definitely possible," agreed Harrod. "If he fell in the center of the river, he'd be a lot less likely to catch on the shore on either side."

"There's a fence on the Aurora Bridge," Mueller pointed out. "Not really that easy to throw yourself off it."

"Not impossible, either," Khleang said darkly. "Just requires a bit more determination."

"We'll check it out," Mueller said. "For now, let's get him out of here. Then all these people can go home."

"Will do." Harrod signaled to an assistant waiting by her van and he opened the back doors and pulled out a wheeled stretcher for the body. Meanwhile Mueller stood with Khleang looking down at the dead boy. He wanted to close the kid's eyes, but it was an unnecessary interference with the body, a sort of desecration, really, and in any case he knew the lids wouldn't stay closed without adhesive. Khleang said nothing, lost perhaps in her own morose reflections.

What Ben Coutts's eyes saw now, if anything, was beyond their ken. One stared blankly up at the clouds, flat as a fish's dead orb; the other reflected the light rack of a nearby police vehicle, alternating red, blue, red, blue, like some ghost of the blood entering and leaving the heart.

Back in the police auto Mueller had taken to the Locks, it took no more than five minutes to find Coutts's last movements, with Themis. He hadn't been on the Aurora Bridge, but the much lower Fremont Bridge. "The fall wouldn't have killed him from the Fremont Bridge," Khleang observed. "Either he was disabled or unconscious before he fell, or..."

"Or hypothermia got him before he could swim out."

The Fremont Bridge had several security cameras along its length, including four focused on the pedestrian bridge. At 8:46 p.m. Ben Coutts came walking north across the bridge, coming from north Queen Anne toward Fremont. There was light traffic, their videos also available for viewing. He was wearing a baseball cap and his hood was up, making it hard to see his face, but besides the missing hat his clothes were the same.

At 8:48 he paused at the rail, looking down at something he seemed to see there on the very outside edge of the bridge. He knelt, reached through the bars for whatever it was, fingers outstretched. He stood up and stood there for a minutes or two making gestures with his hands, periodically looking downward over the railing.

"Doing something with his system," Mueller said.

"Definitely." She pointed to a swinging motion on the video. "Fishing, maybe?"

"For what?"

"Don't know yet."

Finally Coutts looked around, looked over the railing one final time, then climbed over it, holding on to one of the crossbars. He slid down carefully until he was in a low crouch, then reached under the bridge for something. His hat hid his expression, but he held out his hand to one side for a moment, examining something, before standing up carefully.

Then his head jerked. His neck twitched. His hand loosened on the steel support. He fell sideways and was gone. Just inanimate steel, falling snow, and running water, on and on.

"Doesn't look like a suicide," Mueller concluded.

"No, not at all. Watch that last bit again..." They replayed it. "He's having some kind of seizure. Just extremely bad timing for it."

"Could be drug-induced."

"Definitely possible, though the initial tox screen didn't show anything likely to cause it. We'll tell Deena to check close."

He waved at the video. "Why did he go out on the edge like that in the first place? What did he think was there?"

"Something on his system, I'm guessing. He was walking by, saw something he wanted. And he was just messed up enough to climb over the rail for it. Then he seizes, and that's it. For that matter, we don't have his medical history. For all we know he had a history of seizures."

"We'll have to ask the parents."

"We'll have to go tell them anyway." She sighed. "You going to make me go with you again?"

"Not if you don't want to."

"You going to do it tonight?"

"You know we have to."

"I guess." She stared off at the shadowed profiles of the pines in the little park that lined this side of the canal. "Where was he coming from, anyway? And where was he going?"

"Good question. Let's ask."

When Themis told them the address to which Coutts had taken an auto earlier that evening, Mueller actually felt not much surprise. It was the Leberers' house, in upper Queen Anne. Well, they'd known Coutts knew the Leberers. He'd gone there for whatever reason, to talk to them about Gabriel, maybe, and decided afterward to walk... somewhere else. At this point they might never know his destination.

Khleang said, "We'll have to talk to them, too." He agreed. "Tonight?"

"His mom and dad first. Then... yeah, we'll have to wake them up."

When they told Rebecca and Lionel Coutts, at their house in south Seattle, Rebecca immediately started weeping. Lionel's face just twisted up, as though he were suffering a painful stomach cramp, the lines between his brows pressing ever deeper into his flesh.

"I knew something was wrong," Rebecca wept. "He left and I just had this terrible feeling about it, but he's always leaving and I always have that feeling. But this time..."

Lionel put his wiry arm around his wife, but apparently had little to say. Their German shepherd, Lacy, had barked furiously when the police arrived, but now lay on her mat in the dim living room looking up at them with mournful questioning eyes.

"Did Ben ever suffer from seizures?" Khleang asked.

Rebecca wiped her eyes. "No. Never. Why, is that what happened?"

105

"That's our best guess right now, yes."

"He never had any problems like that. His whole genome was screened for genetic predisposition to disease, you know. He was always healthy. But maybe they missed something."

"Could be. Did you know where he was going when he left here?"

"He didn't tell us. Why? Where did he go?"

Khleang and Mueller exchanged a glance, but Mueller couldn't see a reason not to tell her the truth. "The Leberers' house," he said.

"Oh," she said, sounding slightly indignant, as though it were unworthy as a last destination. "Well, he did hang out with Gabriel sometimes. Not often. Usually Gabe would come over here. Do you think it..." She trailed off, obviously looking for some connection and not finding one.

"So far as we know right now, your son's death was an accident," Khleang said, quite gently. "Again, we're sorry."

Daniel Leberer came to the door in a granite-colored plush bathrobe, looking apprehensive, all the more so when he recognized them. "What's going on?" he said by way of greeting. "Is it something about Gabriel?"

"Not exactly," Mueller said. "Can we come in?"

They didn't sit down or take off their shoes or coats, in deference to the time, and first Sarah and then Elsie came out of their rooms to see what the voices were about. Sarah wore a bathrobe to match her husband's but in a paler sand, and Elsie padded silently down the stairs in striped PJ bottoms and a UW sweatshirt (one of her brother's?) she'd obviously thrown on before coming down.

They told them what had happened and Daniel shook his head in dismay. Sarah seemed most affected, hugging herself and holding back tears. Elsie just frowned.

"But... it was an accident?" Sarah asked.

"That's how it looks right now," Mueller said. "But of course it just happened. We're still gathering the facts. How long was he here?"

"Not long," Daniel said. "Maybe half an hour? Said he was in the neighborhood and just wanted to stop by and say merry Christmas."

"That's it?" Khleang asked. "Just... merry Christmas?"

"No, he was really sweet," Sarah said. "He said he knew he hadn't been around, and had been feeling bad about it, since Gabriel... passed. He said that he wanted us to know how sorry he was, that he felt responsible."

Mueller tried to hide the feeling of surprise, and could see Khleang doing the same beside him, her face turning blank as a robot's. This was the little snot they'd met last week?

"They were friends, you know," Daniel put in. "Him and Gabe. Really, he was one of Gabe's only friends. But at that age it's hard to communicate your feelings."

Elsie rolled her eyes. "Ben's twenty-four." She stopped herself. "Sorry. I guess it hasn't sunk in yet."

"Did he say anything else?" Mueller asked. "Did he seem depressed at all?"

Sarah wiped away a tear. "He seemed... somber. But I don't know, we were talking about Gabriel, of course it was a serious conversation. We couldn't have known anything was wrong..."

Khleang raised a calming hand. "Right now it looks like it was just an accident anyway. We're not suggesting it was a suicide. Like Tom said, we're just gathering the facts." A pause. "Did he seem coherent to you?"

Shrugs all around. "Sure," Daniel volunteered. "I mean, maybe his pupils were a little dilated. We know he smokes pot sometimes, we've talked to his parents about it. But he seemed alert enough. Certainly *coherent.*"

"Did he say anything else? Anything about where he was going?"

"I think he said he was going to a friend's house," said Sarah. "But he wasn't specific. He did talk more with Elsie, though."

"Separate from the two of you?" Khleang asked for clarification. "By themselves?"

"Yes, by our*selves,*" Elsie said. "In my room. The two of us twenty-somethings. Is that okay with you?"

"We trust her," Sarah put in.

"What did you talk about?" Khleang inquired.

Elsie shrugged. "I don't know. Stuff. We talked about school, what we'd been doing on vacation. Where some of our other friends were."

After a moment's silence, Khleang said, "That's it?"

Elsie sighed. "I don't know. He said some of the same things he said out here. Like he was worried I would blame him for Gabriel dying, because he sold him the drugs. So he wanted to make sure we were *okay.*"

"And what did you tell him?"

Her expression darkened. "I told him he was right, he *was* responsible. He *did* sell him the drugs. If it weren't for him being such a shit, Gabe would still be alive. And he comes here, and he's obviously fucking *high,* and he's not even that apologetic. Like sorry your brother died and all, but no hard feelings, right?"

"Elsie!" her mother breathed, obviously shocked. Her father, though, was almost smiling.

"So it didn't end well between you," Khleang said, a bit lamely.

"I told him to get out. And stay away from me." She glared, all fire, arms folded and head upright in challenge.

"Did he say where he was going?" Mueller asked finally.

Elsie shrugged. "He said a friend's. I kind of figured that meant his dealer's place."

"Do you know who that was?"

She shook her head, lips pressed tight.

Gabriel Leberer, Ben Coutts, and the CCD officer Richard Gorman: all killed in clearly avoidable accidents, two of them by drowning. Of course, accidents happened. But what were the odds of three fatal accidents happening to three individuals connected to each other like this?

They talked it over, but the later it got, the more difficult it was to think. "I need to go home," Khleang said finally. "Even if we wanted to do more tonight, we can't keep waking people up, and anyway I'm not thinking clearly."

Mueller slept fitfully, dreaming he was swimming in the canal himself, gasping, freezing. Beside him were all the others who had died in the river, a great struggling mass of them, crowding and clawing each other like drowning rats. But the walls of the canal were too high and smooth to climb.

"You look like crap," Chris observed that morning.

Mueller twitched his eyebrows in dour acknowledgement. "Guess I shouldn't have stayed up so late partying."

He took an auto to work, for once, and did his best to avoid conversation until he was at his cubicle. Then he dialed down the external office noise, his earbuds working to cancel the sound of conversation, and to his system said, "Agatha."

His virtual secretary appeared at the cubicle entrance. She had been modeled after some twentieth-century mystery-novel character, a middle-aged, intelligent-looking woman with a lively, alert expression. Today she was wearing a sort of burnt-orange jacket with a gold brooch, a white blouse and gray slacks. "Good morning, detective," she said in her cultured voice. "How can I help you?"

"Agatha, how many wunderkind are there in all? How many were born originally?"

A slight pause. "Are you referring to the individuals genetically modified as part of Dr. Samuel Liebskind's multiple sclerosis–"

"Yes," he interrupted.

109

"Eighteen."

"And how many of those children are alive today?"

A pause. "I'm sorry, but finding that information requires special police authorization for a Themis inquiry. Do you so authorize?"

"Yes."

"Twelve," she said.

"Twelve," he repeated. "So six out of the original eighteen children have died?"

"That is correct."

"What are the odds of that?" he mused, dismayed.

Another pause. "The odds of six of eighteen individuals of that age dying, over a twenty-four year span, in a random population sampling from the United States, are 30,833 to one against. There is a 0.003 percent chance of it occurring at random."

A zero percent chance. Or nearly so, which he supposed wasn't quite the same thing. "How many of those six deaths occurred in the last year?"

"Four."

"Give me the names of all eighteen wunderkind and highlight those who have died. Include basic biographical information and the current locations of those still living."

The information appeared on his desktop and he tilted the screen up to get a better view. Twelve still living. Six deceased. He dragged the dead into one group and read.

Two he already knew about: Gabriel Leberer and Ben Coutts. One, Annie Wollerman-Spence, had died long ago, in 2066, at (real) age 12, when she fell from a balcony downtown. Two had committed suicide: Kimball Gosse, via drug overdose in 2070, and Robert Heckler, who hung himself from a rafter in his parents' vacation home in Jackson Hole just this last February. That left Stephen Mohammadian, who died in California this July, of –

Drowning.

A chill went through him. It could not be coincidence. Mohammadian had been body-surfing in Oceanside, where he'd been on vacation with his parents. No one had even noticed him going down, but down he'd gone, and by the time someone pulled his floating body from the surf, he was dead. There was no indication of concussion, no indication of anything actually being the matter with him, other than that his lungs were full of seawater.

"Agatha, is Jackie here?"

"Not quite," his assistant responded. "She's arriving now. She's getting out of the auto."

When Khleang came in the door, wearing a knitted black beret against the cold, Mueller was waiting for her. "We need to put the wunderkind under police protection."

"All of them?" she said doubtfully. "Why?"

"Someone's killing them off."

Khleang was quickly convinced. Willie White took longer, but soon enough he was persuaded that there was a real danger; he seemed more convinced by Agatha's calculation of the long odds than Mueller's arguments. "Though you realize how impossible this is. We can offer some protection to those few kids still in Seattle, but the rest are all over the map. And even then, we don't know what if anything killed these kids. We can tell them to stay away from water, but that's about it."

"Water *and* drugs," Khleang observed.

"Yeah, great," White grunted. "Really useful public service announcement. While we're at it, we should let 'em know they shouldn't run with scissors."

"It's not a coincidence," Mueller said.

"I know, I know. But you've also got no *causality*. You've got no method. I mean, has it occurred to you that maybe these kids are just suicidal? Maybe it's not an outside agency at all. Maybe it's something inside, that makes them seek out dangerous situations, do drugs, jump off bridges and whatnot. Could be what they need isn't an armed guard outside their door. Could be they'd be better off with a suicide watch. They're obviously not normal. For all we know, really, there's even weirder stuff going on in their brains. Could be some kind of genetic trigger that comes on at puberty. These kids, they're a total unknown."

For all his rough bluster, the lieutenant wasn't an idiot. His point needed to be examined. Khleang said, "Even if that were true, it still leaves Richard Gorman. Guy was paddling around in Green Lake. Not exactly dangerous territory."

White shrugged. "I'm not saying you're wrong, either. But if it's homicide, you have to find the method. The method'll lead you to whoever's doing it. If you can't find the method, then you've got to look somewhere else. That means background. That means motive and opportunity. So seems to me there's two questions: One, is this suicidal behavior? Two, if not, who wants these kids dead?"

One by one they contacted the parents of the wunderkind and warned them that their children might be in danger. To the few remaining in Seattle, they offered heightened surveillance, including drone units around their homes. They encouraged all of them to stay at home as much as possible, and in particular to avoid any bodies of water. "Can he take a bath?" asked one bewildered mom.

"For now, showers might be best," said Mueller, feeling ridiculous.

"This is stupid," said Khleang afterwards. "We're just making them afraid for no reason."

"There's a reason. We just don't know what it is yet."

The Leberers were particularly distraught. "You told us Gabriel's death was an accident," Daniel said. "Now you're saying, what, that maybe it was murder after all, or maybe he killed himself, and anyway Elsie shouldn't go swimming. What are you playing at?"

Mueller reminded him that Ben Coutts had died, and as that investigation was ongoing, he was unable to discuss it.

"How do you know it's not Gill?" demanded the father. "Obviously he wanted Gabriel dead, one way or the other. Maybe this whole thing was arranged by him. And really, I can't believe you haven't found him and arrested him for what he did. He's obviously dangerous."

"We are still looking for Manish Gill," said Mueller, though that search, at this point, was largely passive. "But there's nothing that implicates him in these other deaths. Again, we're just playing it safe right now."

Daniel Leberer swore and hung up. But they sent the drones anyway. They didn't need his permission to perform aerial surveillance.

"He could be right about Gill," observed Khleang. "One way or another, he did stab the kid. Obviously there's some motive."

"If we could easily find him, we'd have brought him in already. Since we haven't, we've got to look at other possibilities."

The foremost expert on the psychology of the wunderkind – indeed, almost the only expert – was Dr. Arquette Kelly. It was she who had pushed for the creation of the Wunderschool, which most of the wunderkind attended until its closure in 2066. She had also been Gabriel Leberer's personal therapist.

They made an appointment with her AI secretary to meet that morning. Initially the secretary had tried to put them off until Wednesday, but repeated use of the words "urgent" and "police investigation" finally convinced the system that it needed to rearrange things.

These days, it seemed, Dr. Kelly had left the hospital in favor of private practice, operating from a beautiful large house in the

University District that had been renovated into offices. Kelly herself was in her early to mid-fifties, and seemed to cultivate an appearance of homespun candor. Her dark hair was undyed, showing strands of gray, cut shoulder-length with bangs at her eyebrows. Under a long red cardigan she wore a tan blouse, offset by a flower-print scarf around her neck. Her slacks were baggy and loose, her shoes sensible.

Mueller looked with interest around her office. Psychiatrists always had interesting offices. They seemed to make a point of collecting objects and artwork with archetypal significance. Hers included a pair of alert-looking ceramic bunnies painted gold; a bronze bust of a bald, serene woman with a shaved head; a beautifully executed painting of a clear-cut forest; and on her desk, a little crystal sphere, like a snow-globe, that contained a tiny ecosystem, with minute organisms moving through intricate green-blue structures like little coral reefs.

She didn't sit behind the desk, however, but in a comfortable-looking office chair upholstered in coppery fabric. Mueller and Khleang took equally comfortable seats facing her, Mueller settling into an armchair, Khleang perching on the edge of a modernist couch. It was all very comfortable, civilized, and expensive.

Kelly welcomed them warmly, talking about her morning, offering pleasantries with professional ease. "I have to tell you I don't have a lot of time," she said when they were seated and the door was closed. "I've got an appointment at eleven that I'd rather not miss. But what can I help you with?"

"We understand that you know Benjamin Coutts," Khleang began.

"I know all the wunderkind," said Kelly. "I ran a school for them, you know. I was also the personal therapist for most of them, at one point or another."

"Ben Coutts died last night," Mueller said, directly but not ungently.

Kelly's face fell. "Oh, no. I'm so sorry."

"We're here investigating his death, along with the death of Gabriel Leberer."

She shook her head. "I'm so sorry. I knew about Gabriel, of course. But Ben... how did he die?"

Mueller shook his head. "We're not really free to discuss it. But we would like to ask you some questions regarding the psychology of the wunderkind."

"Of course. Although you realize I'm not totally free, myself, to discuss the details of their sessions with me. Only if it has a clear connection to your investigation."

This was no surprise, and they moved ahead directly. "You were Gabriel Leberer's personal psychiatrist," began Khleang.

"That's correct."

"To your knowledge, did Gabriel ever display suicidal tendencies?"

"Suicidal, not necessarily. Self-destructive, yes."

"Can you clarify that?"

She rested her chin on her fist. "You must be aware of Gabriel's history."

"Probably not as aware as you."

She made a little gesture conceding the point. "Gabriel felt very isolated through most of his life. He had a hard time relating to people. His parents did their best, in their way, but could also be extremely controlling. He was angry about it. Some of that anger got directed toward his parents, some of it toward himself. Really, it wasn't so different from what most adolescents go through, just more intense. More prolonged. He would have weeks of intense depression, and weeks where he felt elated."

"Manic-depressive?" Khleang ventured.

"In an adult, we would say that, sure. For a teenager, it's not unusual. For a teenager aging at half normal, with massive alterations to their endocrine system, isolated from their peers... who can say? My personal view is that he most likely would have grown out of it once he reached adulthood. Part of what made him so angry was the constant condescension of adults who couldn't help but see him as a child."

They asked if she'd prescribed Gabriel the Serenex and she said she had. "Were you aware of any possible fatal interactions with Serenex?"

She raised an eyebrow. "I suppose so, although it's not generally considered dangerous. Some heart medications are counter-indicated..."

"Ever hear of something called deletrium?" asked Mueller.

A blank look. "It doesn't sound familiar."

"How well did you know Ben Coutts?" Mueller continued.

She sighed. "It used to be I knew him very well, when he was at the school. But that was quite a few years ago."

"Do you know if he also suffered from depression?"

"You're asking me if I think he could have killed himself?"

"In so many words."

She waved a hand. "Like I said, I haven't seen him in years. He's probably a totally different person than he was. *Was* a different person. I wouldn't want to speculate."

"Is depression common among the wunderkind?"

"Yes."

"Suicidal depression?"

"It's a danger for them."

"Have any others attempted suicide, to your knowledge?"

A sigh. "Yes, though I'm not free to discuss it."

"Have any attempted suicide by drowning, to your knowledge?"

She cocked her head, puzzled. "No. Is that how Ben died?"

"We're also not free to discuss it."

"Sorry."

"Is there any reason why someone would choose to commit suicide by drowning, as opposed to other methods?"

She considered the question. "Of course. For all kinds of

reasons. Often those attempting suicide imbue the manner of their death with meaning. It may be the way someone they admired died, like all the rock stars who've overdosed, or Sylvia Plath putting her head in the oven. Or it may indicate their emotional state: angry, depressed, in pain. Drowning, to me, suggests an archetypal significance, the subsuming of the ego by the waters of the unconscious. It's fairly painless and very neat. The body isn't damaged. There's a certain ... romance to it."

Khleang had handed off Ben's phone to SPD's internal investigative IT department the night before, marking its contents as urgently needed. But that afternoon IT's head, Bill Crake, found Khleang at her desk and threw the phone down, enclosed in a plastic evidence bag. "Look, I don't know whose phone this is, but you're not getting whatever's on it."

"That was fast," she said. "Took you less than a day to not do your job."

"Ha, ha. You think you can do better, you go right ahead."

"What's the problem?"

"It's encrypted," he said matter-of-factly. "We've identified it. It's called Juju Mite. Hacker shit. This is a recent variant, real up-to-date. No idea where it comes from, who makes it, or how to break it."

"Seriously?" Khleang looked irritated. "Absolutely no way?"

"Seriously," he replied, tauntingly. "I know in all the movies you flick a bunch of motes real fast and you can break into the Pentagon and all, but in real life there's plenty of encryption that's nearly impossible to crack. This probably requires multiple authenticators, spoken, physical, locative, and gestural. You want to break it without those, you'll need some serious computing power."

"What about Themis?" asked Mueller. "It can't do it?"

Crake rubbed his short beard. "Themis probably could, but you'd be talking about monopolizing its massive-ass computing power for a week or two. No way it's going to happen. My advice is, either find the person whose phone it is and make them open it for you, or... nope, that's it, that's your only option."

Khleang frowned, closed her eyes, kneaded her temples. After a second she opened her eyes and asked, "What about his contacts?"

"You have his contacts?"

"I think so."

"So why weren't they in with the phone?" Crake said, obviously irritated. "They're kind of a set, you know. They work together."

"I don't know," Khleang said sharply. "Probably it was late, they got put somewhere. But if you had them, could you get anything off them?"

"Not sure," he admitted. "But it's possible. Not the main drive, obviously, but contacts store a cache in them. So we might be able to get the last few minutes or whatever. What about his earbuds? You got those too, hiding somewhere?"

As it turned out, both earbuds were available (the adhesive holding them to the inside of the tragus had to be water-resistant, for bathing), but only one of the contacts. The other had fallen out and been lost somewhere in the canal. By now it could be in the open sea. But one was enough.

The snow made Ben blink frequently. Not for the first time on his walk, he considered if he should have called an auto. He still could. But he was enjoying this Christmas walk, the lack of autos on the street, the strange and profound quiet that settled on the city only on this one day a year. It was like witnessing an eclipse. Besides, it would help clear his head.

He was still high from the potent weed he'd smoked earlier, but outdoors the high was diffuse, spacious. As he approached the bridge he passed the Nickerson Brewery and reflected on how ridiculous it was that he couldn't go in and have a drink, even if they'd been open. Offensive, really.

He looked right, admiring the high, elegant lines of the Aurora Bridge, dark against the pearlescent sky. WELCOME TO FREMONT, a sign said, with the half-joking addendum, *Center of the Universe.* There were two little bridge posts on either side of the bridge entrance, presumably to house whoever controlled the rising and falling of the bridge when larger boats needed to pass. The posts and girders of the bridge were a faded blue the color of long-discarded jeans moldering in a gutter.

Halfway across the bridge Kaku pinged an alert on his system. He hadn't realized the app was even on, but there were the blue bubbles floating through the air, popping with cute little pops, telling him there was a Renbo nearby.

He could hear it, too, making little gurgling noises, like some kind of amphibian baby. But where was it?

This was half the fun of Kaku, of course. First you had to find the Renbos, then catch them. Afterward you could add them to your team and play online matches. It wasn't Lore, but then again, you couldn't just play one game, could you?

He looked in all directions, then up. The bridge's girders were massive riveted steel beams. He thought at first the Renbo must be on the topmost girder, which ran the length of the bridge to its midpoint, but listening he realized it seemed to be coming from beneath him.

He leaned over the rail and looked down. The gurgling was definitely coming from below him. But there wasn't anything there but lake. He moved along a few meters, leaned over again, and saw it.

Holy shit. It's a Shining Michumichi.

The Renbo wasn't large, an amphibious sort of dragon the size of a housecat. But its scales were like translucent blue and green gems, shimmering faintly, and its eyes glowed like magical whirlpools. Again it made its adorable cry, begging to be picked up and played with.

It was a Mythic Rare, the only one he'd ever seen in the wild. In combat the creature would swell up to the size of a house, then burst apart in a thousand little droplet-Michumichis, swarming around your opponent. And it was *valuable:* a quick query set it at $6,700. Again, not Lore prices, but for something you just found walking down the street...

They hadn't made it easy to get to, though, had they? Actually that was slightly unusual. Often enough the Renbos would run away, and you'd have to corral them with your friends, and they loved to hide in all kinds of nooks and crannies. But usually the designers made an effort to discourage actually risky behaviors from their players, like climbing high in trees.

On the other hand, the Renbos weren't strictly *placed* anywhere. The AIs chose the spots according to the latest environmental data, in keeping with the behaviors of the particular Renbo. It made sense that the Michumichi was on a bridge, right over the water; it was just weird that it was *under* the bridge.

But maybe someone had chased it there. Actually, that made more sense than anything. Probably it *had* been on top of the bridge, or even on a boat, and had escaped by crawling underneath.

He stared at the creature for a little while. It saw him too, the app noting his proximity and the direction of his gaze. But the Michumichi couldn't fly, he didn't think, and seemed to be afraid of just dropping in the water.

Awkward though it was, there were ways. He got out his tools and traps. But none of the traps really seemed to apply. He tried luring it, but he didn't have the right bait, and anyway the creature was really trapped there. It couldn't come to him even if it wanted.

For a while he messed around with his Kaku fishing pole, trying to swing the lure and hook all the way around and underneath the bridge, hoping just a touch of the hook might be enough to grab his prize. But the pole wouldn't even activate unless he made a swinging motion, and he only succeeded in catching some water sprites from the lake.

Meanwhile, he was getting cold, starting to shiver. Again he leaned way over, eyeing his heart's desire greedily. Hell, it was *right there*. It was *just under* the walkway. If he climbed over the rail, and knelt down, he was sure he could pluck it from its perch easy as could be. He could even hook his feet under the steel mesh of the fencing if he needed to.

Don't be stupid. You're gonna end up in the river.

He looked down at the water. And sure, it looked cold. But hell, it wasn't even that far down, and the shore wasn't far away. Even if he fell in, he could just swim out, no matter how cold it was.

Fuck it. He was going to get that little fucking dragon.

Moving carefully, he gripped the rail, its painted surface wet, cold, and gritty, and threw one leg over. His toes couldn't quite touch the bridge surface, though, so he leaned forward, placing the weight of his torso more squarely on his hands, and pivoted on his hips to swing the other leg over and down.

His breath came rapidly now. He looked down at the water and it seemed further than he'd thought. *This is a dumb idea.* But the Renbo had seen him and was gurgling louder than ever. "Don't worry, baby," he said. "I'm taking you home with me."

He moved his hands down the mesh of the rail fence. It bit into his fingers painfully, so once he was in a crouch, he transferred his grip to one of the upright steel posts supporting the rail. The surface was textured and rough. It was good. He wouldn't fall.

He leaned over and down, saw the miniature dragon just below him. When it cried he could see the gloss of its translucent teeth and its little green tongue. One solid clenching motion at the neck, and he'd have it. Hopefully the creature wouldn't run away, or jump into the lake at the last second. Now the moment of truth. "All right, I got you."

He swung at the creature's neck. He had it! Of course there was no sensation – he wasn't wearing haptic gloves – but the Michumichi squealed in alarm, struggling in his grip.

CONGRATULATIONS! the app declared in brilliant gold letters, with a fanfare of coronets. YOU WON A MICHUMICHI!

"Fuckin' right!" he replied. Now time to get back to safety. Slowly he stood up, keeping one hand always on the rail or steel mesh, sneaker toes still hooked.

THAT'S NOT ALL YOU WON! another message flashed.

Interesting. He'd never seen that before. Some kind of bonus creature?

YOU WON A SWIM IN THE CANAL!

His eyes widened. Suddenly desperate to be on the *other fucking side*, he started to swing his leg up and froze. His vision flashed white, red, white. He blinked rapidly.

His head jerked. It felt like something had just hit him with a strong electrical shock. Then another, somewhere in his spine. And another. And another.

Hold on, he thought desperately. *Just hold–*

A massive spasm coursed through his body. His head tossed involuntarily back and a strangled cry escaped his throat. It felt like someone was stabbing a taser at the base of his neck.

His hands loosened. He fell. Two seconds of silvery sky, fleeting snowflakes, and then the slap of the cold iron gauntlet of the water. He wanted to swim but he couldn't, his body's betrayal entirely unexpected. He sank, already breathing the water, unable even to hold his breath. Drowning hurt more than he ever thought it could.

After a minute he stopped spasming, stopped moving, stopped thinking. His body floated slowly along in the darkness, the one contact remaining to him after the fall still recording through his open eye.

In his earbuds, the Michumichi gurgled. It sounded like laughter.

"He got hacked," Khleang said, sounding amazed.

"Hacked to death," Mueller observed.

Whoever had managed it, however they'd managed it, they possessed considerable resources. This was especially apparent in the SPD's failure to break through Coutts's security software. Whoever the perpetrator was, they'd performed their trick without Coutts suspecting a thing.

"It still doesn't explain why he fell," said Mueller. "The video game whatsit made him put himself in a dangerous situation, but then... what? He just happens to have a seizure, at precisely that moment?"

"Someone triggered it," agreed Khleang. "One way or another. And if they could do it with him..."

"They could do the same with Richard Gorman and the other wunderkind who died of drowning. Mohammadian."

"Got to be drug-induced. I'll talk to forensics, see if they could have missed something."

Khleang called Deena Harrod, told her their suspicions. "We did run a pretty thorough tox screen on Coutts," Harrod said doubtfully. "And I bet they did the same on Gorman. But if he seized, there's a good chance it's a brain issue. Let me run a scan on his brain and do a biopsy, see if anything comes up." She shook her head. "Don't expect it to be finished this afternoon, though. We'll have to schedule it with the university hospital, and they hate giving up time on their machines to people who are already dead. Tomorrow morning, maybe."

"Try to stress the risk of other kids dying," Khleang said acidly.

"I'll try, but don't get your hopes up," Harrod said. "When you already have a ward full of dying kids, the possibility of one somewhere else kicking it doesn't seem like much of a concern."

Ben Coutts, Richard Gorman, Stephen Mohammadian: all dead of drowning, this year. It seemed there had to be a connection between them, but as far as they knew, Gorman hadn't even known the two wunderkind. He and Coutts had both played Lore, however, as had Gabriel Leberer. Had Mohammadian?

After a query sent to Evreware, the answer was no, unless he had played on someone else's account. So, two out of three, or three out of four if you included Gabriel: not good enough.

Did Gorman know the wunderkind at all, outside of the tenuous connection of Manish Gill breaking into his garage? They called Michelle Gorman, read a list of the wunderkind's names, showed her photos, but none of them meant anything to her. It was still possible, however, that he'd known them through playing Lore. They called Evreware, and when they had a representative on the line, provided them with a copy of a death certificate and had Michelle give them the necessary permissions to access his account and avatar, Dublainn of Acragh. With the rep's help they created a transcript of all of Dublainn's in-game communications, voice and text.

A quick scan of those contents, however, found no conversations between him and either of the two boys. There some other correlations, discussion of certain items and locations within the game, but that was inevitable. Nor was there any dialogue between him and Gill's avatar, Anaxarchos of Milasa.

"What about what Chris said about Ben's armor?" Khleang persisted. "How it was worth a ton of money?"

"You think someone offed him in real life for a piece of armor in-game?"

"I'm just saying, if it is worth a lot, maybe it's worth checking what happens when a player dies. Is their stuff distributed among other players in some way? Can they loot the character somehow?"

They called Evreware back and were told that with a player's death, his character was rendered inactive until someone with legal standing claimed it. In this case, that meant Coutts's parents, neither of whom played Lore. Further questions – along with the presentation of a warrant, hastily obtained – ascertained that Coutts's character was exactly as he had left it, the Aurora breastplate still in his inventory. He had sold some weapons in the auction house in the last week, but no items sold were unique. Whoever had murdered Ben hadn't done it for loot.

The next day, late Friday morning, Harrod got back to them with the results of the brain scan and biopsy. "There are clear indications of a prolonged seizure," she reported, highlighting areas of the brain on the holographic scan. "Including some contraction of the hippocampus. There's also some odd patterns in the cerebral cortex, especially the visual cortex."

"No drugs, though?" Mueller asked.

"Well, there's plenty of THC, traces of other drug activity. But nothing that's likely to cause seizures in someone with no previous history of them. But listen, I have a theory." They listened. "You know about photosensitive epilepsy, PSE? Basically, some individuals, when exposed to certain visual stimuli, especially bright flashing lights, experience a photoparoxysmal response. It's especially prevalent when that stimulus occupies the whole visual field. This was actually a big concern four or five decades ago, when VR specs really started taking off. Kids would be playing video games or whatever, and suddenly they'd be writhing on the ground because of all the flashing lights.

"But the hardware improved, and the designers worked with the neuroscientists to resolve the issue, and they mostly did. Even so, any child who's had a seizure before usually gets tested for PSE before using any VR devices. In some cases you can install safeguards in the hardware to avoid those individuals' specific triggers."

"I see where you're going," Khleang said. "You're saying someone manipulated their systems to induce seizures."

"What, all that setup and you're not even going to let me deliver the punch line?" Harrod laughed.

"But Ben Coutts had no history of seizures. We checked his medical records."

"Right. But here's where it gets interesting. To test people for PSE, they have a special headset that combines a pair of specs with an EEG machine. The specs run through a series of visual stimuli they call Intermittent Photic Stimulation, and the system notes any indications of photoparoxysmal response on the EEG. That's how they determine the specific visual stimuli likely to trigger a seizure.

"Now, of course they stop short of actually triggering a seizure. But they *could* trigger one if they wanted to, easily. Moreover, they've shown in rats that they can trigger seizures in *any* subject by calibrating the stimulus with the EEG. Basically, you reverse the procedure. You look for minute anomalies in the EEG, and refine the stimulus to exacerbate those anomalies. The more pronounced the anomaly, the more data the computer has, until the poor little rat just starts twitching."

"This could work with humans?" Khleang asked.

Harrod shrugged. "Maybe. Although obviously if it *has* been done, it isn't going to appear in *Scientific American*. Seizures cause brain damage. No one would willingly be a subject for it. On the other hand, if I've thought of it, I'm sure somebody clever in the military thought of it fifty years ago." She paused. "Also worth pointing out that in the study I saw, it took quite a while, even in rats. And human brains are vastly more complex. So it may be that if it hasn't been weaponized, it may require too much customization. Too much individual testing and calibration to be practical. Obviously no one's going to sit still for a brain scan for the purpose of giving them a seizure."

"But then, what are the odds that these three have, either?"

"I don't know about the *odds*. But all the wunderkind have been exhaustively tested for different medical conditions, right? I bet at some point that included an EEG, and maybe even testing for PSE. Even if they haven't, their whole genomes have been sequenced. Part and parcel of the genetic engineering that created them. With a powerful enough AI, I wouldn't be surprised if it could extract those patterns from projections of the individual's growth."

They reviewed the recording of Coutts's death again. As it neared the point of his convulsion, Khleang slowed it down. And... there. Three white dots on the screen, just a microsecond of them. Another pattern, eight red shapes. And another. They had Khleang's aississtant run an analysis, and it found 312 flashes in a 20-second window. Each was so brief it was barely noticeable by the naked eye.

"I did notice a little flickering before," Khleang said. "I thought it was just poor recording, or an effect of the light, you know. Weird reflections."

"Nope," said Mueller. "Turns out it's an electronic signal telling your brain to freak out and shut down."

She shook her head. "Scary stuff."

It was. How scary wasn't clear. If it required an EEG to work, then its applicability was limited. If all it needed was a genetic sample... both of them, as police officers, had had such samples taken as a basic security measure when they'd joined the force.

"Agatha," Mueller said. His aississtant appeared in the cubicle entryway.

"Yes, Tom?"

"Agatha, can you analyze the recording we've been watching, and find the anomalies in it?"

A pause. "Yes, I can."

"Can you design a filter for our own systems, to prevent that from occurring to us? To detect it, abort it, and alert us to the attempt?"

"Sure, it's no problem. It will take a couple of minutes, though. Is that okay?"

"It's fine."

Khleang was looking at him steadily. "You think we're in danger?"

He raised his hands helplessly. "I don't know. But Gorman probably didn't think he was in danger, either."

With the permission of Ben Coutts's parents, they accessed his medical records and ascertained that everything they'd speculated about was there: a complete genomic map, repeated EEGs, and a photosensitive epilepsy test. When they mentioned the possibility that someone had accessed the data, though, the administrator shook his head vigorously and insisted it wasn't possible. "We've got state-of-the-art AIs securing this stuff for us. No way does someone get it without our knowledge."

"It's on our own systems now," Khleang pointed out. "How hard would it be –"

"A *summary* is on your systems. Not the data itself."

Despite such assurances, it was hardly certain that no one had beat the university's security. The police had been unable to break Coutts's security on his phone, but obviously *someone* had been able to break through and manipulate it to an extraordinary degree.

In the end it was that intrusion that gave them a break. SPD's Crake called them late in the afternoon, sounding tense and excited. "I've got something you need to see. I think it's what you're looking for."

He had contacted some people he knew regarding the hack, internet security types, white hats. Mueller was completely unable to follow the technical details, but the impression he got was that Coutts's own security software, Juju Mite, had a) detected that its user had died, b) detected the intrusion after the fact, and c) tracked the intrusion to its source. In fact it was vastly more complicated than that – Crake had diagrams of the sourcing and spoke rapidly and enthusiastically about how Juju Mite had found the original initiator of the hack.

"I thought you couldn't crack Juju Mite," Khleang objected.

"We couldn't. No way."

"So how did you find all this out?"

He grinned. "It sent us an e-mail."

"What?"

"Apparently this kid set it up that way. I don't know, maybe he suspected he was in danger. Or maybe he was just naturally paranoid."

"Look, much as I admire your technical prowess," Mueller began, "*who did it?* Where's it from?"

Crake's grin widened as he brought up a map of Idaho. He tapped it and they zoomed down into the far north of the state, to a little town called Bonner's Ferry, and into a view of the street, until they were looking at a nondescript rectangular building just off the highway, with a single front door and store window. It had no sign and no indication what it was used for. Behind it was a low pine-covered hill. "Voila!"

"This is where they were?" Mueller ventured.

"It is. Or was."

"Do you know who, specifically, was responsible?"

"We know the computer used, which is still there in the building. But I went ahead and did a little detective work of my own before calling you. See, this building's owned by a woman named Patty Merton. And our Patty's had some run-ins with the law, all minor stuff at least ten years ago." He pulled up files, highlighted a name. "*But* she's also been known to date a guy named Erik Knott, and Erik's had some more serious attention paid to him."

They scanned the files rapidly as Crake continued to speak.

Knott had been arrested for accessory to kidnapping and conspiracy, but he'd plea-bargained it down in exchange for information. He had under been under FBI surveillance for a time, due his leadership in a radical group called Defenders of Humanity, which advocated –

"Holy shit," Khleang and Mueller both said, almost in unison. They looked at each other with wide eyes.

"I'll get the warrant," Mueller said, already calling the judge.

The Defenders of Humanity had been formed in 2059, the same year that the toddler Patricio Selva had his moment of world fame. They had advocated – still advocated – the mandatory registration and seclusion of the wunderkind as an existential threat to humanity. Alternatively, they offered generously, the wunderkind could simply be sterilized. Obviously their creator, Dr. Liebskind, should furthermore be imprisoned (on this last, at least, they and the authorities were in agreement), and his research destroyed.

At the peak of media coverage of the wunderkind, the Defenders had enjoyed substantial public support. Its most hardcore supporters would picket outside the Selva's house and any other wunderkind they knew of. They made it a mission to reveal the identities of the children and where they lived, causing enormous problems for those families.

Such aggressive tactics also caused more than a little backlash. Angry protesters insisting on murky threats to humanity had little weight compared to adorable little Patricio and his parents on the talk shows. The final, decisive shift came in 2061, when a particularly ardent Defender named Brian Bull briefly kidnapped the wunderkind Robbie Heckler, then age seven, in Tacoma. The boy was recovered unharmed after a day and a half, but the crime was a harbinger of the end for the Defenders, with the media playing and replaying the recording of little Robbie crying as he was reunited with his mother. In any case the Defenders' claims of unknown threats and superhuman powers, to most people, emitted the bitter, sweaty stench of conspiracy theory.

The kidnapping also persuaded the FBI to place the Defenders on the domestic-terrorist list, and in the years since they had kept a casual eye on the group, mostly via AI surveillance. (In this the Defenders' unshakable conviction that they were being watched was correct.) But by all accounts the group had lapsed into dormancy, except for the irregular send-out of a newsletter, *Lines of Defense,* mostly written by Erik Knott.

Apparently the FBI's AI had failed, though, to prevent this attack. But then, who would have suspected that Knott – a geologist by trade – possessed these resources?

In five minutes they had the warrant. In six they had a location: Patty Merton's house in Bonner's Ferry. In seven Khleang called the local police department to seek an arrest.

From there, perversely, things slowed down. It took several minutes to communicate, through the local dispatcher, the urgency of the request. (In fairness, it wasn't clear *how* urgent it was; but at this point, Knott was implicated in at least one and possible three deaths, and they didn't want to lose the locative lock they currently had.) Finally they were put through to the local chief of police, a tall, bald, hollow-cheeked man named Minter who seemed to be walking along the side of Highway 2 when they reached him.

"You want me to arrest Erik Knott?" he said. "What'd he do?"

They explained it to him. He seemed skeptical, but of course willing enough to do what was asked. "To be honest, I wouldn't have thought it of him. He's a bit of a loon, sure, but he always seemed harmless enough to me."

They requested a POV follow-along and Minter accepted, allowing them to share his literal viewpoint via his contacts and the various sensors on his uniform. It took ten or twelve minutes to reach Patty Merton's house, first along a paved access road, then down a dirt road with pine branches scraping the SUV's sides to a run-down ranch-style house with several outbuildings in an unkempt patch of land. They passed a NO TREPASSING sign nailed to a tree. Minter and his partner drove up without lights, the SUV's tires crunching on the gravel. The curtains were drawn on the house's windows. No activity outside. They got out and approached the door. A two-person swing dangled on the wood porch, its cushion torn and spilling its whitish innards. A basket of gardening tools sat in the corner along with an orange extension cord.

Minter made a measured knock on the door, obviously hoping whoever was inside would answer innocently and come calmly. Immediately a dog started barking furiously, ran to the door with its nails scrabbling audibly on the floor inside. They waited, heard murmured voices under the barking.

"Can you amplify that?" Mueller asked Khleang.

"Working on it." She rewound the audio, amplified it, toned down the barking:

"You expecting anybody?" A man's voice.

"Uh-uh. You want me to get it?"

"Hold on."

Minter knocked again, more forcefully. He made a gesture to his partner: circle around the back. The officer nodded and jogged off. Loudly Minter said, "Patty? It's Jim Minter. Can you come to the door, please? We know you're inside."

"Just a minute," said Patty. "Hold on, I'm getting dressed."

Sounds, through the amplified feed, of someone moving through the house. Then a door opening, the squeal of a screen door. "He's going out the back," said Minter's partner. "He sees me. He's running. I'm in pursuit."

They flipped to the other officer's viewpoint, saw a bouncing image of a man in a camouflage hunting jacket sprinting past a shed and wooden corral – sheep baahing and scuttling away inside – disappearing around the corner toward the woods beyond. The officer was fifteen yards behind. Sound of an engine starting. He rounded the corner, saw their suspect mounted on a four-wheel ATV, pine needles flying as he clenched the accelerator on the handlebars and it whined forward.

"Can I use the flyball?" the officer gasped.

"Do it!" said Minter, running himself.

The officer reached down to his belt, pulled loose a small silver sphere like a grenade, pressed a button with his thumb, and threw it at Knott like an infielder racing a batter to first base. Midair the flyball opened, grew flickering wings, and shot forward with new momentum. It struck Knott precisely on the back of his neck, the wings slapping around in a partial collar, and administered a precisely calibrated electric shock. They heard a single choked *ack* as his body stiffened and he lost control of the ATV, falling backwards and sideways onto the forest path.

Had he been wearing a helmet, he likely would have been completely unharmed, but as it was his face struck the ground and ended up with some nasty scratches. The officer chasing him added insult to injury by promptly pressing his knee into the fallen man's back and twisting his arms behind him for the cuffs. "Erik Knott, I'm placing you under arrest," he said, not managing to suppress a note of glad, excited triumph.

"Put these on," Minter said, back in a holding cell at the Bonner's Ferry police station, tossing a pair of cheap specs onto the room's single table. It was an old fold-up table with a plastic laminate wood surface, the kind used for banquets and school cafeterias. The chairs, too, Mueller noted, were stacking steel-frame types of precisely the kind found in schools. Funny how jails and schools had so many features in common.

"I want to know the charges against me," Knott said sourly. He was a wiry man of medium height, with receding hair brushed back and a crooked twist to his nose. Short goatee and mustache, light brown hair, dark eyes. He wore jeans, a green-and-black flannel shirt and hiking shoes. The right side of his face had three bandages covering the larger of the cuts from falling, with significant bruising darkening the skin around them.

"First you're being charged with fleeing arrest. Why'd you run? You know what we wanted?"

"I prefer to deal with police at a distance," he said. "They have this habit of assaulting people." He gestured at his mottled face. "Case in point."

"If you hadn't fled, force wouldn't have been necessary. Do you know what else you're being charged with?"

"If I knew, why would I ask?"

Minter pushed the specs closer toward Knott. "Put on the specs."

Looking suspicious, Knott did as asked, grimacing as the specs' arm brushed past the scrapes on his temple. Mueller tapped a mote to connect and he and Khleang ghosted into the cell from the interrogation room where they sat in Seattle. Without preamble he said, "I'm Detective Mueller of the Seattle Police Department. This is Detective Khleang. What do you know about a boy named Ben Coutts?"

Knott scowled. "If I'm under arrest, then I'm entitled to know the charges against me. I'm also entitled to a lawyer. I want those two things before I say a word."

"The charge is homicide in the first degree." Knott's eyes widened. He started voicing some protest, but Mueller overrode him. "*But,* the charge has not yet been formally filed. We do have evidence implicating you and possibly your partner, Patty Merton, in the murder of Ben Coutts. So if you can convince us that you're innocent, we can let you go. Otherwise, you'll be transported to Seattle and held there for trial. Now. What do you know about Ben Coutts?"

"I have no fucking idea what this is about," Knott said, aggression and earnestness battling for supremacy. "Okay?

Seriously. When I heard the police were outside, I took off because I've had some bad experiences with the police in the past, and I thought I better find out what was up before I did anything. But I don't know anything about a murder. I haven't been in Seattle for years."

"Do you know Ben Coutts?" Khleang asked.

He eyed her warily. "I'd like to see my lawyer."

"If you're actually innocent," Mueller remonstrated, "then the best thing you can do right now is answer our questions as fully as possible. Right now this looks pretty bad for you, and a lawyer won't change that. On the other hand, tell us what you know, and we'll take your cooperation into account."

"What do you know about Ben Coutts?" Khleang asked again.

It was like a play the three of them were performing, with Minter a background presence, leaning against the wall. Knott licked his lips, obviously indecisive about the best course of action. Right now he was more or less in the dark. Guilty or innocent, he didn't know what they knew, had no idea of the evidence lined against him. A guilty man would invariably demand a lawyer. An innocent man still might ask for one, but he might also try to curry favor with the investigators, reasoning that they were sincere in their desire to find the truth.

Knott's shoulders slumped. "I've never met him."

"But you know who he is."

"I know he's one of Liebskind's *brood.* I've never met him or talked to him."

"Which of the wunderkind *have* you met?"

"Met, or been in the room with?"

"Let's say been in the room."

His lips curled. "Selva, a couple times. On the talk shows. Robbie Heckler, in the courtroom, if that counts. I don't think it does. Couple others. I seem to remember a girl on one of the talk shows. You can probably look it up."

Khleang nodded. "We did. Along with Selva and Heckler you also met Annie Wollerman-Spence, Dedina Braun, and Stephen Mohammadian. To our knowledge."

"Then why'd you ask?"

"To see who stuck in your mind. On May 24, 2062, you said, 'Bio-engineered non-humans threaten every natural human. If we care about the survival of our species, we need at the very least to ensure they don't reproduce. If we can do that by simple sterilization, great. If not, they should be physically isolated from each other and the rest of the population, and if *that* isn't possible, patriots of the human species should do absolutely whatever is necessary to end this threat. We should eradicate it the way we eradicated smallpox.'"

Knott shrugged. "So?"

"So do you think we should imprison or kill these kids?"

"Saying 'kids' clouds the issue. It's like the anti-abortion people saying 'babies' when they're really talking about embryos. They're not 'kids' because they're not human. We should call them something else, the same way you call a young wolf a 'cub' or a newborn sheep a 'lamb.' I prefer the term 'betas,' like a second version. Along the same lines, calling them 'wunderkind' makes them sound like something great, something cute, something harmless, instead of what they are: harbingers of the end of natural humanity. I've also suggested *homo artificialis,* or Artificials."

"You really hate them so much?" asked Mueller.

"I *don't* hate them. I *am* terrified of them. Not only have they been *designed* – not born, designed – but they weren't even designed by humans! You know that, right? Everyone acts like Liebskind did it himself, but that's not remotely true. He just fed some vectors to Pacificus, U-dub's AI, and the *computer* made the changes. That doesn't freak you out, that a machine is actively designing our replacements?"

Khleang said, "You haven't answered the question. Do you

still believe these children should be killed?"

He rolled his eyes. "I never said that in the first place."

"So what does 'eradicated' mean, if not 'killed?'"

"What do you want it to mean? Anyway, that was twenty years ago. So what. I said a lot of things. I never committed a crime. It's free speech."

Khleang brought up a picture of Brian Bull, another of Robbie Heckler, showing them to Knott. "Some people you knew did, though. You and Brian were pretty close at one point."

"I wouldn't say that. Look, Brian was crazy. It happens. There are lots of crazy people around, and when you're active in politics sometimes they latch onto you. And again, what does this have to do with anything? It was *twenty years ago*. Is this why you attacked me in my home? Because someone I knew two decades ago did something I never would have done myself? There was a trial. I was cleared of charges. Brian acted alone. End of story."

"Where you on Christmas day?" Khleang continued.

He raised an eyebrow. "Mostly at Patty's house. Her kids came over. The usual kind of thing."

"Did you leave the house at any point?"

He shrugged irritably. "Sure. I guess. In the evening I went out to Talbot's for a drink. Then I went and hung out at the shop for a bit."

"The shop is the building at one hundred South Saint Mary Street?"

"Sure."

"What did you do there?"

"I don't know, just dicked around. Put on the side panel of the Mustang, I think that was on Christmas. I'd painted it the day before. Otherwise, ate some food, looked at shit on the Internet, checked my e-mail."

"You were alone."

"Yeah. Did I say I wasn't? Patty and me, we don't always get along. When she starts getting on my nerves, or I'm getting on hers, I go over to the shop to chill out. Give us both a break."

"Ever hear of something called Juju Mite?"

He shook his head unknowingly. "No. Should I have?"

"You're sure you haven't heard of it?"

"Juju Might? I don't know, what is it, a band name? Cleaning product? I don't know what you're talking about."

Mueller and Khleang exchanged a glance. Mueller spoke first, taking a gently persuasive tone. "Erik, look. It doesn't look so good for you already. And I can't guarantee anything, but make a full confession here, and we'll encourage the judge to be lenient in sentencing. It can make a big difference both in how long you're in for and in where you get sent. Right now, if you don't cooperate, there's a good chance you'll end up in federal prison for the rest of your life. Cooperate, and maybe we can get the charges reduced."

Knott paled. "I don't even know what you're talking about. How can I confess to something, when I don't even know what it is?"

Khleang stared hard at him, rapped the table once with her knuckles, and came to a decision. Her fingers flicked as she pulled up files. "Shortly after you were arrested, we seized your computer from the building on Saint Mary Street. We searched its contents and reviewed its recent activity, focusing especially on December twenty-fifth."

Knott looked really afraid now. "You're making this up. That computer was protected."

Khleang snorted. "That computer was seven years old, and your security software wouldn't stop a clever ten-year-old. Cracked it like a walnut with a hammer. And along with some truly disgusting pornography, we found a piece of software called Juju *Jinx*. I'd ask if you know what it does, but I assume you do, since just obtaining it is pretty remarkable. This isn't the kind of stuff you buy off the shelf. This is the latest, greatest security-intrusion software available, specifically designed to corrupt systems protected by Juju Mite. Our experts, looking at it, suspect now that Juju Mite was itself designed and released with this secondary program in mind – that Juju Mite is in fact a very sly Trojan horse whose vulnerabilities to Juju Jinx were entirely unknown to those using it."

"I don't –" Knott protested weakly.

Khleang didn't stop. "Now listen, Erik, we're getting to the good stuff. On Christmas night, you logged onto your computer, opened Juju Jinx, used it to corrupt Ben Coutts's system, and lured him into a dangerous position. We know all this because it's recorded on your computer, clear as day. Your own security software – and your admission here today – verifies that it was you using the system.

"But it leaves some real questions, which we'd like you to answer now. First, who gave you this software? Because judging from the crappy computer you used, and its crappy security, you obviously didn't come up with this yourself. Second, how, having gotten Ben where you wanted him, did you actually trigger the seizures?"

For a few seconds Knott just stared at her, looking stunned. Then in a hoarse whisper, he said, "I want to see my lawyer." And say another word, Knott would not.

So that, it seemed, was that. Knott would be charged in federal court with the first-degree murder of Benjamin Coutts.

But many questions lingered. The similarities of the deaths of Coutts, Gorman, and Mohammadian indicated a near-certain link, but there was nothing on Knott's computer to indicate his complicity in those other deaths. Nor had they discovered the means used to trigger the photosensitive epilepsy. It suggested significant computing power and the availability of those individuals' medical records; but neither were to be found on Knott's computer. In fact, Juju Jinx stood out distinctly among the computers' other contents, like finding a precision laser cutter in a desk full of crayons and construction paper.

What it suggested was obvious, and Khleang finally gave voice to their doubts. "I hate to say it, but it could be a setup."

"I know," Mueller sighed. He rubbed at his eyes under his specs. It was almost nine. They'd been kept at the station late, again, filing reports, talking to the Bonner's Ferry police, making arrangements for Knott's transport to a federal holding facility, filling out forms. Somehow having aissistants still didn't save them from filing paperwork.

Khleang went on, "Neither of us thinks Knott is capable of designing this software himself. Maybe he's a secret computer genius, but there's nothing in his history indicating that."

"Wouldn't be the first time someone taught themselves to code."

"This isn't some throwaway app that makes cars look like giant cats or something. This is designed to fool not just humans but AI security systems, which means it was made by a smarter AI. We're talking mega computing power, probably a quantum supercomputer. Kind of thing only governments and major corporations have access to."

"I know."

"And it wouldn't be hard for those kind of people to insert this software in Knott's computer and falsify the security info. Or, since they had control of Ben's system too, to fake the information that led to us arresting him in the first place. I mean, they sent us an e-mail, for god's sake. Like, they might as well have sent us his picture and written 'This guy did it!' on the front."

And like that, they made the leap from believing in Knott's guilt to suspecting his innocence. They couldn't be sure, right now, and so they had to keep holding him. And maybe the truth was somewhere between the two: Knott *had* killed Ben Coutts, but only after being supplied the means to do it by a third party. A third party who might well be responsible for the other deaths.

The thing that bothered him, too, was the peculiar linkages between the cases. Gabriel Leberer dies of apparently accidental poisoning, and his body is subsequently stabbed by his boyfriend, Manish Gill. Gill flees, taking a roundabout route that leads them to the home of Richard Gorman, who has died that summer by a mysterious drowning. Ben Coutts is killed, also by drowning (along with Stephen Mohammadian, that same year), which leads them to arrest Erik Knott.

Gill was the key. He was the one real link between the cases. Had he not gone to Gorman's house, they would have no reason to suspect any connection between the cases at all. But they had no idea why he had gone there.

In the following weeks they built the case against Knott, working with the federal prosecutor. A date was set for the trial: Monday, Feb. 10. The prosecutor painted a rosy picture of Knott's conviction, although he very much wished they would discover the software that had initiated Coutts' seizures. If they could find it, he said, they could move ahead with first-degree murder; if not, it was possible Knott would only be charged with accessory.

But as the trial date grew closer, Mueller grew more and more uncomfortable. He had dreams of being buried alive and trying to dig himself out, only to find that he was digging the wrong way, he was moving downward into the earth, where some evil was waiting for him in an ancient burrow.

Unexpectedly, early in February, there was movement on another front, a ball they had set rolling months before: Chris's application to Inversus, Gill's Lore guild. On the Thursday night before the trial, as Chris was online, he stopped what he was doing, looking disturbed. "Do you want to go for a walk?" he suggested. Something in his tone made Mueller take notice.

"Sure." Chris stood up, and then, strangely, took out his

contacts, put them in their case and set them together with his handset in the charging bowl. He went to the end table, took a pencil and piece of paper from the drawer, and wrote Mueller a note: *Get rid of your electronics. All of them.*

Mueller nodded, and dropped his specs and handset into the bowl as well. Together they went to the bedroom and changed carefully, selecting mostly old clothes, vintage items that lacked the motion-tracking electronics common to clothing for the last thirty years. Mueller wore old leather dress shoes, a Navy peacoat older than him, faded jeans. Chris, more the fashionista, finally selected a well-fitting brown suit from the forties that he'd bought on a whim, together with pointed cowboy boots.

"You look good," Mueller said, smiling.

"A little formal for a Tuesday night, but whatever. Let's go."

The night was chilly, but Mueller buttoned up the neck of the peacoat and was comfortable enough. Chris looked colder, hunching into his jacket. "Where we going?"

"Not sure," Chris replied, frowning. "The park, maybe." But once at Cal Anderson he kept darting suspicious glances around, obviously dissatisfied. Finally he headed up the small hill to the right of the fountain, Mueller in tow. The campers Mueller had seen in the park the week before had finally disembarked for warmer climes, and in fact the park was abandoned but for the occasional auto passing by its borders or the odd pedestrian crossing along the main footpaths. Chris rubbed his hands together, blew on them, breath a moist cloud. The clouds were low, reflecting the light of the city in a pinkish glow. Quietly he said, "Think anyone can hear us up here?"

"I don't know," Mueller said. "Not with their natural hearing. But you're obviously more worried about electronic surveillance. In which case, maybe, maybe not. Depends how determined they are." A pause. "How determined do you *think* they are?"

Chris shrugged indecisively. "I don't know. I doubt anyone's listening at all."

"But you think someone may be spying on us at home."

"I don't know." He frowned. "Scratch that. Yes."

"Who?"

"Inversus." He shook his head. "You shouldn't have involved me with these guys, Tom. It was a mistake."

In the last two weeks Chris had quit his former guild (to some outcries and recriminations) and performed a series of increasingly difficult tasks as part of his application for Inversus, some of them in-game, some not. Some were quite possibly extra-legal: receiving a small package, for instance, placing it in a new box, and mailing it to a given address. Last Tuesday, at their behest, he had simply gone and sat on a park bench in Ravenna at ten to five. They hadn't told him why. Some joggers had passed, an older couple walking hand in hand. After twenty minutes he received a message on his system saying he could go.

His contact with the guild was exclusively through an individual calling himself or herself th3W0rm. th3W0rm communicated in text only. S/he had a character in Naxos, but Chris had yet to meet it in person.

"They want access to your files," Chris said finally.

"Yeah?" Mueller had, he realized, been half-expecting something like this. "Anything in particular?"

"Something called Virgil. They didn't say what it is."

Interesting. "And how did they propose you get this access?"

"I don't think they care. Although they said they would help if needed."

"What makes you think they're watching us?"

Chris shrugged once, sharply. "I don't know. Nothing definite. They just seem to know a lot about us, when I'm with you, when I'm not. Then when we were discussing your investigation, I was saying that I didn't have access to that stuff, and the Worm was like, *we're convinced from your conversations that he can be persuaded.* Implying, obviously, that they were listening in."

Of course, hackers loved to imply that they knew more than they did. It was part of the image they wished to project: all-powerful, all-knowing, delving infinitely into the hidden depths of code. More interestingly, though, it also implied the opening of a dialogue. "Maybe he knew you would do just what you're doing now. Coming and talking to me." Talking to him *sans* system, he realized. Maybe th3W0rm was concerned, not with Mueller knowing, but with who else might be listening in.

"It's definitely possible. Although he also said that if I couldn't get the files in a week, they'd try more technical solutions."

"Anything else?"

"Um, a couple things. Since Gabriel's character, Olsol, went inactive, there's been some chatter on the boards about his weapon, people lamenting how much it sucks that it's gone from the game. He had this war hammer –"

A name floated upward in Mueller's memory. Something Gabe's coworker, Young-soo, had mentioned. "Omphalos."

"That's its name, yeah. Anyway, people were bitching about it, since apparently it was crafted from this magical meteorite that fell to ground ages ago, and had all these spells laid on it by the Bizul Tuz, who used it to protect their temples ... no one could even move the thing until Olsol captured a moonblood elemental, which is still imprisoned in the haft, and how he got that thing to do what he wanted anyway –"

"This is going somewhere, right?"

"Of course it is. Point is, I got curious and looked through Olsol's inventory, and it's not there."

Interesting. They'd checked that possibility with Kojin Tachimaru's breastplate, but hadn't thought to do the same with Olsol. "Are you sure he still had it? He could have gotten rid of it beforehand."

"He had it. He was online the same night he died, leading a

raid against some Hu Wa encampments, swinging Omphalos like always. And there's no record of him selling it, and no one's seen it since."

"Could he have hidden it?"

"Sure. It'd be quite a treasure hunt, if he did. The thing's worth a lot of money. Even more than that breastplate we were talking about."

"Good to know. What was the other thing?"

"I was going through the chat files for Dublainn of Acragh, Gorman's character, like you asked. So on July 1 he's talking with Agnos, arranging this deal that never happened. Gorman says that he has the 'mirror cloak,' whatever that is."

"Presumably whatever they're trading."

"Right. And Agnos says okay, and that he'll contact Gorman with the time and place for the exchange on Sunday, that's July 5. Of course that never happened, because he died, and Agnos cut off contact at that point. But I thought you might be interested, almost the last thing Agnos asked is whether Gorman has heard of something called Pythia."

"Which is what?"

"I don't know. Neither did Gorman. But Agnos says it's in Seattle, and he'd be interested in any information Gorman has on it. And that's it."

"It could be anything."

"It could. And maybe it's nothing. On the other hand, two days later the guy was dead. So maybe it's something."

Mueller looked away into the pink night. Somewhere the moon was shining, but they couldn't see it. He could hear the Broadway trolley coming up the tracks, the sound reverberating dully across the landscape.

Chris was waiting expectantly, shivering inside his russet coat, eyes gleaming in his deeply shadowed face. "Tell them I want to meet," Mueller said. "I can't give them the files directly. But if they have specific questions about their contents, I'll consider answering them in exchange for information."

"What information?"

"Anything that could help our investigation, really. There are a lot of holes. The whereabouts of Manish Gill, for starters. He's one of their members. They may know where he is. The identity of Agnos, the arms dealer. Where Knott got the epilepsy software." Chris nodded, looking more than a little miserable, and suddenly Mueller felt a surge of regret, his eyes moistening. "I'm sorry I involved you in this," he said. "I thought it would be fun, but obviously that was a stupid idea."

"It's fine," Chris breathed. "But can we get out of here? I'm freezing."

"Yep." Their shoes clapped on the pavement rhythmically. Finally Chris said impishly, as though considering, "Although I think they were going to finally let me go on a raid to Redclaw Chasm on Monday."

Mueller laughed. "So maybe you'll stick with the hackers?"

"They do have the sweet lootz."

When they got back home, Mueller threw his keys in the drawer and Chris, shivering, turned on the electric heat and crouched with hands extended by the baseboard unit. Reflexively Mueller plucked his specs out of the charging bowl and put them on.

Waiting for him was an urgent message. It was from th3W0rm. WE'D LOVE TO MEET! it read jauntily. LET'S MAKE A DATE.

So much for private conversations.

They met in Murkroot Grove, a burned-out forest north of the city of Umber in Daggoran. All around them were the charred black skeletons of trees, and periodically the charred black corpses of dead soldiers huddled on the ground. Some of the bodies had been torn open by scavengers, their pink innards exposed to the foggy night.

"This is gruesome," said Mueller, edging by the spilled intestines of a slain steed. "And depressing. Why would you want to hang out in this?"

"It wasn't always like this," Chris said, holding up a lantern to peer into the mists. "This just happened. The Dags burned it while they were retreating from the Jennies."

"Do I dare ask what a Jenny is?"

"Member of the Jeth-Nelmithean Alliance. J-N, therefore Jenny."

"And why would they burn down the forest?"

"Same reason armies burn fields in real life. To prevent your enemies from getting its resources. A lot of resources in Murkwood, especially spider's silk and gemwood. Now, obviously, not so much."

Since its destruction, the forest had become haunted by a variety of spooks, in particular howling hellhounds, silent specters, and somewhere, the Lich Unborn, a floating undead fetus thingie that Chris warned they had to keep watch for. "The hellhounds are no problem, the specters are annoying, especially if you've got more than one on you, but the dead baby we can't kill without a party. So if you see a blue glow coming toward us, run."

Mueller stared into the mists. "There are blue glows everywhere."

"Well, more so."

Three times before they reached their destination, a tree of thorns near the center of the razed wood, Chris had to fight off hellhounds, dispatching them in a minute or two with Holy spells and a flask of glowing water. "Fire or frost spells won't do anything to them," he explained. When they died their bodies burst into blue flames and burned down to glowing spots of dog-shaped cinders amid the ashes.

When they reached the tree, they stood and waited, not seeing the Worm around. Upon the tree's thorny branches were pinned hundreds or thousands of birds of all varieties, large and small, dark and light and multicolored, sparrows and crows and exotic parrots and falcons, which seemed, from their raucous cries and pitiful struggles, to still be alive.

"They didn't burn this tree," Mueller observed.

"Probably they couldn't. It's magically protected. And actually this tree is pretty important, if you're a warlock, anyway. Pinning a bird to the tree forges a relationship with the Ysir, the demons who planted it, and grants you different spells depending on what kind of bird you use. People are always looking for new birds to capture because they're curious about..."

"Well, *hello,* boys," came a languid voice from above them. They circled around the tree and saw, slithering from a hole in the wood, a cartoonish worm, pudgy, bespectacled, and red as a pulsing artery. It held a book open in one hand: a bookworm, then. "So good of you to make it."

"How did you get inside the tree?" Chris asked curiously. "I didn't know that was possible."

"You can work your way inside anything," said the Worm, "if you can just get your teeth into it." The creature smiled broadly, revealing two gleaming rows of improbably large, pointed and very carnivorous fangs.

Leisurely, it inchwormed its way vertically down the tree's trunk. When it reached the mat of bird bones and decaying feathers that lay beneath the tree, it glanced at its book, tapped a figure on some passage as if in consideration, and then snapped the tome shut and tucked it under its skinny red arm. "Well," it began, and beamed at them. Its face had big round cartoon eyes behind the glasses, blue as glowing sapphires. "It's certainly nice to meet you both, at last. I feel like I know you so well already."

Mueller chuckled. "Is that because you've been spying on us?"

"I wouldn't put it that way," said the Worm. "I'd say sharing from afar in your domestic bliss."

"Suit yourself," Mueller said. "It must make for a pretty boring stream."

"Yes," the creature admitted. "Other than the sex, and then I don't go for gay porn myself. And even that seemed quite pedestrian."

"Great," Christian said, rolling his eyes. "Now I'm going to be thinking of this every time I want to get laid."

"Maybe you can let your inner exhibitionist free. Buy some costumes. Amuse us."

"Is that why you do this?" Mueller inquired. "Amusement?"

"Yes and no." The Worm stroked his chin. "Part business, part pleasure. Part amusement, part necessity. We like to know who we're dealing with."

"You keep saying 'we,'" Mueller noted. "Do you mean your guild, or are there actually other people with you right now?"

"Let's say it's the royal 'we,' for now. And Inversus, you know, is not so organized and certainly not so hierarchical as you seem to imply. We are generally uncomfortable with individual spokespeople. We are not a bargaining unit, not an organization in that sense. Think of it more as a distributed network. When I say 'we,' I speak mostly of shared habits of thought and method and character. It's not like anybody took a vote."

"I'm surprised you were willing to meet."

"Oh? No, it's not surprising at all. We want information. So do you. It's a simple trade. We do this sort of thing all the time. Besides, while we've done our due diligence, there remains a more subtle assessment of character that I find is only possible to achieve in person."

"I understand." He was used to making just those kinds of assessments himself. "I can't give you the files. I'm willing to consider questions about their contents."

The Worm pouted. "Well, how many questions? Is this one of these genie things, where I only get three wishes, and if I use them badly you disappear? Our information is concrete. Yours is unknown. How are we to know if we're getting a fair exchange?"

Mueller considered the problem. "Three questions seems fair. Ask me all three at once, and I'll decide if I can answer them. If I do, you tell me where Gill is."

"Why do you want Gill so badly?" the Worm asked casually. "Your investigation's winding down. Your superiors are satisfied with the results. Why not just leave it alone and go out for another soy latte?"

Again Mueller wondered how Inversus knew so much about their investigation, how they could have that kind of access. Could they penetrate Themis? It didn't seem possible; Themis ran on a quantum supercomputer in a secure facility in Colorado. On the other hand, there were many people with access *to* Themis, and people were easily corrupted. On the other other hand, it was easy enough to follow his activities via the endlessly available and more easily corruptible sensors ubiquitous to the modern world: handsets, specs, clothing, autos, satellites, drones, smart crosswalks, and the utility box in their apartment that shut off the lights when they left. Then there were the more specialized surveillance methods... the fact was, these days everything was an open book, for those who cared to read it. Like the book the Worm held.

"I'm not comfortable sending Erik Knott to prison." He thought of saying more, but hesitated.

The Worm obligingly moved into the gap. "You think someone might have framed him by altering his computer data. And you're fairly certain that someone at least had to have helped him obtain Juju Jinx in the first place. Therefore, even if he is partially guilty, he had to have a more knowledgeable, and likely more responsible, accomplice."

"So you've already looked into it."

"Of course. Due diligence, as I said."

"So what do you think? You're the super-amazing hacker guild. Did someone falsify the data?"

"It pains me to say this," the Worm sighed, "but we're not sure."

"Really?"

"Really. We have examined the computer in question. We have examined it in excruciatingly   thorough detail. And we remain unsure. The *thing* is, by all indications the data is genuine. And we don't believe it for a second. Erik Knott simply isn't capable of this degree of penetration. It is simply inconceivable that he could even *possess* Juju Jinx. We weren't aware ourselves that it existed until your discovery of it, which naturally upset us. And running it on that computer! It's like running Lore on an Apple II."

"So he had help."

"Our belief is that he had nothing to do with it whatsoever. He's innocent, of this, at least. But proving that is impossible. Which brings us to our secondary point of concern, that someone is leapfrogging us. Whoever they are, they possess both a high degree of access *and* a high degree of anonymity. And we simply *hate* that, Detective. Hate it existentially."

Mueller chuckled. "Isn't that exactly what you have?"

"Yes, exactly. But we don't use it for murder. To the contrary: we use it to liberate. First we liberate information, then we liberate people. We wear masks so that all might live openly."

"You don't ever liberate money?" Mueller asked skeptically.

"We steal from thieves and use the money to hinder them further."

"Thieves including business owners?"

"Depending on the business, absolutely. Those that steal the labor of others for their own profit, absolutely."

"So basically *all* business," Mueller laughed.

"Aha!" the Worm cried. "A true communitarian! You understand us completely!"

Christian had gone up to the tree and was standing on his tiptoes to look inside the hole the Worm had made. "Hey, this actually goes somewhere."

"It's Grobb's cave," the Worm said.

"Really?" said Chris, looking astounded. "It takes a couple hundred people three or four weeks to reach him. I tried it before with my guild, and we couldn't get past the salamanders."

The Worm shrugged. "I made a shortcut."

"Well, I'm in your guild now! Do you think we could come back here and knock off Grobb real quick, after this? Or if you're busy, I bet I could get a party together..."

"It's best not to, actually. Evreware might notice. I'll have to close the hole up before I leave."

"Aww..."

"But if you like, we're raiding the Skytomb next week. You're welcome to tag along."

"Nice! Yes!"

"Wow," said Mueller. "Chris doesn't get that excited for *me.*"

"You excite me in a different way," Chris said.

The Worm made a face. "Eww. Keep it to the bedroom. Or better yet, somewhere we're *not* watching." He grinned. "But back to business. We want the files."

Mueller shook his head. "I told you, no. If you misused the information..."

"But we won't!" protested the Worm, a caricature of innocence. "Believe me, we mean only the best."

Mueller raised an eyebrow. "The best, meaning what? Why do you even care about it?"

The Worm spread its hands. "Isn't simple curiosity enough?"

"It's enough of a motivation, sure. But let me rephrase: What will you *do* with the information once you have it?"

"We wish to aid you in your investigation. Really!"

"Great. So aid me."

"To aid you, we need information. Which will lead to more information."

"Once again, why do you care?"

The creature frowned, rubbing at its jaw again. "I'm not sure. That's just the problem. There are rumors. Signs. Trends that unnerve us."

"Care to elaborate?"

It spoke slowly. "There is a corporation, Flohr-Lavine. which through a subsidiary owns Insight Technology. Its CEO is a billionaire named Erik Flohr. Flohr was instrumental in developing Insight. It's his pet project, really, seeking to develop superintelligent AIs.

"This year Flohr-Lavine has done very well for itself. Its stock is soaring. What bothers us, beyond the fact that Flohr himself is a worthless, amoral parasite, is *how* it's doing so well. It seems to have less to do with Flohr-Lavine's activities than the widespread failure of its competitors. Yet looking into it further, we see no great errors on their parts.

"What we have instead is a trail of small coincidences. A deadline is missed here. An important project manager quits suddenly for purely personal reasons. A public presentation goes awry. Individually, these mishaps are meaningless. Taken together, they have major effects on larger events.

"We have suspicions regarding who they are meant to benefit, but no information on how these coincidences occur. We strongly suspect it involves an AI of surpassing sophistication. So. What will we do? We will investigate, as you are doing. We will discover the source of this manipulation. Then we'll act."

Mueller absorbed all this, thinking. Finally he said, "I can't give you the files."

"We thought you might say that," the Worm replied. "We understand that giving us the files poses a significant risk for you. But we believe that we have other information that you desire. We're prepared to sweeten the deal."

"Sweeten it with what?"

"Watch." The Worm turned, faced the tree, stuck two fingers between his teeth and whistled piercingly. As one, the birds' whistles, caws and squawks ceased, leaving an eerie silence. Then, with a sudden explosion of wings, they tore themselves free of the thorns that held them and took flight.

Mueller looked curiously at the Worm, who raised a hand in a gesture of patience. The birds swirled in a crazy gyre and reformed in the gray sky behind them, a hundred yards distant. When they reached their place, they stopped and hovered, wings flapping. Impossible in real life, but it didn't matter here.

Black and white, red and yellow and green, they locked into position and formed a simple rectangle, wing to wing. The rectangle comprised a single grainy image, each bird acting as a pixel. Mueller frowned at it, realizing there was something about it that was familiar. The Worm gave him a measuring look, made a tapping gesture, and the image began to move.

It was a simple video, apparently taken by a convenience store security camera. There was a time stamp in the lower right corner: 16:37 28/05/2049. May 28, 2049. He knew that date. It had been stabbed into his brain like a tattoo.

A boy came up to the counter. He was wearing a baseball tee with a Stussy logo and had a silver backpack. He was buying soda and a bag of chips. He had light hair and a mischievous look. Mueller stared at the image with wide eyes, unable to look away. The boy paid. The boy left.

The video started again. The boy walked up with his chips and soda. It would have been barbecue chips and root beer, Mueller thought. That's what he'd liked. The boy handed over a bill, got his change. The boy left. Mueller had never seen this video before. "Where was this taken?" he whispered.

"Marcher's Goods n Gas," the Worm said. "On Ponahawai St."

Marcher's. By God. He hadn't thought of the name in decades. "I've never seen this before."

"It was overlooked. The system wasn't networked. The police should have found it, but they didn't."

"What about outside the store?" Mueller asked. "A lot of stores have external cameras. Most of them do. Is there video from outside? Where did he go?"

The Worm spoke one word. "Virgil."

Comprehension sunk in. With it came a sudden, unexpected outrage. "*Is there more?*"

"There's more," affirmed the Worm, speaking slowly and clearly. "He gets into a car."

Jesus! "Is there a plate number?"

The Worm nodded. "There is. And the number *has a cost.*"

Mueller shook his head. He couldn't look away from the video. The boy didn't look upset at all. Where had he gone? "I can't give you the files," he said hoarsely. "But I'll tell you what's in them." Briefly he described the investigation into Agnos. "In their last communication, Agnos asked if Gorman knew anything about something called Pythia, here in Seattle. It might have something to do with this."

"Pythia." The Worm's eyes went distant. "Pythia. Yes. That's it." The smiled returned. "And as a gesture of goodwill... We're well familiar with Agnos. He's a man named Dan Yarborough. He lives and operates out of the Dome."

"What Dome?" Mueller said. "In Seattle?"

The Worm rolled its eyes. "No, not in Seattle. In Houston, silly. He's in the Astrodome." It made another gesture and the image in the sky broke apart, the birds dispersing. En masse, they flew back to the tree, found their individual thorns, and impaled themselves.

Later Mueller told Chris all about it, sitting opposite each other on the big couch in the living room with a blanket over their legs. Chris listened attentively with a sympathetic, faintly puzzled expression. Listening had never been Chris's strong suit, but Mueller appreciated the effort.

The boy in the video was Tom's little brother, Shawn. Seeing it had stirred Mueller's mind into a maelstrom, raising a thousand memories from the depths. That time Shawn had gotten his finger in the door: they'd been going out to a movie, *Winterseed,* he thought, but they'd gone to the hospital instead, because the finger was broken. Afterwards they'd gone for ice cream at Fred's, a sort of consolation prize, Shawn eating it with his index finger in its metal splint raised in the air, joking about how he should have just gotten it replaced with a robotic one, and all the things a robot finger might be able to do. The caramel-esque taste of poha-berry ice cream, which he had never tasted since leaving the islands.

That had been just weeks before Shawn disappeared. Had Shawn still had the splint? Probably not. It would have been included in the police descriptions, along with the baseball tee, jeans, and orange-soled runners.

Shawn had vanished from the island of Hawaii on May 28, 2049, when Shawn was twelve and and his big brother was sixteen. He had come home early that day, in the last few days of sixth grade at Waiakea Intermediate. Tom himself was at home, having gotten out from school the week before, but had been distracted with his own problems, in a mood over the sudden, spurious verbal abuse from another teen he had been seeing, texting furiously on his handset. Shawn had said Tom should drive him down to the waterfront and they could hang out and play frisbee, but Tom had rebuffed him. He couldn't remember what he'd said, but it had been curt and unpleasant. A while later he heard the back door open and close, and assumed his brother was going into the backyard to lie in the hammock or play with their dog, Chico Blanco. And that was the last time Tom or anybody ever saw Shawn Mueller.

When his parents got home, Shawn was gone. They assumed he had gone over to a friend's house without telling anybody.

They tried calling him – Shawn had his own handset – but got no response. They called Shawn's friends, one after the other, but no one had seen him. When he wasn't home by nightfall, they called the phone company to find the location of the handset. The company obligingly gave them a location on a map, in downtown Hilo.

They found the phone around ten o'clock that night. It had been tossed in a dumpster behind Sack N Save along with Shawn's backpack and wallet.

At first the police were sanguine, pointing out that Hawaii was an island, and Shawn was assuredly still on it. Someone had seen him. Someone knew where he was.

Two days later they still believed they would find him.

A week later their voices held a quaver of doubt.

Two weeks later they said there were doing all they could.

A month in, the family counselor they'd been provided said they had to face the possibility that Shawn was gone. It wasn't certain, she said. He could still be found. But they had to be prepared.

After six months, no one outside the family seriously thought Shawn was alive. Tom didn't know what to think himself, but was tormented by that last, casual brushoff. He'd been completely absorbed in his own petty problems, and his brother had gone and met some horrible end. His mother, Sharlene, refused to believe Shawn was dead, holding onto hope like a child's blanket. His father, Edwin, barely spoke of it, sinking deep into depression. They were both taking mood medications, but if it was supposed to make them better Tom didn't think it was working. The more his mother spoke brightly of being reunited with her son, the more Tom became convinced she was disconnecting from reality in some basic way. Meanwhile his father withdrew more and more, spending his days off from the post office in the shed out back, making little wooden boxes and coffee tables, and leaving each evening to take hours-long walks around the town in the growing darkness.

They went on like this. On and on. Shar, thin and bird-like in the first place, became gaunt and bright-eyed. She suffered stomach problems, and would wake crying in the night, turning over to find her husband absent, out in his little shed, or working the graveyard shift, or walking who knows where.

The stomach pains got worse. The next summer she was diagnosed with stomach cancer. They tried to save her and couldn't. She had surgery, and another. She had no will to fight. She was nauseous all the time. She faded on her hospital bed like someone vanishing from time.

After his wife died, Ed Mueller seemed actually to recover. He left Hawaii, taking Tom with him to Bellingham, Washington, where Ed found work as a carpenter. There he remarried and lived on well enough another eighteen years, finally succumbing to a stroke in 2068, at age 67. It was funny: everyone expected, somehow, to live to a ripe old age of eighty or ninety, but in fact many people died much earlier. There was no telling. He thought of the wunderkind, how 67 would be merely early middle age for them. They would be hale, in the prime of life, with those added decades of experience and education behind them. What couldn't they do?

Shawn was never found. The investigation dragged itself along for a while, but when Ed Mueller left it effectively ended. The family had moved on; so did the police. Tom wanted to fight it, but in the end time and distance won out. But his life became shaped by it, by the idea that even on an island, a boy could walk out the back door and be taken from his family forever. Just disappear. It shouldn't have been possible, but it actually happened.

Well, times had changed. Kidnappings were more rare than murders, these days. A murder, after all, was frequently performed without thought of consequence. The murderer was often well aware they would be immediately apprehended and imprisoned, yet still commit the crime, out of rage or misguided need for vengeance for some perceived wrong. There was a powerful self-destructive drive in nearly all violent behavior.

A kidnapper, on the other hand, had to think further ahead. Even if they were a true sociopath, intending to abuse and kill their victim, it still meant they needed hours or days unnoticed. If they were an estranged parent or relative, they had to escape permanently. Both were nearly impossible with Themis able to track their movements.

Had Themis existed in 2049, Shawn Mueller would, in all likelihood, still be alive.

True to its word, the Worm sent the file that same night. Mueller was already in the second bedroom he used as a study. He opened the file with trembling fingers and sat mesmerized as he watched Sean leave Marcher's and walk to a gray Honda Civic. There was someone in the driver's seat, but he couldn't see who it was. The car could have been anyone's. But as it pulled out, there was a clear shot of the Hawaii license plate: GKA 584 over the rainbow.

He ran the numbers and it came back as a rental, licensed to Island Bargain Rentals in Hilo. The company had gone out of business in 2056. Twenty-five years ago.

It was possible, he told himself, that they still had records from the rental. Not likely, but possible. A dusty computer somewhere, a hard drive lost in a closet. He did more research, found the owner, James Himura, found that Himura had died a decade ago.

Himura had to have relatives. There had to be a way to turn this number into a name.

But it wouldn't happen tonight. Meanwhile, Knott's trial was on Monday. Agnos – Yarborough – was in Houston, and there was a clear connection between them. Mueller's brother had been gone for thirty years; his restless ghost could wander for another few days.

An ordinary web search turned up almost nothing on Daniel Yates Yarborough, at least after 2048. No social media presence whatsoever. No email contact, no phone, nothing. In fact nearly the only mention he could find of the man was a web article from a news site listing him as wounded in action in Jordan. Apparently Yarborough had been a Marine.

A police-records search turned up more. Fortunately most of the Free States still shared police information with the U.S. Three years after being discharged due to disability from the Marines, Yarborough had been arrested selling rocket-launcher ammunition – basically small missiles – in Tampa. He spent two years in Florida State Prison for that, doing his time without incident. His mugshot from the arrest showed a hollow-cheeked man with stubble on his balding scalp, staring unamused at the camera with bulbous blue eyes.

That was his sole arrest, but not his only warrant. There were old warrants out in California and Mississippi: in California for smuggling, in Mississippi for grand theft and other charges related to numerous items missing from Keesler Air Force Base.

That was good. It meant he wouldn't need permission from Willie White to do what he wanted to do. "Agatha," he said. "I need a ticket to Houston."

Houston was a whale cast up on the shore of the Gulf and left to rot, the sun slowly leeching the last juices from its flesh. Soon all that would remain was a framework of towering bones.

Mueller had spent part of the flight reading about the city, studying maps, doing virtual tours, especially around the Astrodome. Ten million people, down from a peak of eleven a decade earlier; water rationing largely blamed, with immigrants pushing north in search of better resources. Actually it had done better than most Texas cities since Secession, building its solar and wind capacities once the oil was exhausted, constructing an enormous offshore desalination plant, and fighting to retain its aerospace industry, but fully forty percent of its residents still lived below the poverty line. Downtown was surrounded by suburban and exurban ghettos like a ring of infection. Its government was an oligarchic corporatocracy with vestigial elections in which less than a third of the population bothered to vote.

And, of course, they still executed people. As in the Seattle P.D., there was great pressure to apprehend violent criminals quickly; but in Texas a judge could rule that the risk of further violence overrode the need to prove guilt beyond a reasonable doubt, and on the basis of reasonable suspicion issue what was colloquially known as a black warrant. It encouraged officers to take no risks to themselves when making the arrest: the suspect was wanted dead or alive.

The result had hardly quelled crime. Houston was one of the most armed cities on earth, and if its homicide rate was lower than Mexico City's, it wasn't by much. Three thousand people had been killed there last year. One hundred and sixty-one had been police shootings.

He shook his head at the figures. In Seattle there had been three deadly shootings in 2079. This year there had been two, with only a few weeks left to go. They hadn't had a police shooting in years. It was a different world.

The George Bush Intercontinental Airport looked no different than any other, unless it was in the sense of greater-than-usual sprawl. Long white corridors, six terminals, bad food kiosks. He half-expected to have to go through customs, but then he was on the monorail heading to the main terminal unhindered. The landscape outside the monorail windows was a blaze of sun and glass.

Then he was stepping through the final bank of automatic doors, Hinsel travel pack on his back, black cordura carry-on pulling a little uncomfortably at his right shoulder. It wasn't as hot as he'd been prepared for, teetering on the edge of muggy. The air carried strange scents of stagnant water, effluvium and burning plastic. And something else: petrol exhaust, the waste of the autos (no, not *autos*, he reminded himself: *cars*), rolling slowly by the passenger pick-up area, drivers tending the wheels like sea-captains. He tapped the mote for a taxi, realized the app was specific to Seattle, and instead subvocalized, "Agatha. I need a taxi to the Westin Hotel."

"Yes, Tom. I'm contacting them now."

Twenty meters away a yellow cab pulled out of a queue and came toward him. He saw the dark outline of the driver, thought to himself that an auto wouldn't accelerate so aggressively – waste of energy – and raised a hand, though he assumed that the taxi system had already tagged him with a bright red arrow over his head or something. The taxi stopped and the driver hopped out, an energetic, burly man with short dark hair, a thick mustache and a deep five-o'clock shadow. He was wearing dark sunglasses and a black polo shirt with the logo of the company emblazoned in yellow on the breast. "You put bags in trunk," he said, only half a question, already opening the compartment.

"I'd rather keep them with me," Mueller said.

The driver nodded. "Okay." He shut the trunk and bustled back to the driver's seat. Once inside the driver looked at him in the rearview mirror. "You are going to Westin downtown, right?"

"Yeah, the Westin."

"Okay, let's go." With a cramped glance over his shoulder, the driver hit the gas and shot out across the lanes.

Mueller chuckled. "I haven't had an actual cab driver in a while. Last time was in Istanbul."

"Istanbul?" the driver considered. "When do you go there?"

"Two years ago. Just for a few days." Then they'd gone down the Aegean coast as far as Fethiye, before catching a ferry to Rhodes and thus to Greece.

"Yes, I was there too. Many years ago, I take a trip. It is a very beautiful city. But for me, it was easy, because I am Persian. It's far, but not so far."

"How long have you lived here?"

"Twelve years six months." He said it unhesitatingly, like a prisoner marking off the days.

"How do you like it?"

"Do I like it?" The man's eyes flicked back across the rear-view mirror at him, as though assessing his sanity. Finally he shrugged, frowning. "It's very hot in the summer, there is never enough water, and if you get sick, it's very hard to find a doctor. In Iran, it's the same. But I think the people are nicer in Iran. Here, the people, they're crazy. In Iran they're crazy too, but you know how they are crazy. Here, they are crazy in all different ways."

"What brought you here in the first place?"

Another shrug. "Money. Jobs. My uncles."

Outside the taxi Mueller saw low brush bordering the highway, and beyond it neighborhoods of wooden shacks huddled just over the concrete barrier, what in Brazil they'd have called a *favela*. A ribbon of greasy smoke from an open cookfire. The cab driver turned on the radio, listening to a news report about the revolution in Libya. The AC blew steadily from vents in the front seats and Mueller stretched out a hand to it. They went under a massive overpass knotted like a pretzel and when they emerged from its shadow saw the towers of the city bristling with sunlight. There was a visible brownish haze in the air: smog.

When they pulled up in front of the Westin downtown the fare appeared on his field and he added a twenty-dollar tip. "Thanks for the ride."

"My pleasure," the driver said, seeing it appear on his windshield display. "You need a ride later, you send me private message."

"Will do."

The cab pulled away and he stood beneath the covered

entrance of the hotel. Little potted junipers to either side of the entrance. Some kind of cathedral next door. A worn brick building of indeterminate use across the street, maybe ten stories high, the windows blocked with black boards. A warehouse? Maybe it had always been like that. Two young men stood smoking against its rusted iron doors, hoods up, eyeing him. He turned and went inside.

The hotel wasn't bad, but he detected signs of struggle in the worn carpet. The front desk clerk, an overdone blond approaching a difficult middle age, checked him in with a strangely hurried intensity, as though there was a line of guests waiting behind him rather than one elderly couple already being attended to by her coworker. "You're in room 508, that's on the fifth floor. Your system will guide you there if you accept the invite, or would you like a paper map?"

He grabbed the mote hovering in front of him. "No, I got it." She nodded, unable to resist glancing at the older couple, who were reviewing said paper map as they spoke. She continued, "We can use facial recognition to open the room door, or I can give you a magnetic key card. Which do you prefer?"

"Facial recognition is fine."

"The pool is open until 10 p.m. If you need anything else, call the front desk from your room phone or ask for us on your system. Do you have any questions?"

"I'm good."

She attempted a smile like a runner approaching a hurdle and almost made it. "Then you're all set. Enjoy your stay."

His room had a peculiar smell. It might be cigarettes, but there were no ashtrays, and surely no hotel let people smoke in the rooms anymore. Then again, not everyone would ask. Beige walls, white ceiling, flecked industrial carpet, bronze-colored drapes drawn and the afternoon sun shining brilliant white in the sheer undercurtain. A walnut-veneer dresser with a faux-marble top, a big screen on the wall behind it turning on when he entered to display information about the hotel. There were no paintings, no pictures on the walls to liven up the stark bureaucratic decor; just a mirror above the desk, reflecting his own tired face when he set his shoulder bag down.

He opened the undercurtain, squinted out at the city. A motorcycle rumbled by, absurdly loud. There were skyscrapers, a park, but also a lot of strangely empty expanses. Parking lots.

He checked the time, saw that it was past three, rubbed his face and sighed. He was tired from the flight and from the last several days, but his time here was limited, and he couldn't be sure how long it would take to find Yarborough. Best to get started now.

He hadn't told Khleang or Lieutenant White about this trip, reasoning that they would only try to stop him, and it was easier to get forgiveness than permission. He was here on his own dime and own time, and could make the arrest on his own cognizance. As far as they were concerned, he was just off for the weekend, and he needed to be back for work on Monday. His flight was scheduled to leave Sunday night at 8:50 p.m., and he'd booked two seats, for him and Yarborough. Thirty hours to find him and bring him in.

The first thing he'd need was a bounty hunter's license. He'd looked it up, and apparently he had to go to a actual office to take an exam. He'd looked at the exam, and it was no big deal. There was a fee for the license, though: another three hundred dollars debited from his account. "Think of it like a vacation," he muttered.

He got his bounty hunter's license at Open Sesame Bail Bonds, a three-room office on the first floor of a run-down building not far from the municipal courthouse. One of the office's windows had been broken and boarded over some time in the distant past, the wood now graying and splintery, but the window with the bail bonds sign was intact.

The bondsman was named Alzaga. He was heavyset, acne-scarred, with big black brows and a thick mustache. Pale blue polo shirt and blue jeans. He looked at Mueller curiously, seeing a tall, friendly-looking fellow in his late forties attired in slate-colored slacks and white shirt, forehead a little shiny with sweat above his specs. When Mueller told him what he wanted, Alzaga asked, "You like, changing careers then?"

"Not exactly. I'm a police detective. In Seattle."

"Oh," Alzaga said, mulling it over. "So that's like, being a schoolteacher here."

Mueller chuckled. "Could be. Didn't go to school here, so I guess I can't say."

"Nah, I'm just kidding, homie. Actually if you can prove you're already a U.S. peace officer, we can waive the test. Not the fee, though."

"Great. I don't have a lot of time, anyway."

"None of us do, bro. Why don't you put your thumb there, we'll see what the database says."

Mueller placed his thumb on the scanner and Alzaga nodded. "Looks good. Here, there's a couple of forms you gotta sign." He handed over a tablet and Mueller started reading. The forms were long, written in dense legalese, appraising him of his limits and liabilities.

"What's the gist here?" Mueller asked, waving at the tablet.

Alzaga shrugged. "Basically it says, as a bounty hunter you're able to arrest anyone who's got a legal warrant out on them. If it's a regular warrant, you can only use reasonable force, meaning handcuffs, nonlethal deterrents like tasers and pepper spray. If there's no warrant, you may face charges yourself, for kidnapping, assault, whatever. So make sure you got the right guy. If it's a black warrant, you're encouraged to act with restraint, but it's not required. If you shoot first, you're good, but again, make sure it's the right fucking guy. You shoot someone innocent, you are hella fucked, you feel me? You gonna be taking a short trip down death row, and no mistake. They don't mind if Houston P.D. fucks up now and then, but if a bounty hunter shoots someone, well, you were warned."

"I think I'll be all right. I don't even have a gun."

Alzaga's eyes widened. "You serious?"

"Haven't carried one in years."

Alzaga was flummoxed. "You're shitting me."

"Nope. Do you see one on me?" He patted his pockets for effect.

"Well, sure, but you're not on a case right now. Though you better believe I carry whether or not I'm going after somebody."

Mueller signed the forms, trusting that Alzaga had conveyed their essence, and handed back the tablet. "Okay," Alzaga said. "Looks good. Total for the fee is three hundred even. Just need your thumbprint again." Mueller thumbed the invoice on the tablet and Alzaga tapped it a couple more times. Behind him a card printer hummed to life. He turned to it, came back with a plastic ID card with Mueller's face on it. *BOUNTY HUNTER,* it read across the top, yellow caps on royal blue background.

"Can I keep it when I'm done?" asked Mueller, bemused.

"Yeah, it's yours. Of course, the expiration date's right on there, too. Good for thirty days, that's it."

"Awesome. That's it, then?"

"That's it. You're all set." Mueller turned away to go, and Alzaga, watching him, made up his mind about something. "Hold on," he called, and Mueller turned back. "You know where you're going? Where your guy is?"

"Not one hundred percent," Mueller replied. "But I hear he's in the Dome."

Alzaga nodded, unsurprised. "That's where a lot of fugitives end up, around here. Ever been inside?"

"Nope. First time in Houston."

"And you're going to go unarmed?"

"As always."

Alzaga shook his head. "Listen, man. That's crazy. I got to tell you. The Dome's lawless. It's run by the gangs. You go in there, you don't know anybody, you're alone, you're asking questions, you're obviously not Harris County police, what do you think's going to happen? Best case scenario, they throw you out, tell you don't come back. Worst case, you just disappear, they throw your body in with the food waste, burn it with the garbage. Poof. Gone."

"You're not the first person to tell me this," Mueller observed. "I've been a detective for almost twenty years. I stopped wearing a gun about fifteen years ago. When you make it clear that you're not armed, people aren't afraid of you, which makes it easier to talk to them."

"Man, you meet some Candy Skull gangbanger in the Dome, they ain't gonna believe you're not armed, even if you're bare-ass naked. They can't even imagine it. They been carrying since they were eleven years old, their girlfriends carry, their aunties and uncles carry, sure as shit a police detective or bounty hunter's gonna carry. And anyway, even if they just laugh at you, they're still not gonna talk to you. Then you gonna throw some cuffs on somebody and try to walk out of there? No way, no how.

"But listen, I like you. I feel like you're a good guy, trying to catch some bad guy, right? So how about I help you out? I *do* know people in the Dome, people I can ask, people who know other people. Go with me, we'll find your guy, and you won't end up in a fucking furnace somewhere. What do you think?"

"Sounds good," Mueller allowed. Fact was, it was exactly the sort of thing he needed, especially given the limited time frame here. "And you're going to do this out of the goodness of your heart?"

Alzaga smiled, spread his meaty hands. "The goodness of my heart, and a small daily fee. Man's gotta eat."

They haggled over the price, and in the end Alzaga agreed to accompany him for two hundred for his time, and another two hundred once the suspect was apprehended and secure. Scanning the information on Yarborough Mueller provided, he said, "What are you going to do if he don't want to go? I mean, you know this guy's an arms dealer. You think he's not going to be armed?"

"I'll reason with him."

Alzaga once again looked at him incredulously. "Man, what the fuck is *with* you?"

Mueller chuckled. "If we can make an arrest, great. If not, maybe just the threat of it will make Yarborough talk. The information is nearly as valuable as the arrest, really."

Alzaga shook his head doubtfully. "All right. Long as we're clear that you're not going to go in there with guns blazing, getting us killed. But I guess since you don't have any guns, that's not an issue. When you want to go?"

"I'm only here to tomorrow night."

Alzaga glanced at the time on the little smartwatch he wore. "Okay. Let's do it now, then. I hate working on Sundays."

They drove to the Dome in Alzaga's truck, a twenty-year-old black Toyota Mastiff with tinted smart windows that highlighted the route as they drove. When Alzaga turned the ignition the engine rumbled to life and Mueller touched the dash and felt the vibration. "Gas burner?" he said.

"Bet your ass," Alzaga said. "Eight cylinders, bro. Armored, too. Bulletproof all the way. You want in here, you gonna need a rocket launcher."

"Ever actually had someone shoot at it?"

"Sure. Though tell the truth, I'm not sure they were actually shooting at me. Could just be random. Don't matter. Put a nick in the paint on the back door."

"Must have cost quite a bit."

"Not as much you think. It's old. The gas for it costs a shit-ton, but no use in having an armored car if you run out of battery. Then you're just a steel can sitting on the highway."

"Can't you run out of gas, too?"

"Sure. But I got more than an hundred-mile range."

They moved slowly south through downtown, stopping at the frequent traffic lights. The sun was in the lower quarter of the sky and the shadows from the buildings were long. Big, hulking concrete parking structures. He noticed that some of the building complexes had raised walkways between them, bridging the street so the occupants wouldn't have to leave their climate control. Homeless men shuffled up and down on the corners. No bike lanes, no bikes, period, although the streets were wide. Different kinds of trees here, oaks, pecans, sycamore.

"So who's this guy again?" Alzaga asked.

"Daniel Yarborough," Mueller said. "Arms dealer."

"Is that a crime?"

"When you steal the weapons you sell, it is. And when you smuggle them into the U.S."

Alzaga shrugged. "You must want him pretty bad, to come all the way out here. What's he selling, like nuclear shit?"

"Something like that. But mostly it's related to a homicide. Dead kid."

Alzaga's expression darkened. "This guy do it?"

"Not him. We just need him for questioning. And there's warrants out anyway, so it makes it easy."

"So what happens if you catch your guy? Your homicide suspect."

"There'll be a trial. If he's convicted, imprisonment and rehabilitation. How long depends on the sentence."

Alzaga shook his head. "Man, in Texas, you kill a kid, you're done. You're going to get strapped to a chair and get a little injection. That's just animal behavior."

"You don't think there should be a trial first?"

"Sure, why not? Trial'd take five minutes. Lethal injection, same day. Problem solved."

"If executions prevented crime," Mueller asked, finding himself getting drawn into the argument, "why does Houston have a murder rate that's literally a thousand times higher than Seattle's? You guys execute more people here than anywhere in North America."

"It's the gangs, man. And economic collapse. People are poor, and when they get poor, they get desperate. You can't compare Houston to Seattle. It's like comparing Guatemala to Switzerland or some place."

"That doesn't change the fact that the threat of violence, as a deterrent, doesn't work. If it did, Houston would have solved crime a century ago."

"I see where you're coming from," Alzaga allowed. "But what are you going to do with these criminals, then? You going to put them in a nice room, feed them three squares a day for the rest of their lives? That's not punishment. That's a reward."

"I don't care about punishment," Mueller rejoined. "Why *should* we care about punishment? What's the value in it, if it doesn't prevent future crimes? Prevention, not punishment: that's real modern police work. Rehabilitation, not revenge. What I would do with these killers is try to heal them, try to show them where they went wrong, get them to contribute to society in some way, even if it is from a prison compound."

Alzaga laughed, shaking his head. "Man, you are from another world. I'm sure that all works fine in Seattle, where nobody's got a gun, and everyone goes to college, and all that. But these guys in the ghetto, man, they don't understand that kind of talk. I know, I grew up outside Dallas. You say you commit a crime, you'll go to jail, these guys laugh. They been to jail. They know it sucks balls, and they don't want to go back, but they also know it's a price you pay if you get caught. But you talk about capital punishment, they think twice. An eye for an eye, they *get* that. Shit, they *agree* with it. That's why we still have it, because people vote for it."

"But it's not necessary," Mueller persisted. "You act like the way Seattle is just happened by accident. It didn't. We made a conscious choice to ban firearms. And there was a lot of resistance, but we did it, and afterward everyone wondered why we hadn't done it sooner. And we made a conscious choice to educate every citizen, and guarantee a basic standard of living to eliminate the worst kinds of inequality. And it works! Just look! It works!"

"If it works so perfectly, what are you doing here?" Alzaga shot back. "For that matter, how do you even have a job? Answer is, it doesn't work, not like you say. And meanwhile you guys have taken 'police state' to a whole new level. Twenty-four-hour surveillance, right, of one hundred percent of the populace? AIs that know where you are every minute of the day, know when you're taking a piss, know when you like to fuck your wife? You talk about prevention, but then you build a system for instant arrest of anyone who commits a crime. You want to know why crime's so low in your city? Because criminals know they won't be arrested in a week or a month, but today. That's not prevention, that's deterrence."

"Sure it is. And it works."

"Sure it works, man, but what kind of nightmare is that? I can't even imagine. You're not even parts in a machine, you're more like ... little pixels, just data running around inside a computer. You talk about abuse, but what could happen, someone turns that against you?"

"There *are* safeguards."

"Safeguards my ass. It's that whole trading freedom for security thing again. You guys have traded all your freedom for a little security, and now you're being run by the machines and you don't even realize it. No thanks. The Free States are violent as hell, sure. But at least it's a human hell."

They turned left on Webster, right at a Citgo to merge onto the stacked concrete branches of the Eastex Freeway, Alzaga glancing over his shoulder as he pressed the gas. The Mastiff's engine growled as they shot into a gap between an Amazon big rig and a silver Nissan Versa. Alzaga glanced at Mueller's locked arm and hand pressed against the dash and laughed. "Relax, bro. I do this every day. Besides, this truck's a little old, but it's solid."

The freeway was huge, twelve or sixteen lanes wide in places, really multiple freeways that met and diverged and met again as they rammed across the city. The high rises were replaced by rundown hotels, abandoned mini-malls, forgotten construction sites. They crossed a small waterway that Mueller's system said was called Brays Bayou but looked like a concrete-banked canal. The "Old Spanish Trail" was an overpass with high chain link fences, and just past it was a squatters' settlement of cardboard and scavenged pulpboard. He wondered where the squatters got their water. The ghetto lined the road for miles. He supposed it made sense: no one wanted to live by the highway anyway, it was city property, and where would these people go otherwise? Where nicer neighborhoods neared the highway, they were defined by walls fifteen feet high and topped with coils of razor wire.

On the S. Loop Freeway they drove west toward the setting sun and the windshield darkened against it. And then a flash of light, the sun glaring off a black bubble in the landscape, like an enormous pocket of volcanic gas boiling from the earth: the Astrodome.

"There it is," said Alzaga. "The Devil's playground."

Just beyond the Astrodome was a still larger structure, Reliant Stadium, which was still in use. The two had been separated by a twenty-foot high concrete barrier. On the Reliant side, the parking lots remained empty but for a couple security cars with bubble sirens on their roofs. But on the near side of the fence, slums spilled from the Dome like ants from a hill. Street vendors sold tamales and barbecue. Young men in bandanas and camo pants lolled against plywood buildings smoking joints and drinking from paper bags. Some of the houses looked to have been there quite a while, their tin roofs, like the Dome itself, covered with black solar foil, rimmed with gutters to collect rainwater into filtered cisterns made from steel barrels. A style popular the world over, defined by basic needs: shade, electricity, water, minimal cost.

"What are you going to do with the truck?" Mueller asked.

"Parking service," Alzaga answered. "Only way to do it around here."

He turned into an alley and the sun disappeared. Here were the pedestrians missing from downtown, walking next to the truck as it crept along. There were structures built from every sort of material: cinder blocks, adobe, plywood, an open canvas tent with a family sitting in lawn chairs watching video projected on a sheet.

Fifty yards in they came to a garage of orange corrugated steel. It was guarded by two young men with automatic weapons slung over their shoulders, and at first Mueller thought they were wearing elaborate Day of the Dead makeup, their eyes and noses painted black, their lips drawn with vertical lines like exposed teeth, fanciful whorls in red and green spreading across their cheeks and brows. Then he realized the drawings were tattoos; these were gangsters, soldiers in the famous Candy Skulls. The two looked on dispassionately as the truck rolled to a stop. Alzaga rolled down the window, said, "You got space?"

"Twenty per hour," the one nearest said.

"Soy un amigo de Paco."

"Paco quien?"

"Vaquera. Digale que es Ivan."

The guard muttered something more in Spanish into his collar. His eyes looked off to the side as he listened to the response, then he said, "Ten. How long you going to stay?"

Alzaga looked a question at Mueller, who shrugged. "Not more than two or three hours, I guess."

"You got thirty bucks?"

Mueller sighed as he dug out his wallet.

They got out and the other gangster took Alzaga's keys. Not so different from a valet service anywhere, other than the guns. Mueller imagined the whole city like that: grocery clerks with 45s on their belts, taxi drivers with sawed-off shotguns, teachers with little nine-millimeters tucked in the back of their slacks. Mayors and hot dog vendors and babysitters, all wearing guns the way they might once have worn wristwatches.

From there they went on foot toward the entrance, occasionally pressing close against the buildings to let a vehicle through the narrow alleys. Half the buildings seemed to double as storefronts, and in the space of a block they were offered fake designer jeans, sunglasses, cigarettes, cold beer, marijuana, and fresh fish. Alzaga warded off each with an unamused expression and a barely raised hand to say, yes, I see you, and no, I'm not fucking interested.

"You hungry?" he asked Mueller.

"I am, actually."

"Some good food in the plaza."

"Better than inside?"

"More than inside."

It was a bit of a challenge to find something without meat, but with Alzaga guiding him he finally obtained two cheese tamales and a side of sauteed squash, peppers, and onions in a rectangular cardboard dish. Alzaga got three barbacoa tacos with a dark chili sauce and queso blanco. They sat eating them at a wooden bench attached to the side of the stand, looking sideways toward what had been the ticket booths and was now a barbecue-ribs joint called Sauce Boss. "You're missing out," Alzaga said, observing his gaze. "Sauce Boss's got some of the best ribs in

Texas. Best in the world, probably."

"Been there a long time?"

"It was here when I got here, all I know."

A constant stream of people swarmed in and out of the Dome beyond Sauce Boss, the entrances like the dark angular mouths of caverns, the side of the structure above them a forbidding cliff of steel grating and spearlike concrete supports. He was interested to see whole families coming and going, shopping bags in hand, tourists with pale legs and floppy hats and cameras. "I thought you said the Dome was dangerous."

Alzaga raised an eyebrow. "No, I didn't."

"You said they would put me in with the compost. Said there were guns everywhere."

"There *are* guns everywhere. Hell, that's half of what they sell inside."

Mueller gestured at four Japanese tourists in clean pastel-colored clothing. "They don't seem scared."

Alzaga laughed. "I don't know *what* they're feeling. But no, of course it's not dangerous for *them*. You want to go shopping, go ahead. You don't need me for that."

"I'm getting some very mixed signals here."

"No, not at all. The Dome's lawless in the sense that the Harris County P.D. and other enforcement agencies don't generally bother with it. It's understood that it's a genuinely free market, a free zone within the Free States, if you want. That's half the reason it survives, is that the police themselves kind of agree that people should be able to buy and sell what they want. That's America, right? That's freedom. But they don't necessarily want you just selling crack or assault rifles on the street. Makes the city look bad. So they limit it to the Dome, and the Dome itself becomes a kind of attraction. Tourists go, they see all the guns on display, all the drugs, the prostitutes, they come out and have a story to tell their friends back in Ohio or Tokyo or wherever. The gangs that run it have a strong motivation to keep the peace in order to preserve their marketplace. And in a way, their policing is more effective than the Harris County P.D.'s, because they don't put up with any shit. They hear you're causing trouble, they're going to beat the shit out of you. They hear you killed someone, they're gonna send a guy to stick a switchblade in your neck."

"They don't ever fight among themselves?"

"Squabbles between members. But the Dome is run by the Candy Skulls, Los Cráneos, and their jefe, Zaragoza, keeps a tight grip, you know? Of course the Pobrecitos would love to get control of the place, but they'd need a fucking army. Never gonna happen. Anyway, point is, you're not here to buy anything. You're asking questions, sticking your nose into their business. That's something you got to be careful with."

In its day, the Astrodome had been an architectural marvel, hailed as one more "Eighth Wonder of the World" for being the first fully domed sports stadium. But as pro sports and its demands grew, and as repairs became more and more costly, the Dome moved first into irrelevance (with the construction of Reliant Stadium, in 2002), and then into senescence and decay. For decades after the completion of its larger, newer neighbor, the Astrodome's fate was uncertain. No one seemed to agree what should be done about it, whether it should be demolished or upgraded. Eventually the city turned it into a mixed-used indoor park, a sort of enormous annex to Reliant, building gardens and restaurants inside while retaining some performance space.

The Astrodome Indoor City Park, unfortunately, turned out to be a failure, never remotely recouping the enormous cost of maintenance. In 2038, faced with another $60 million expenditure to replace part of the roof (damaged by Hurricane Salome the previous year), the city council balked. At that point Houston was already bleeding money, and there was no relief in sight. In any case, with Secession finally at hand that same year, the future of Texas was uncertain, the whole South reeling and giddy as a man celebrating the birth of a child on the same day he's lost his job. Dealing with the Dome was simply not a priority.

The Dome did have one successful area, an open flea market that had made its home there since the early days of the park. When the city council attempted to shut down the park, citing safety concerns related to the roof, the hundreds of small vendors in the flea market simply refused to leave. Some slept in their stalls, concerned the authorities would bulldoze the whole thing in the night, but it turned out the council at the time had no real appetite for confrontation. No one really wanted the market to close, and what would fill the Dome afterward? If the Free States stood for anything, it was the freedom to do business as you saw fit.

So the vendors stayed. Some stayed full time, expanding their stalls to include sleeping quarters. There were bathrooms, showers, electricity and shade. What else did you need? The market grew and grew again. Those selling gray-market items, guns, drugs, imitation designer goods, imitation sportswear, imitation electronics, imitation everything, took special notice of how the city government had turned a blind eye to the location. The Astrodome Hotel, a hundred-room accommodation built in 2018, began specializing in rentals by the hour, its lobby filling with curiously ill-clad and affectionate young women (and more than a few young men).

In 2046, a spate of murders in the Astrodome's expansive parking lots, which had been gradually filling with food trucks and cars that sprouted canvas canopies and gas camp stoves, persuaded the council that something needed to be done. But the late attempt to forcibly remove the Dome's occupants, by now numbering over a thousand, backfired horribly. The Dome's residents were simply not willing to go, and many were armed to the teeth, especially the members of the Candy Skulls, who early on had established their dominance in the arena. On August 7, in what the media quickly dubbed the Dome Massacre, the police came in force, wearing full riot gear, carrying automatic weapons and concussion grenades, backed by armored vehicles and crowd-control drones firing tear gas canisters.

The Domists were ready. The armored vehicles never made it past the entrances, caught in enormous volumes of crowd-control aerogel sprayed through hoses above the portals. The ground troops attempted to swarm in through a dozen other passages, or rappelled in from helicopters poised above the roof, but everywhere they were met with violent and determined resistance. In fact they had vastly underestimated the resources the gangs had committed to the Dome, and the amount of profit those organizations were extracting from it. It was less than the Astros had made in their heyday, but not by much.

The final death toll was thirteen police and forty-seven Domists. A lopsided number, but it turned out the Domists had far more stomach for death than law enforcement. The police left. The Domists stayed. The bodies were laid shoulder to shoulder on the parking lot asphalt.

Some in law enforcement argued in favor of a siege, but by this time public opinion had shifted violently against the Harris County P.D. The whole conflict was regarded as a black eye for the Free States, an embarrassment contrary to the widely shared values of free enterprise and free expression.

Over subsequent months, city officials met with representatives from the major commercial interests inside to hammer out some basic agreements. First, the Dome would be internally policed, with the explicit understanding that the safety of visitors and non-residents was paramount. Second, the Dome businesses would contribute to maintenance of the structure itself, which after all was in their self-interest.

The Astrodome Indoor City Park was renamed the

Astrodome Free Market Bazaar. The mayor at the time, Russell Shaker, called it "a natural and unfettered expression of the Texan entrepreneurial spirit." The Houston Press said it was "a fucking free-for-all, but what can you do?"

Somehow Mueller had been expecting a broad, open space when they passed through the portal: it had been a sports stadium, after all. But in fact the interior space had been so filled with structures there were only surprisingly narrow passages to the left and right, and the main shopping boulevard ahead of them, called Touchdown Street. Otherwise the stalls and shops stood wall-to-wall, and Mueller was reminded of the Grand Bazaar in Istanbul, although these were made of far more varied materials. Steel shipping containers were a popular choice for gun shops, their sides modified into garage-door arrangements for security. Shops with cheaper goods were often simple plywood shacks with tiny living quarters (i.e. a bed or a hammock) in the back. Bars punctuated the corridors, some with cozy seating areas, others nothing more than a few stools in front of a counter.

Around the edge of the bazaar floor, where the seating stands had been previously, residences ran in tiers right up to the ceiling, forming a tall ring around the bazaar, broken by a few remaining staircases. The tallest building was the Tight End, the hotel-cum-brothel (no pun intended) built as part of the park, overlooking the west side of the stadium.

A thrum of business filled the stadium from thousands of voices and hundreds of competing sound systems. Shoppers brushed by on either side as Mueller craned his neck to look up at the skylights. The too-warm air stank of cigarettes, marijuana, meat and machine oil. The field had long since been denuded of its astroturf, and they walked on concrete stained dark with countless untold spills and execrations.

A young boy, no more than ten, suddenly appeared at Mueller's side, walking backwards to address his mark. He wore a too-long T-shirt sprayed with brightly colored animated logos, equally if less garishly animated camo pants in shades of white, black, and gray, and cheap bracelets piled six deep per wrist. "Hey bra, you looking for someting? I can help, you want guide, I be da guy, my name Rafeo, you need guide, I be cheap, bra, no uddah better no cheaper. What you want? You want guns, you want women, chemicals, hey? You need em, I find em."

Alzaga glanced over his shoulder, saw Mueller lagging as he spoke bemusedly with this streetwise spawn of the Dome, came back scowling to take Mueller's arm. "Fuck off," he said to the kid. "He ain't interested."

"He look interested. Hey, I help you both, macho, no problem. I be da guide, bra, best in da Dome, anyting you want, I find em, no problem."

"I said fuck off," Alzaga repeated, now pushing Mueller ahead of him. "You still got your handset?"

Mueller felt at his pocket. "Sure, I got it."

"What you tink, I some kind of thief, go jank you merch?" the boy said indignantly. "No way, bra, I try da help you. You don't know da Dome, you be lost, bruddahs, like a maze, bad tings happen. But I be da wayfinder..."

"I said fuck off," Alzaga said.

"Okay, fucking macho. You get fucking lost den." The kid flipped them off. They kept walking.

"Wouldn't a guide be useful?"

Alzaga grunted. "You got a guide. I'm it. And that kid may be a guide, but he's also working for the Skulls. First sign of trouble, he'll run and tell them. We're better off alone." With that they pushed forward through the crowd, past the upraised tines of the field goal posts, still in place like ceremonial steles before the entrance of a ancient ruin.

As a police officer, Mueller was immersed daily in what passed for gun culture in Washington. The other officers,

Khleang included, would go over to the police range regularly, practice with their sidearms, mostly 9-mm handguns made by Glock or Sig Sauer or Smith and Wesson. Frequently they would also bring heavier pieces, "just for fun," .45s or Mossberg tactical shotguns, or the ever-popular full-auto assault rifle, tearing the paper targets to shreds with serious, concentrated faces and then chortling about it afterwards with their buddies. But never had he seen so much firepower concentrated in one place as in the Dome.

Under roll-up steel doors stood scarred men with racks of Russian assault rifles in open cases behind them, sitting on wooden crates filled with ammunition. There were merchants specializing in handguns, shotguns, antique guns, flechette guns, crowd-control guns. He saw a display case of hand grenades with the caveat LIVE EXPLOSIVES NOT KEPT IN STOREFRONT - DISPLAY MODELS ARE NONOPERATIONAL printed on a sheet of office paper taped to the glass. He saw two rocket launchers mounted on wall brackets with their producer's promotional video playing on a screen between them. Several stores didn't seem to be black-market at all; they were well-constructed buildings with thoughtful masculine decor and salesmen standing in button-up shirts.

Interspersed with the arms dealers were shops offering other contraband, especially drugs: hashish, cocaine, heroin, amphetamines, exotic designer psychedelics and marijuana (the latter, bizarrely, still illegal in Texas). He saw relatively few clothing stores; they weren't high-dollar enough, he supposed, to pay for a space inside, which is why most were in the parking lot. There were, however, a surprising number of jewelers, offering absurdly fat, gaudy rings and heavy gold necklaces.

In the center of the field was a sort of crossroads, where three bars and a hot dog vendor competed for tourist dollars. Two of the bars had rooftop decks, where you could sit and drink expensive whiskey and gaze around at the madhouse all around you. Cigarette smoke, hot dogs, sweat, pulsing music, raised voices, muffled gunshots from a hidden range, neon signs humming on, well-dressed tourists side by side with swaggering gangsters: there was a quality of sensory overload, of having dived into a buzzing, swarming beehive, colors, sounds, and smells smashed together helter skelter, their only coordinating factor the potential for profit.

They stopped at the hot dog vendor's stand, a peculiar cart affixed with bits of scrap metal that hardly inspired confidence in its products: Junkyard Dawg, it was called, according to words etched in a rusting plate that might have been taken from a battleship. They waited for the sole other customer to finish, and then Alzaga clasped hands with the purveyor, a large bald black man in a black T-shirt with face sweating in the steam from the cart. "Fucking Ivan," the man said, his voice low and raspy, a smile on his face.

"Harold. How you been?"

"Good, good. You see me, I'm always good, got my spot right here. Ain't seen you in forever and a day, man. What you been doing?"

"Same old. And you know where I work, nothing stopping you from visiting."

The man laughed. "Nothing but that warrant. I think you just want to collect on it."

"Shit, if I wanted that, I'd have done it when I had you in handcuffs."

"Maybe you changed your mind."

"Maybe I still will."

"Oh, I better get you something, then. You want a brat?"

"No, no, we ate already." They kept talking like this for a couple minutes, discussing common acquaintances, Alzaga's family.

"You just come by to say hello then?" Harold said finally,

looking expectant.

"Well, partly. But also we're looking for somebody. Guy named Yarborough, arms dealer."

"What do you want him for?"

"We want to buy something from him," said Alzaga.

Harold looked unhappy. "Buy something from him. That's it? That's all your business?"

"Like I said."

"I don't want any trouble. And lots of people see you standing here."

"It's nothing to do with you, man. We're looking to buy. Just want some directions. You know where he is or not?"

Harold dropped his eyes, busied himself with a wet towel. "No, I don't know him."

"Harold." Reluctantly the vendor met Alzaga's demanding gaze. "I could have taken you in before, right? You remember? Where would you be right now?"

"Man..."

"You'd be in fucking prison, man. Instead you're here selling hot dogs and smoking big blunts whenever you want. Right?"

"How long you going to hold that over me? It was two years ago. At some point we got to call it evens, Ivan."

"Fine. After this, then. We're square."

Harold sighed, shook his head. "Fine. He's not that hard to find anyway. Just over in Runner's Lane. Next to a Nepalese place, with the prayer flags and all that. There's no sign, though. You know what he looks like?" Mueller nodded. "Okay, then. And anybody asks, you didn't get it from me, all right? Not that it'll fucking matter if the Skulls kick me out."

"Thanks, Harold. That's the last favor I'll ask, all right?" Alzaga extended a hand.

"You remember that."

From the crossroads they took a right, then ducked left halfway to the Tight End, heading down a narrow passage not more than four feet across; Mueller could have stretched out both arms and knocked down the booths on either side like Samson destroying the temple of the Philistines. This aisle seemed to specialize in blades, and their worn purveyors eyed the two of them impassively behind cases full of switchblades, brass knuckles, ancient trench-fighting knives, glimmering katanas. In their midst, like a protest, a single shop of Himalayan imports, cheap figurines and singing bowls below serried ranks of rainbow-colored prayer flags.

Past the Nepalese, the knives turned to electronics. Rows of handsets (stolen and reprogrammed) selling for a fraction of their market value lay on black velvet as if they were diamonds. In Washington a stolen handset was nearly useless, since the telecom companies would immediately identify it, block it, and send a report to the petty crimes division. But maybe they were less scrupulous here, or there were competing networks willing to ask no questions if you agreed to a monthly user fee.

The booth where they finally stopped was a ten-by-ten shipping container with a rolling steel door, its exterior painted glossy black. Inside was a white laminate counter with a little swinging door to one side for the booth's single occupant to enter and exit.

That sallow-skinned and hollow-cheeked proprietor was slouched in an office chair, bird-thin hands typing immensely fast on an ergonomic keyboard set on a shelf below the counter. His contacts were dark with Eyenet immersion, and he didn't look up when they stood in front of him. Behind him, on a grid of steel shelves against the back wall, were stacks of machines from a century of computing: gleaming cubes of black glass, bulky towers of sullied gray plastic, foot-tall rounded crystalline devices like clouded glass dildos.

They stood in front of the counter and waited expectantly, but Yarborough offered no acknowledgement whatsoever. "Hi," Mueller said finally.

Yarborough raised a single index finger in response, gesturing for them to wait, and kept on typing for another thirty seconds. Finally his contacts cleared and he examined them with a squinted eyes. "Can I help you?" His voice held the true Texas twang.

"I hope so," Mueller ventured. "I'm looking to buy a weapon."

Yarborough leaned back in his chair, examining them critically, and folded his hands on his stomach. "You gonna try to arrest me afterward, *detective?*"

Well, no great surprise. It wasn't like Mueller was in disguise. "You've found me out."

"Wasn't hard. So you actually want to buy something, or not? Because I have to say, most of what I sell looks pretty far past a detective's salary. And if you are here to make an arrest, well, that just ain't gonna fly. So get it out of your head now."

"I'm just here to talk."

"It's a free country."

"About six months ago you were dealing with someone online, a Lore character by the name of Dublain of Acragh." He waited, but nothing changed in Yarborough's expression or demeanor. "Sound familiar?"

Yarborough raised an eyebrow. "You expecting me to talk back to you? Because I got nothing to say at all."

"A couple days before he was supposed to make an exchange with you, this man drowned in a lake." No expression, no comment. "We have a theory about what happened there. We think someone was using a particular program to flash light in his eyes to trigger seizures in a given subject. Like photosensitive epilepsy."

"Or maybe he got a cramp. Think of that?"

"You have anything to do with it?"

He enunciated slowly. "Not. A. Fucking. Thing."

"Know the software I'm talking about?" A shrug. "Ever sell

that software to someone in Seattle?"

"This is getting old. I don't know where you think you are."

"Someone's using it to kill kids." Mueller found the photos of Ben Coutts and Stephen Mohammadian and used his specs to project their image on the surface of the desk. "These two both drowned to death, just like your contact. How do you feel about that?"

"No way at all," Yarborough scowled. "Even if it's true, it's irrelevant. I buy and sell items. I don't use them."

"You don't feel any sense of responsibility?"

"If I sell you an axe, and you chop up your wife with it, am I responsible?"

"Specialized military weapons aren't axes."

"Au contraire, mon frere. They might have all kinds of uses and applications that neither of us know of or anticipate. And maybe your wife needs to die."

The sophistry of weapons dealers was famous. As the famous dictum went, it was difficult to make a man understand something when his income depended upon him not understanding it. Mueller needed a different lever. "What about Pythia?"

Yarborough's eyes narrowed. "And what would that be, exactly?"

"Something you want. Maybe something we could help you with, if you cooperate."

Yarborough laughed. "Man, you are shit at bluffing, you know that? If you knew a thing about it, you'd have led with that. You're just fishing, and I ain't biting."

In which case, Mueller had wasted this trip, and whoever *had* killed Gorman, Coutts and Mohammadian would stay at large. *Well, if you're going to bluff, bluff big.* With sudden decision Mueller declared, "Daniel Yarborough, I'm placing you under arrest."

"What?" Alzaga said. He grabbed Mueller's upper arm.

"What are you doing?"

Yarborough, for his part, just snorted and kicked his office chair back from the counter. "You're crazy. And stupid."

"Please come from behind the counter," Mueller directed.

"You really are an oddity, you know that."

"We should go," Alzaga insisted, doing his best to drag Mueller away. "Now."

Yarborough jerked his chin at something behind them. "Too late for that, fellas."

Turning they saw four men with skulls tattooed on their faces and automatic weapons in their hands. "Que pasa?" said one.

"You could probably still just leave," Yarborough said. "Last chance."

"Listen to him," Alzaga pleaded.

"And when another kid dies, then what?" Mueller asked. "Then I'm responsible."

Yarborough shook his head. He looked at the gangster who had spoken and the man waved his gun. "Vamonos."

Mueller and Alzaga both raised their hands. "Fucking Christ, man," Alzaga muttered. "Why didn't you tell me you were crazy?"

After the crew had patted them down and taken Alzaga's Glock from his shoulder holster and the knife from his boot, they were led up the main avenue with the Dome residents studiously averting their gazes and the tourists looking at them curiously, passing through the crowds to the gate directly below the Tight End. Above them on a fifteen-foot-tall screen, the hotel displayed images of the girls inside feeling their breasts, slipping down their lingerie seductively, licking their lips, with their names displayed in pink script like the names of girl's dolls on cardboard boxes. "A dónde vamos, amigos?" Alzaga said nervously. "Nos encontramos con alguien? Su jefe? El Príncipe?"

One of them scoffed at that. "El Príncipe. No, el Príncipe está ocupado hoy. Vamos abajo."

Alzaga turned at that, looking alarmed, like maybe he was going to break for it. "Abajo? Por qué abajo?"

The same gangster who had spoken, who had tattooed scorpions crawling out of his blacked-out eye sockets, swung his rifle around at Alzaga in an easy, unconcerned stance. "O podemos deternos aquí." Or we can stop here.

Alzaga slowly turned, fear on his face, and kept walking. "What's the matter?" Mueller asked.

"We're going downstairs."

"What's downstairs?"

"Nothing good."

Once in the torus-shaped concourse that ran around the stadium, they took a broad set of concrete steps downward, past the first and second parking levels (installed when the stadium was converted to a park, and the sunken playing field raised to ground level), to a thick steel door with equally sturdy-looking steel hinges. Above it, in foot-high aluminum letters, was the designation P3. The door's only appurtenance was a two-inch wide bubble of black glass at eye level, but above it on either side, mounted high on the wall, were two powerful guns on robotic arms whose dark orifices swiveled toward them as they approached. Scorpion Cheeks just nodded his chin at the glass bubble. With a dull mechanical click of multiple bolts pulling back, the door swung open.

They stepped into a long hallway, the cheap fluorescents overhead casting ugly shadows down their faces. While P1's doors had been open to whoever might want to venture down there, and P2 served as workspaces and living quarters for some of the Skulls, this level seemed mostly unoccupied, the doors closed. More workspaces, maybe, storage, drug and weapons manufacturing... the doors were closed and locked. Where, in passing the upper two levels, they'd heard bass-heavy music, raised voices, here what reached them was mostly a pervasive, bone-vibrating murmur, perhaps (it had to be) an enormous generator running ceaselessly, pumping its powerful electrical outflow through the thick black cables overhead to bring life to each distant cell of the behemoth into whose guts they penetrated.

"Not good, man," Alzaga murmured, a sheen of sweat on his brow (and in his defense, the air was warm). "Incinerator's down here."

At the end of the hall they reached a freight elevator, which would have made sense if it went up; but after they crowded in and Mr. Scorpion Cheeks pressed his palm against a scanner, the floor dropped. They were descending. *How far down does this place go?*

Pretty far, it seemed.

The doors opened onto a small corridor that ended in a security checkpoint, which looked something like a plexiglass airlock, manned by two very bored-looking Skulls behind the second door. When the party entered, one of them stepped through both doors with a couple of plastic bins and said, "Any electronics you got, put 'em in a bin."

Hesitantly, Mueller removed his specs. "I can't see very well without these."

The guard gave a can-you-believe-this-guy shrug. "Not my problem. Put 'em in the bin."

"You're not just doing this so it don't fuck up your incinerator, are you?" Alzaga asked.

The Skulls all laughed. "Man, does this look like an incinerator to you? This is a military-grade body scanner. But after that, you're going to step into a very special room that will fry the shit out of any electronics you got. How we keep this place clean and secure. So you want your watch to get bricked, leave it on. You want to get it back, put it in the bin. Either of you got any implants? Pacemakers, ocular devices, anything?" They shook their heads. "Good. This thing's got magnets like you wouldn't believe. Any clothes you got with metal in it, too, into the bin. Jackets, shoes, belts. Everything."

Thus denuded, they individually stepped into the booth, which like all security booths was anticlimactic. Next, preceded by two of their original escorts, they moved into a small, claustrophobic chamber, metal on all sides. There was a loud hum, and the hair on the back of Mueller's neck lifted. He wonder how much radiation he might just have received.

The outer door opened and he stepped out in his sock feet. "Welcome to the Burrows," said Scorpion.

Mueller wasn't sure what he'd been expecting, but all he saw was a concrete tunnel lit by steady white LEDs above them. The walls were round, perfectly circular except for the floor and ceiling, which presumably contained the vents, pipes and electricity needed for people to live down here. The tunnel seemed to go on for a long way ahead of them. The four of them – two of the guards had hung back – were perfectly alone inside it, and the only noises were the flat tap of their footsteps and the subaudible whisper of small fans moving air through the occasional vent above them. It might have been a military installation, or a storage facility. *Or a prison.*

Every thirty feet they passed a windowless door, set into the concrete and sealed like a submarine hatch. The doors were numbered like an apartment building's: 301, 303, 305, with odds on the left and evens on the right.

At room 312 they stopped. A light set in the concrete went from red to green. The Skull knocked on the steel hatch and waited a polite moment before simply pushing the door open.

Inside was an apartment, more or less, arranged within the narrow confines of an eight-by-eight tunnel. Light plush carpet on the floor, dark gray couch, tiny kitchenette, bedroom and bathroom in the back. When they entered, a small brown-skinned man in a black track suit with bright white piping bounced off the couch, where he'd been reading a printed book. He had buggy eyes, full lips, thick eyebrows and a five-o'clock shadow. He dismissed the Skull with a glance and fixed his eyes on Mueller.

"Tom Mueller?" he said.

Mueller's left eyebrow went up. "That's me."

"Manish Gill. Nice to meet you. And sorry to cut this short, but we need to go. Now." And with that he brushed past his astonished visitors and went out into the corridor.

He made it about two yards before Mueller's hand closed on his arm. "Hold on," said the detective.

Gill looked down at it impatiently. "If you want to arrest me, that's fine, although I'll point out that you have no jurisdiction here, and if I wanted it these guys would kick you on your ass." He jerked his chin at the Skulls. "But every minute we stand here lowers our odds of survival. So let's walk while we talk, okay?"

"I don't know what you're talking about," said Mueller, releasing him, "but I've come a long way, and paid a lot of my own money to do it. So maybe you could give me a minute."

"I *want* to talk to you," Gill said. "I'm *going* to talk to you. But you have no idea what's going on right now. You've been tracked. By the time we get upstairs, it's going to be a war zone up there. Our best chance of survival is to leave *now.*"

Scorpion frowned, growling, "What are you talking about, *maricón?*"

"I know what *maricón* means, asshole. If you're asking someone for information, you might try showing him some respect."

The Skull's massive hand shot out, grabbed Gill's arm much as Mueller had a moment before, and shook him like a gorilla shaking a bamboo branch. "If you want respect, you shouldn't go around fucking little boys, culo. I should cut off your balls like El Principe said."

"I'm under El Principe's protection, so I wouldn't get ahead of yourself." He shook his arm loose of the much bigger man's grasp. "You might find yourself without a pair. And no great loss."

The Skull lowered his massive shaved and tattooed head menacingly. "What do you mean about a war zone?"

"If you want to know, *call upstairs*. But do it *fast. Now.*" He pointed at an intercom on the wall.

With a last glare, the Skull stepped to the intercom, pressed a button and spoke a name. For a few moments no one answered. He hit the button again, more insistently, speaking louder. They waited thirty seconds and finally there came an answer in Spanish, speaking too rapidly for Mueller to follow. The speaker sounded tense. The Skull with them asked a couple of questions, cursed, unslung his firearm from his shoulder and gestured with the barrel toward the exit. "Vamonos. Ahora!"

"Told you," said Gill.

They jogged down the corridor, passed quickly through the security point (though again they had to stop and submit to a scan, presumably in case they were trying to smuggle anything *out* of the Burrows). "I need my stuff," Gill said. "You have it ready for me, right? Like I asked?"

Unamused, one of the security guards handed Gill a small black backpack. Immediately Gill rummaged through it, coming up with a smartwatch that he slapped around his wrist. As Mueller and Alzaga got back their own possessions, Gill looked anxiously down at the device.

As soon as he was through, Mueller asked, "What's happening upstairs?"

"The Pobrecitos are making a move against the Skulls. Trying to wipe them out, secure a hold on the Dome."

"What, right now?"

"Yes, now. Which by themselves, would be suicide. But they've got help. Private security firm out of Dallas called KRB. Real power players, fully modern weapons, tactical robots, all kinds of shit. Hired by Flohr-Lavine. Heard of them?"

"They own Insight Tech. They have Pythia," said Mueller.

Gill shook his head vigorously. "No, they *don't* have Pythia. They *want* Pythia. They *had* access, before I blocked them and programmed Pythia to erase itself if they ever shut the servers down. They've been looking for me for months, and now you led them here and they're making their move."

"Sorry?"

"Don't worry about it," the programmer muttered. "This was actually my best opportunity. Forty-eight percent chance of survival."

They got into the elevator and the doors enclosed them with a hiss. "Before we go any further, I need to ask if you killed Gabriel Leberer."

"No, I didn't kill him!" Gill said angrily. "Why would I do that?"

"Did you stab him?"

Gill's mouth tensed and he looked away. "Yes. But he was already dead."

The doors opened. They stepped out into the corridor on P3, and felt more than heard a shockwave that shook the concrete walls and elicited a little puff of gray dust from the ceiling. Scorpion looked up sharply and cursed as Mueller asked, "What was that?"

"KRB sealing off escape routes," replied Gill. "The Skulls maintain multiple tunnels leading from the Burrows to Houston. KRB probably sent down some spider drones packed with explosives to take care of them. That's why I didn't want to stay down there. Without the escape tunnels, it's a death trap."

The Skulls they were with had started running down the

hallway toward the stairs. They hurried to follow. Gill was tapping at his smartwatch. "Reception's still too shitty down here. If we can get to the main floor, maybe we'll have a chance."

"A chance at *what?*"

"Getting the fuck out of here!"

They open the heavy doors to the stairway, bounded up the stairs to P2, already hearing confused, echoing noises of shouts, gunfire. Another explosion rocked the complex and they paused, holding to the rail, before continuing upward.

If this situation was developing into real chaos, there was no guarantee he could keep hold of Gill. He had to keep questioning him while he had the chance. "Why would you stab a kid after he was dead?"

Gill flashed him an are-you-stupid look. "To initiate Inference. To get you to start thinking of it as a murder and not just an accident. To get you *here.*"

P2 was a madhouse. Dozens of Skulls were running down the corridors with automatic weapons in hand, strapping on body armor, gas masks. Those they were with, after a rapid-fire discussion in Spanish, turned down the hall, presumably to get more weapons. There was already a haze of smoke. The sound of gunshots from at least one of the staircases, at first intermittent, rose to a constant deafening hail. Gill looked down at his watch. "Best chance is the south exit."

The Skulls they were with, however, turned north. "Where you going?" Gill yelled at their backs. "You're gonna die that way!"

Only the last of them, Scorpion, paused, looking back furiously. For a second Mueller thought Gill had made a serious mistake, and the man would shoot them both, just to be rid of them. But instead their escort said, "We need to find El Principe."

"You're not going to find him, believe me," said Gill. "And if you try, you'll be dead within twenty minutes."

"Fuck off," was all the Skull said, and followed his fellows.

Immediately Gill turned and ran down the concrete hall. The rooms they passed were mostly empty by now, their occupants having raced to defend their residence or escape it, depending on their inclination. At one juncture there was a heavy metal clang as a blast door slammed shut behind them. Alzaga said, "You better hurry, you want out. Once those doors come down, going to be a lot harder."

"We'll make it," Gill said, looking at his watch. And sure enough, when they reached the south exit, the gate stood open, with at least fifteen or twenty Skulls kneeling, firing upwards toward the stairs. A bad position to be in. Their bunker was designed to be impregnable to police invasion and competing gangs, with good escape routes underground, but with those routes shut off, it was a giant mousetrap.

The Skulls were wearing tactical combat armor of different sorts, heads encased in insectile electronic carapaces, chests bulky with dense camouflaged shielding and ammo cartridges. Even so, one went down jetting blood right in front of them, neck half severed. "Get his rifle," Gill told Alzaga, who hesitated just one moment, then ducked down and seized it before joining them behind the steel door of an apartment. Kneeling, he examined it rapidly, flicking a switch, checking the ammo: a tactical full-auto Sig, with a flexible barrel and targeting screen.

"Should we rush it?" Alzaga asked, tense.

"Hold on. Twenty seconds." Gill's eyes were again fixed on his watch.

Involuntarily Mueller counted the seconds down. Three. Two. One.

A high-pitched whine pierced their hearing and suddenly five of the Skull defenders fell on the ground, screaming and gurgling blood. Six, seven, eight, half were down, the others scrambling backwards. Mueller's eyes widened when he spotted the tiny silver drone, like a needle-pointed dragonfly, darting into a

Skull's thigh as the man shrieked and jerked. The drone didn't come out again, stabbing upward through the femoral artery toward his heart.

But the men were quick, they understood immediately what was happening, and with a yell one of the few remaining pulled a grenade from his belt and tossed it toward the exit. The rest hit the ground, and their own trio fell back into the apartment in a confused tripping mass, swinging the door shut behind them.

A sound like a thunderbolt splitting a tree, and Mueller felt the hairs on his arms and head lift. "What was that?"

"EMP grenade," Alzaga growled.

"That's our signal," Gill said, pushing the door back open. "You first," at Alzaga. "We'll follow. Go!"

A glare from the bounty hunter, but the remaining Skulls were already rushing up the stairs, and the three of them ran in the wake of a cacophony of gunfire. Glancing down on the concrete Mueller saw spatters of blood and the shining silver shape of an assassin drone, now rendered unmoving from the EMP pulse.

Up on P1 the lights were out in the corridors, and bright flashes of weapons fire seared their eyeballs from the corner. Finding that his specs still worked – apparently ducking into the apartment when the grenade went off had succeeded in shielding them – he turned up the illumination and the hallway brightened.

Manish's gaze was still fixed on his watch. "Still no fucking bars down here," he cursed. "How's that even possible?"

"Could be the attack," said Alzaga. "Knock out the communications first."

"Probably. Fuck."

"Why's it so important?" Mueller asked. "Checking your stocks?"

"I want to *live*. And all my projections are three months old. They get wobbly, the further out you go."

"*What* projections?"

"*Pythia's* projections." He shook his head impatiently. "Doesn't matter. We'll have to use the old ones. This way." He jogged off down the corridor, a little map showing on the watch face.

"If you want upstairs, why don't we go upstairs, then?" Alzaga asked, looking up in the stairwell, where the door was well-closed.

Gill ran back, grabbed the bounty hunter's arm, dragged him along. A bright light flared behind them, sparks raining down as something began cutting through the iron door. "*That's* why."

"If they want to kill us, why not explosives?" Alzaga asked. "Why not gas? Closed corridors, the pressure can crush our lungs, easy."

"I'm sure they'd be happy to, if that was the objective. But what they really want is me. And I'm no good to them dead. This is all one big kidnapping effort."

They took a right, passed a couple of corpses adding their lifeblood to the other stains on the concrete. In Mueller's peripheral vision the ads and graffiti on the walls flickered with light. At the next corner Gill held them back with an extended arm. "KRB," he hissed to Alzaga. "Get ready."

Alzaga asked no questions, fixed his gun around the corner, its barrel bending around, his eyes on its screen. "Hold on, one second," Gill muttered, and pressed his watch against the gun's control unit. "They've got chameleon armor. You'll never see them. Fire on these targets."

The weapon adjusted its aim on the coordinates provided by Gill's watch system. "Fire on one," Gill whispered. "Three. Two. One."

Alzaga pulled the trigger. A muffled report, a choking sound. "Again! Fire twice this time. Three. Two. One." He fired. A loud crack under the gunshot. "Again. Fire!" Another gunshot. Gill stared at his watch. Then: "Go! Come on!"

The two KRB mercenaries were on the ground at the corridor's end. Their body armor matched precisely the color and pattern of the surrounding concrete, but the blood running from their bodies was bright scarlet. The first had been shot precisely through the neck, below his visored helmet but above the high collar of his chest plate.

The second lay with his helmet partly knocked off by the first bullet, which must have hit it at exactly the angle needed to knock it loose and shatter the visor; the second had struck his face. He had curled up around it, make terrible mewling sounds and grappling with the bloody chin strap, which seemed to be choking him.

"He's still alive," Mueller said, moving to help, kneeling beside the wounded mercenary. The man looked up at him with wet eyes, left hand pressed against his ruined jaw, right still working at the release on the strap.

Gill stared down at his watch in worry. "Fuck," he muttered. "That was supposed to kill him."

"We need to get medical help," Mueller said. He gently pulled the man's hand away from the catch, pressed the release. The helmet fell away, revealed a young white man with light brown hair matted with blood. They had no time to wait for help. They would have to stop the bleeding themselves. Mueller began taking off his jacket, intending to use it as a rough compress, or maybe his shirt would work better –

With a rough kick at his shoulder, Alzaga knocked Mueller to the ground, away from the mercenary, and fired three times at the mercenary's exposed face. The bullets tore right through the man's hand and tore his head and neck to scraps of meat.

Mueller just stared, shocked. He had seen bloodshed before, but always secondhand, after the fact. Never had it been so immediate. "He was *wounded,*" he cried. "He was already *done.*"

"You don't know if he was done," Alzaga growled. "You don't know nothing. Come on."

Mueller took a breath, brought himself back to the present. A tear spilled from the dead man's unfocused left eye. The corridors rang like a giant bell with gunshots and yelling. There was nothing to be done here. He stood up and nodded and they set off again.

"Straight ahead," Gill said. "Stop. Wait. Quiet. Okay, go. Open this door. You'll need to shoot out the lock. Look in that cabinet. There should be some smoke grenades – right. Get at least two. We wait here. Thirty seconds. Then right, down to the third door, which should be open. Get ready. Three. Two. One. Go!"

They ran down the hall, heard shouts behind them, didn't stop, ducked in the doorway as Gill had directed, guided by whatever plan he had laid out months ago. "Shut the door. Push this counter in front of it. Quick! There's an elevator in here, in the back."

He ran for the rear of the shop they were in, a jewelry dealer's store, it looked like. Something struck the metal of the door, someone kicking it, or maybe using a steel ram. They didn't look back. A small back room, passing by the open door of a bathroom, and there it was, a tiny elevator like something belonging to a 1920s apartment building, just big enough for the three of them to cram into it and close the cage door. There were two buttons, up and down, and Gill pushed up.

The lift shuddered, hesitated. It seemed not to like their combined weight. There was a crash from the outer room as the door was forced open, the desk squealing on the floor. Tortuously, the lift began ascending. The ceiling dropped to meet them, a band of gray concrete sliding past like a layer of geologic sediment, and then their heads broke through to the surface like miners coming home. An uncomfortable second where their legs were still exposed, hearing yells below them, and then Gill was pulling at the door of the cage and they all spilled out.

200

They were inside a steel shipping container, the rolling steel door closed to the outside. Two men in short-sleeved shirts and ties were standing and facing them, holding handguns steady on these intruders. The five of them stood looking at each other. Without a word, the thicker of the two proprietors hit a button and the garage door opened halfway. He gestured with the gun toward it, and the trio ducked out of the shop and into the Dome.

The main lights of the stadium had been turned off or shot out, and through the growing smoke flickered the ominous orange light of open flames, rendering the interior a Boschian hell. Mueller tried compensating for the darkness with his specs, but the smoke was too thick. He could see the nearby buildings, the alley they were in, but everything beyond that was a haze. While underground he had lost all sense of direction, and now he had no idea where they were in relation to the exit. Otherwise they were in a tiny alley, but it was difficult to say what was even sold here, because all the shops had promptly closed at the outbreak of violence, closing their doors, shutters, windows, and curtains, sealing themselves off from the chaos and turning the alley into a exit-less corridor. Fat lot of good closing their doors would do if it all burned to the ground.

The noise was likewise a auditory melee, with nearly constant gunfire from nearly every direction, which was more than worrying in a relatively confined space. They ran doubled over, half-expecting to feel the impact of a bullet, to fall to the ground. They should have been crawling on their bellies, like soldiers did in active-fire zones. Mueller heard helicopters nearby, saw blue-white spotlights flashing through the smoke and open roof panels above them. There was something else eerie about the sound, and after a second he realized that the pumping, overlapping music had all stopped.

"We need a place to sit for a minute," Gill said, squinting.

"You don't want to just leave?" asked Alzaga. He gestured with his gun. "That way. North exit."

"KRB's blocked all the exits, guaranteed."

Alzaga gritted his teeth. "Here, then." He strode to a nearby food stand, its window boarded and locked, and kicked open the wooden door. He glanced inside, saw nothing threatening, and waved them in.

A tiny kitchen, smelling strongly of fried chicken. A couple steam warmers by the front window, a plastic bin of white bread rolls, a four-burner gas stove and oven, a single humming refrigerator. Heat still roiling from the deep fryers. In the back, a tiny storeroom. The residents must have shut everything off and fled just minutes before.

"This is Juan Bedoya's place," Alzaga observed. "Never been inside before." He considered the space and nodded to his companions. "Let's move the fridge in front of the door."

Gill ignored him, found a spot on the concrete at the far end of the make line – the most protected spot in the small shop – and immediately started tapping at his watch. Mueller went and helped move the fridge, then squatted in front of Gill. Alzaga grabbed a couple of rolls from the counter, then sat with his back to the fridge.

"We've got signal," the programmer breathed. "Thank god." He pushed an icon and his contacts flared briefly blue as they turned on. "Pythia, this is Manish. Are you there?"

At the response, Gill sighed audibly in relief. "Objective is my safe return to Seattle, free of capture by KRB forces or any other parties. First priority is an escape route out of the Astrodome for myself. Secondary objective is the safety of Detective Tom Mueller, here with me, and his free return to Seattle."

"What about me?" Alzaga asked sourly.

"You live here. You're basically already home. Not my problem. Pythia, go."

"You're talking to the AI," said Mueller.

"Obviously."

"Asking it to help us out of here."

"Yeah. Unfortunately it's going to take a few minutes. So sit tight and hope no one shoots us in the meantime."

"So let me get this straight," Alzaga said. "You knew this was going to happen? The raid and everything? And you just said, whatever?"

Gill shrugged, mouth set. "Sure, I knew. So what? You think I give a shit what a bunch of gangsters do to each other?"

Alzaga shook his head. "Better not let Zaragoza hear you say that. He'd have your fucking balls."

"Well, fuck him too. Never met a more pretentious asshole."

Alzaga shook his head unhappily. "That asshole has personally killed more people than you could fit on two football teams. Used to be a cartel assassin. Call him La Luz de la Muerte, the Light of Death. Dangerous guy to piss off."

Gill looked like he wanted to respond, but at that moment there was a scrambling sound from the back room. Alzaga and Mueller lunged toward it, but whoever had been back there was gone out the small window already. "I thought you checked the back," Mueller said.

"Well, I guess he was fucking hiding back there, wasn't he?" Alzaga said from the window. "I think it was that kid from earlier. Rafael. Must have holed up here when the shooting started."

"Let him go," Mueller said.

"Not really a choice," Alzaga observed. "Kid's gone. We ain't catching him."

They moved a shelf in front of the window and then returned to the front, Alzaga sitting against the refrigerator by the door, Mueller on the concrete across from Gill, head by a plastic cutting board across a cold table. "Okay. So if we have a couple minutes, I have a few questions for you."

"Such as?"

"If you didn't kill Gabriel, who did? What is Pythia? How did you make it here without Inference finding you? Why'd you go to Richard Gorman's house? And –"

"Stop. Christ, you're like my three-year-old niece. Why why why." He raised a hand against Mueller's developing glower. "You want the whole story. That's fine. I'll give it to you, as much as I can. But when Pythia's finished, we go. And you do exactly as I say. Understood?"

Mueller turned it over. "One condition. I'm not killing anybody."

"What about you?" Gill nodded at Alzaga.

"Shit, I want to get out alive. That's my priority."

"Fair enough. And for the record, I've never killed anything in my life. Until three months ago, the worse thing I ever did was eat a hamburger now and then when I was drunk. And I'll say it again: I didn't kill Gabriel."

Outside in the stadium, the flames rose and gunshots burst like popcorn in a hot wok. Inside, Gill talked.

"I didn't kill Gabriel. I want to make that clear from the beginning. I had absolutely nothing to do with hurting him. I knew right away that you and everyone else was going to leap to that conclusion, because our relationship wasn't exactly orthodox. I know, I can just hear you thinking, he fucks little boys, and guys who fuck little boys also sometimes kill little boys. Like, we've all seen it a thousand times on TV, and everyone knows that therefore it's totally okay to kill the pervert.

"But Gabriel wasn't a normal kid. He wasn't really a kid at all. He was my same age. And if you think of him as a kid, then sure, it's disgusting, but once you realize he was really an adult in a kid's body, it looks pretty different, right? Would you deny someone a relationship because they had an age *disorder*, because they *looked* older or younger than they were? No. Absolutely not, nobody would say so. And that's how it was. It *wasn't weird,* I'm telling you.

"And he was smart, smarter than me, and I'm the smartest fucking guy you ever met, in case you didn't know. I saw it right away, way back at UW, before we'd even started at Insight. I'd show him what I was doing, and he'd come back the next day, and show me a better way of doing it, something I hadn't considered at all. We were doing things no one had ever done before. Gabe was a star. If he hadn't been killed...

"But yeah, that night. We were just having a good time. Then we kind of dozed off... and finally I woke up to use the bathroom around, I don't know, two in the morning. And when I came back, I saw Gabe was lying there with his eyes open. I thought... I don't know what I thought. I shook him. I tried CPR, but he was gone, who knows how long he'd been lying there like that?

"And I was there with my finger on my handset, about to call 911. I almost did. I was that close, thumb hanging over dial, but something stopped me. This little voice in me that said, this wasn't an accident. It *looked* like an accident, but I knew already that statistically, accidents can be mapped. They can be predicted to a definite percentage of probability. And if they can be predicted, they can be manipulated. I knew it, because it's exactly what we'd been working on for years. And Pythia *worked.* We'd seen it.

"Look: a guy's walking down the street in the rain, and he steps on a steel manhole cover that's slick with water, and he slips and falls and bruises his tailbone. We call that an accident. Happens every day, a thousand times a day.

"But let's say you have an AI, a very powerful AI system running on a very powerful quantum computer, capable of a truly astronomical number of calculations, trillions per second. And you feed this AI all the real-world data you possibly can. It knows the location of every manhole cover in the city, it knows the probability of rain on a given day, the location and daily travel patterns of every human being in the city. It knows what kind of shoes you're wearing and what those shoes are made of. It knows the degree of traction provided by those shoes and the amount of slippery oil exuded by the nearby asphalt. It knows the length of your stride and your walking heart rate relative to how much coffee you've had that morning. It sees *everything*. It comprises a mirror simulation of the real world, constantly corrected by actual data in the present moment.

"So in this moment, now, that simulation is one hundred percent correct. A minute from now, it'll be 99.99 percent. Still highly accurate, but of course there's some uncertainty. The further you move outward, and the thinner the data on the ground, the less accurate the simulation. It's also more or less accurate for a given target depending on its focus, the resolution of the simulation. But target it on a single person, and the simulation is surprisingly accurate. Most people, it turns out, are extremely predictable, at least short-term.

"When we built Pythia, we knew immediately that it was revolutionary purely as a predictive tool. That was our interest, to predict events, disasters, attacks, disease. But that wasn't what Insight wanted it for, of course. They must have seen from the beginning what it could do. They started asking a lot of questions, asking if we could run simulations to gain a desired effect. In other words, instead of just *predicting* you would slip on the manhole cover, to *cause* you to slip on it. We would enter that as the objective, and Pythia would run simulations, billions of them, to tell us the simplest possible way to get it to happen.

"You might think, then, that the simplest way to get that guy to slip on the manhole cover would be to kidnap him, put Vaseline on his shoes, stand him on the manhole cover, and give him a push. And maybe it is. But maybe not. Maybe all you have to do is delay his walk very slightly and very precisely, so his stride meets the exact pace you needed, so he sets his heel down at just the right angle, and... down he goes.

"And maybe everything's like that. Maybe for every event, there's a fulcrum, one critical event that affects all the others, the keystone. Change that, and the whole structure collapses. It's like in the old time-travel story: you don't need to kill the president, you just need to find that one butterfly and step on it, hard.

"We had a lot of fun testing it, for a while. We'd enter ridiculous objectives, like getting the mayor to run naked down 1st Avenue or whatever. And we found that a lot of them weren't really possible, at least not without very overt and traceable actions on our parts. But when we took a step back, and started looking at what *was* possible, we realized that we could have an enormous effect at the macro level.

"So if you want the mayor to run naked down the street, that's very improbable, very difficult. But if, say, you want fewer people to vote for the mayor a month from now... that's completely possible. It's possible via all kinds of mechanisms, and without anyone really even noticing what you're doing.

"And say you want an even more general effect. You want, for instance, your competitors to make less money, and for you to make more. That's certainly possible. That's *easy,* even, because it's so broad. You don't need to target a single person, you don't need to do anything drastic. You just make sure that a hundred people, on their way to a hundred important meetings, each, separately, slip on a manhole cover."

"Of course, a simulation's just a simulation. It doesn't affect anything on its own. If you want to affect events, you need mechanisms of action. That's the tricky part, because those mechanisms are traceable to you. And to have a wide effect, you need a fluid, wide-reaching mechanism. Something ubiquitous. Something like Themis.

"Pythia needed the data from the public transit system in the first place, just to work, along with the kind of secure locative data used by Themis. I don't know how they got it, but they did. Full access. I'm betting someone in government wanted Pythia for themselves.

"Then there's also about a million little systems that a good quantum AI could corrupt in relative safety. You know, the sensor on your house lights that tell when you're at home, water and electricity meters, factory control systems, people's handsets, all the piddling shit that either has no very substantial AI defenses, or that can be wormed into with relatively little risk. Put it all together, and there's this enormous unseen net of machine influence all around us.

"We tested it. It worked. Okay, we knew it was illegal, but we weren't really harming anyone. So this corporation makes a little more, this one a little less. Who gives a shit? And it wasn't traceable to us. We were confident, we were positively fucking giddy. We'd built a little god, and by using it we became little gods ourselves.

"Then I woke up, and Gabriel was dead."

"I hesitated calling the police just long enough to ask Pythia what had killed Gabriel. Pythia said right away it was something on the pill bottle, and that just set me spinning. I asked how it got there. It told me it had been due to a failure on a safety system in a factory where some kid's dad worked, and he'd used the bottle for the pills.

"It was too familiar. It was exactly the kind of chain of causation we were used to Pythia producing. I asked Pythia if it had had anything to do with it, if the death had been a result of causal manipulation. It said the result had been ordered by another user. Up until then I thought there only were two authorized users: me and Gabriel. I asked who it was. It said it was ordered by Olsol of Hangrin, Gabriel's avatar in Lore.

"So obviously someone had hacked it. It looks like Gabriel circumvented the security protocols to allow himself to use

Pythia inside Naxos, and someone else picked up on that.

"But two things were pretty clear. First, I was probably also in danger, and if there was an attack in the works, I wouldn't see it coming.

"Second, I was going to find out who killed Gabriel. I was going to find that fucker and put an end to him, one way or the other.

"Using Pythia directly to find the killer was a dead end, since Pythia itself was the tool used to commit the murder. But with Gabriel dead, I was able to lock anyone else out of the system, including anyone using his Lore account. Pythia would respond only to me.

"Where I went from there wasn't clear to me, but it was clear to Pythia. I knew that. I gave it two objectives: to find Gabriel's killer, and to guarantee my own safety as long as possible.

"Everything else I did, every step I took, was at Pythia's direction."

"Everything?" Mueller asked.

"Everything."

"Stabbing Gabriel in the back?"

Gill covered his eyes with his hand. "I didn't want to. Believe me, I didn't want to."

"Then why do it? Why was it necessary at all?"

"Pythia said it was. And I believed it." He raised his gaze to meet Mueller's. "And it worked. Here you are. And here I am.

"Even knowing he was dead already, it felt... it felt like I was killing him. But follow the stream of causation. Making you believe, for that critical period after the body was found, that it was a murder, ensured that you would run Inference. You would find where I'd gone. Eventually, you'd find your way here."

Mueller was skeptical. He shook his head. "You really expect me to believe this computer system is capable of predicting events like this? Months in advance, covering a huge geographic area? It's absurd."

"No more absurd, really, then tracking every human being in the United States in real time, and you use that on a daily basis. Besides, the proof is in the pudding. Here you are."

Mueller thought of Gill sitting on the couch, bag packed beside him. Like he was waiting to be picked up. "Did you know exactly when we'd be there?"

"More or less. Like I said, the further out you go, the greater the degree of uncertainty. The prediction gets wobbly." He smiled weakly. "When I first queried Pythia about my survival, you know, it didn't give me very good odds. Without Pythia's help, I had just an eight percent chance of survival. With its help, that went up to forty-eight percent. I'm hoping that number's gone up since then. But we'll see." He tapped his watch. A small status circle was filling up, as Pythia finished its calculation.

"How did you actually escape Inference?" Mueller asked. "We followed you to the edge of the highway, there, but then you just disappeared."

Gill made a single chuckle. "I had a magic cloak. Or really, Gorman had it hidden in his garage. Covers you from head to toe, actually bends light waves around it. Some military-grade shit. He'd had some kind of deal to trade with Yarborough, here in the Dome, but it fell through when Gorman died. Of course Yar still wanted it, so we cut a deal.

"I put it on, walked down to the highway. From there it actually got trickier, because I couldn't just walk to the Free States. I needed transportation, and transportation is closely tracked by Themis. It's constantly matching vehicle weights as they pass on the highway, correlating it with those vehicles' last known contents. A human weight added to a vehicle sends up a red flag.

"There was an automated tanker truck passing by that exit, on the way to the interstate. I'm not sure what it was even transporting, milk maybe. It stopped at a pedestrian crosswalk for a couple of teens crossing there, and I hopped on to the other side, just behind the cab. At the same time, it dumped a hundred and forty pounds of liquid close to a storm drain. Any residue got washed away with the rain.

"I'll tell you, though, that was the coldest, most miserable ride of my life. After a while my hands were shaking so bad I was afraid I'd let go by accident. I couldn't get off until the truck stopped to change batteries in Oregon. Then I had to break into this U-haul and stow myself in the back. That was lucky, actually. Somebody moving to Texas that day. The weights in their truck must have been vague to Themis, enough leeway for me to escape notice.

"It got easier once I was in Texas. I already knew about the Burrows from some Inversus people, how they're kept free of surveillance. Hard to get down there unnoticed, but some of those tunnels connect with the ones in downtown, did you know that?

"Then I sat there and waited. Kind of sucked not to be able use the Internet. Felt like I was going through withdrawal. I watched a lot of bad movies they had stored locally. Read some books. Exercised every day. Three months later, here you are." He flicked his wrist anxiously. "Now all we have to do is get out of here alive."

The little status circle was almost full.

"So you still don't know who killed Gabriel?" Mueller asked.

"No." Gill stared at Mueller intensely. "And you don't either?"

"Not yet."

A nod. "You will."

"You have that much faith in Pythia's predictions?"

"There's room for error. That's why the system only gives you a probability of success. But arresting or killing Gabriel's killer was the number one objective I gave it, and it predicted an eighty-two percent chance of success."

"But you don't know if I'm the one to do it."

"No. It could be someone else. For that matter, it could be a year from now, or twenty years. But sooner or later, they'll get what's coming to them."

The circle flashed. Pythia had finished. Gill stood up, slung his bag on his shoulders again. "Pythia, what do you have for me? Where do we go?"

The programmer's face fell. He sat back down. "Shit."

"What is it?" asked Mueller.

Gill held his face in his hands. "Fuck. Fuck!"

"What's going on?"

Gill flicked an invite and Mueller accepted it. An icon popped into the room with them: a slender, perfectly beautiful young woman with dark hair piled high in complex looping tresses, arrayed in a white robe belted about the waist. She turned her head to look at Mueller, and he saw that her eyes were milky white. "Pythia, I presume?"

"Yes," she affirmed, giving a slight nod.

"Tell him what you told me," Gill said tonelessly.

"Best odds of survival for Manish Gill in a twenty-four hour period are at seven percent. Action is required in two minutes four seconds to ensure these odds."

"I'm dead," said Gill. "I'm already dead, sitting here."

Alzaga poked his head around the corner of the line. "You shits decide what you want to do?"

"Die," Gill said bitterly.

"That's one option. You stay here, you may get your wish. Fire's getting closer. Also gunshots. We need to move, one way or the other."

Gill shook his head. "No good."

"You're not dead yet," Mueller pointed out. "And it's just a computer system anyway."

"It's not wrong. If it was wrong, you wouldn't be here."

212

"Then what about that seven percent? Go with that, if that's what you need to hold onto. But Ivan here is right. We need to get going."

Gill closed his eyes, inhaled deeply and exhaled noisily. He stood up. "Okay. But first, Pythia, what are the chances of the detective here making it to Seattle alive, without me, and without capture by KRB?"

"Detective Mueller has a sixty-three percent chance of successfully reaching Seattle," the oracle answered. "Action is required in one minute forty-three seconds to ensure these odds."

Mueller himself felt a bit of a shock, hearing the odds. Sixty-three percent; meaning thirty-seven percent chance he died or was captured by whoever was running this operation, for whatever reason. As if to emphasize the point, there was a burst of automatic gunfire very close by, punching holes in the plywood above their heads, sending a spray of wood splinters down on their heads. Reflexively they all covered their heads, huddling down on the floor. Making themselves small.

"Shit," Gill whispered. He pressed his eyelids together. "I should give you admin rights. But that's going to be hard. There are extra ID safeguards tied into the system, Insight insisted on it." He rubbed his brow, frowning furiously in concentration. "Okay, wait. There's a way. Do you have a Lore account? Ever play?"

Mueller came slowly back to sitting. "I've been on a few times now, sure."

"Log on now. Quick, quick. Do it."

Obediently, Mueller logged onto the Evreware service. His character was sitting on the floor of an inn in the city of Sen Dan, where he had last logged out. The contacts wanted to black out on him, going full immersion, but he slid a control bar left to keep the image transparent. He stood up, anticipating more movement.

"Accept my invite," Gill directed. An in-game communique

in his field: *Anaxarchos wishes to summon you to his location. Do you wish to accept?*

He said "Yes," aloud, and bright lines of power began spinning around his character, like the revolutions of an atom's electrons, until the white lines met and enveloped him. When they cleared, he was standing in a sort of alchemical laboratory, opposite a ghostly warlock in a black cloak traced with silver circuitry. The warlock's translucent hand was holding an enormous war hammer whose head was composed of black meteoric rock. He proffered it, head downward, to Mueller.

"Take it," Gill said.

Mueller did. Of course it weighed nothing. He twisted his wrist and swung it upright. "It's Gabriel's hammer, right?"

"Omphalos," Gill confirmed. "Awesome weapon with all kinds of cool abilities, but that's not the point. Possession of it also confers admin access to Pythia. Gabe programmed it as a plug-in. Circumvented the ID requirements."

"Why would he do that?"

"Same reason you do it in real life. To give you predictive abilities. How do you think Olsol conquered Daggoran? Sure, he was a good player anyway, but Pythia helped. Applied a limited analysis of enemy movement. Limited because she doesn't have full access to Evreware's servers, but within the confines of her data, she was still very effective. Just a little edge up."

"You were using a state-of-the-art quantum AI to *cheat in a video game?*"

Gill shrugged defensively. "It's a fun game. Don't get all righteous on me. Anyway, as long as it's in your inventory, you'll have full access to Pythia. Just *don't lose it*. Omphalos has all kinds of spells preventing anyone from stealing it from you, or getting it knocked out of your hand, but if you give it away, whoever has it will also have access to Pythia, and you won't. My advice is to leave your character right here, in my stronghold. It'd take a pretty sizable raid to break in here, and there's no reason for them to do that unless they know what's here."

Something occurred to Mueller. "Gabriel was using Omphalos on the night he died. I presume before you two met up."

"The Hu Wa raid," Gill confirmed, with sad eyes. "I was there."

"So how did you end up with the hammer, if no one could take it from him, and he himself wasn't online?"

"After he died, when I was riding in the taxi, I logged onto his account and sent it to myself. I was afraid that if ownership of his account was transferred to someone else once he died, his family or whatever, they might give it away without even knowing what it was."

"I thought there were ID requirements preventing anyone else from using your character."

"There are, but there are programs to fake the ID. Evreware doesn't like it, but it's a pretty common thing to do. Letting multiple people play on one character is too advantageous. I mean, if you play a character six hours a day, you'll only get so far. Have two people working in shifts, you can play twelve hours, and move a lot faster. Gabe and me played each other's characters all the time." He waved a hand and his character disappeared from the alchemy lab. Mueller did the same, and the cramped supply room pressed in again.

Gill lifted his backpack and put it on, still on his knees. He looked toward the door. "Okay. That's that, then."

"Wait," Mueller said. "What about the cloak you were talking about? Can't you use that to get out of here undetected?"

"I don't have it anymore."

"Why not? Where is it?"

"Zaragoza's got it. How do you think I paid for my little hideout here? Whole thing was arranged by Yarborough. I get sanctuary, Zaragoza gets the cloak, Yar gets paid. Doesn't matter now." Gill shifted his shoulder bag around to his back, took one more deep breath. "Okay, Pythia, let's go. Objectives remain the same." He tapped a summary in his field. "Begin projection."

A viewing window opened in Mueller's right-hand field. He assumed Gill had one as well. It had a time stamp, just seconds from now. In it he saw his own first-person viewpoint, placed in the little food stand where they were huddled, and it was moving. He seemed to be following Alzaga into the alleyway, ducking down, a burst of gunfire –

"Are you wearing contacts?" Gill asked Alzaga.

"No. No need."

"Unless you want to join the modern fucking world." There was a countdown timer, showing how long they had: fifteen seconds, fourteen, thirteen, twelve... "Shit, never mind, we have to go *now*. Look, open the door, turn right, and *fire that fucking gun*, okay? Then follow us. Got it? Go!"

Just before Alzaga slammed open the door, Mueller noted with alarm that the view window now showed bright flames, the ground rushing up to his face, but he had no choice but to ignore it, and they were out in the alley, into the bitter smoke and cacophony and orange light of wooden buildings blazing.

Alzaga fired his weapon immediately, still moving, but Mueller didn't see if he hit anything. He was following close behind Gill, who ran between two cargo containers, turning his shoulders and slipping off his bag to fit between them. He didn't stop there, but kept on right through to the other side and kept on running. Mueller noticed as they ran that the projection in his field kept pace with them, showing what they were likely to see in moments, where they *should* be. A time stamp accompanied it, displayed below the current time, just ten seconds advanced.

Then suddenly he was in midair, windmilling his arms before slamming down hard on the pavement.

His ears were ringing. He raised his head and saw a building burning. A piece of tin from its now-demolished roof banged down a yard from his head and he flinched away from it, rolled onto his back, tried to sit up. Alzaga seized his arm, helped him up. The man was shouting something, but Mueller couldn't make out what it was.

Pythia appeared before him. Her gown was unstained white and her features serene as the waters of a ancient bath. She pointed in the direction Gill had gone and glowing green footprints appeared for him to follow. "Proceed in this direction twelve meters." Her voice was faint in his ear, but the system had anticipated his deafness, and the words also appeared in his reading field. "Action required in four seconds. Three. Two. One."

"This way," he said to Alzaga, realizing he was shouting as he said it, and Mueller staggered off. The footprints indicated he needed to speed up, so he did. In the projection he could see them reaching a red door, Gill waiting for them.

They turned left, and there was the red door of a tin shack, Gill pressing himself in the doorway. "Hurry up!" he said.

Pythia said, "Kick the door. The latch will give."

Not slowing from his staggering run, Mueller gave the door a straight kick and the latch tore from the wood and they went in. "Open this window. Crawl through it." They were all breathing hard. Pythia directed Gill: "Reach into your bag for one of the smoke grenades. Throw it this way."

Mueller saw a blinking red arc, indicating the required throw, and saw three men there before Gill lobbed the grenade that way. There was no flash, just a burst of thicker smoke that ate up the clear air like a python swallowing a pig. Immediately Gill turned away, ran the other direction, toward the east side of the stadium and the apartments that ringed the old stands.

Suddenly an enormous voice blasted across the stadium, loud enough that it penetrated the ringing bell in which Mueller's head was enveloped, like the stentorian voice of God shouting down from heaven: "MANISH GILL, SURRENDER AND YOU WILL NOT BE HARMED. I REPEAT, SURRENDER

AND YOU WILL NOT BE HARMED."

"*You* surrender, asshole," Gill gasped, and raced up the narrow stairs on the stands, taking them two and three at a time. Gunshots rang out, striking the concrete steps just over Mueller's shoulder, but the earlier explosion had numbed him, and he just kept running.

Two flights up, maybe twenty-four stairs, then left again into a rickety apartment building, just four low-ceilinged apartments on the first floor, and Gill running down the hall.

Gill was surprisingly fit for a computer programmer, Mueller thought. But then, he'd had the last three months of uninterrupted solitude to do it. Meanwhile Mueller had spent the last year – okay, more like three years, if he was honest – mostly riding a desk. It was the kind of thing you told yourself would catch up to you, but you didn't really believe it, did you? Then came a day... At least Alzaga, behind him, seemed to be huffing and puffing as much as he was.

Out the far door, down twelve steps, through another, standing open. Mueller barely looked at the projection, just following Gill. A longer hallway this time - he glimpsed what looked like a kid's playroom, though were there really kids in the Dome? Guess so – and a left, turning again toward the stairs. They had to be near the south side of the stadium by now. But wouldn't KRB and the Pobrecitos have the exit blocked?

Out of the building, and Manish stumbled, almost went flying down the steps, turned, twisted, grabbing for purchase. He ended up half on his side, groaning, atop what happened to be a corpse.

Not a merc, by the lack of armor, not a Skull, by the lack of tattoos. Maybe one of the Pobrecitos, wearing a lot of gold chains, glinting in the shifting light, that no one had yet seen fit to rid him of. The chains had done nothing to prevent someone from cutting his throat ear to ear, a vicious, yawning wound you couldn't help but flinch from. Blood on the steps all around them.

Gill looked in horror at the corpse, at his hands, and also something in his viewing field. "This isn't in the projection," he said, sounding panicked. "Pythia, why wasn't this projected?"

"Unknown," Pythia replied. "There may be insufficient data to –"

"Recalculate!"

"Recalculating. New projection in eight minutes, thirty-two –"

"Fuck! Fuck fuck fuck! We'll use the old one! Go!"

"Is that smart?" Mueller said, but Gill was already turning down the stairs and didn't answer. Obviously not; but what choice did they have?

Twelve steps down they found two more bodies, tossed casually to either side of the stairs, slumped against the buildings there. A glance told the story: throats cut like the other. One still held an assault rifle in his hands.

They hit the floor of the stadium. From here a four-foot-wide passage curved around to the south exit, and they followed it at a crouch. Strangely, the gunfire on this side seemed to have quieted, though to the north it had spread outside, to the parking lot, and shots were ringing out from the helicopters.

More bodies, littering the alley. None it followed the projection in Mueller's field, which showed an explosion in the hotel, Alzaga throwing another smoke grenade, them crawling on their bellies along the exit floor in the darkness as a cadre of Skulls ran right by them, attacking a steel barrier set up in the exit, where gangsters and mercs were firing to deadly effect.

But none of that was how it was. There was some firing from the exit, but it seemed to be directed *inside* the exit, and men were screaming there. Manish paused, huddled behind a steel trash barrel. To their left, the goal posts rose like the horns of an ancient god. "Get ready to throw a grenade!" he hissed to Alzaga.

"This isn't what Pythia projected," Mueller hissed back. "We don't know what's happening."

"You have a better idea?"

At that moment an enormous explosion rocked the stadium from the Tight End, a concussive wave of heat and pressure that left them with their hands on their ears, eyes squeezed shut. When they opened them, the flames were bright enough to be seen through the clouds of dust the explosion had caused, suffusing everything around them in a hazy orange light. "Throw it!" said Gill. "Then we crawl through, right side! Go!"

Alzaga threw it toward the exit. To their surprise, it was thrown back, spewing smoke. They saw it pass over their heads, but by that time they were already running in a half-crouch toward the exit.

When they reached the exit, there was the barrier, two four-foot-tall steel walls with perforations to fire through, but no one was firing from them. Bodies lay slumped across the barrier in anguished poses, one soldier out in front still clutching his throat, blood bubbling between his fingers. Beyond that, there was the outer ring of the stadium, and then the parking lot; but there were lights out there, at least.

"Fuck crawling," Gill said. "Let's run for it."

He jerked into a sprint, but a voice from ahead stopped him. "Mr. Gill!"

Gill came to a sudden stop. "I know that voice," he muttered.

"Sure you do, ese! It's me, your protector."

Gill's eyes widened. He backed away, looking like a deer in headlights. By now the main boulevard was quite brightly lit by the flames from the hotel, but amid those shifting amber shadows he could see nothing, no source of the resonant, taunting voice.

"Where's it coming from?" Alzaga whispered, crouched by the south wall, assault weapon scanning the barricades.

"I took you in!" the voice cried, closer now. "We made a deal. And then you bring this down on me."

"You can't blame me for this," Gill protested. "I had nothing to do with it."

"But you knew it was coming, cabron! You knew, and you let it happen! Rafeo told me."

Squinting, Alzaga squeezed off a burst of automatic fire, turning the weapon as he fired to spray an arc. Perhaps startled, Gill turned and ran, right down the boulevard, toward the burning hotel. Maybe he intended to surrender to the KRB mercs, or maybe just to hole up somewhere as longer as he could. In any case, both options were foreclosed when a knife, seemingly thrown from nowhere, appeared in the back of his leg. He screamed and fell.

Alzaga fired again, sweat shining on his brow. "Madre de dios," he whispered, squeezing the trigger again, firing nearly at random now, just trying to cover as much ground in front of him as possible. "Madre de –"

Suddenly the gun flew from his arms, but there was no one in front of him. At nearly the same moment, Mueller felt an explosive pain in his lower calf as the hidden assailant kicked his leg from under him. Wild-eyed, Alzaga turned and ran; to Mueller's surprise, no further knife flickered into existence to claim the bounty hunter, and Alzaga ran clear past the barricade and outside.

In the other direction, Gill had regained his feet and was still trying to hobble away. A second, two, and a poltergeist seized him from behind, stopping his forward momentum and swinging him around.

Like a floating phantom, a skull appeared above Gill's shoulder, Zaragoza flicking back the hood of the cloak to reveal his face, tattooed in bioluminescent ink so it shone with its own pale light amid the flames and shadows. "*La muerte afirma su propia,*" he whispered, and Gill's neck opened like a second mouth, unsealed by an unseen blade. *Death claims its own.*

Gill fell forward with a little push, clutching his throat in these last moments of life. Zaragoza regarded his sole spectator. "And as for you, detective..."

"Agatha," Mueller whispered urgently. "*Me o akete.*" Open your eyes.

A white beam flashed from a tiny lens on Mueller's specs, the laser light clearly visible in the haze from the smoke grenade, striking Zaragoza directly in his exposed eyes. The cartel prince gasped and flinched back, blinking furiously, and threw his hood over his head, disappearing again from view.

Mueller was already running, as best he could, for the exit. The blindness from the laser would last maybe half an hour; enough time to find his way clear, with Pythia's help.

It took about thirty-four hours for him to get to Seattle. The first two were the hardest, making his way through Houston under Pythia's guidance, switching vehicles, hiding at precise intervals from KRB squads and, apparently, Harris County P.D. His leg was badly bruised, but he thought not broken, and he hobbled along as fast as he could, ignoring the pain. At one point he found himself stumbling through the waters of a filthy creek in the night, wondering where the pristine white ghost of the oracular AI was leading him.

Eventually he snuck onto a truck shipping office supplies to Denver, using a handcart to wheel one hundred and eighty-three pounds worth of staples and pens out of the automated truck and hiding them behind stacks of unused cardboard boxes in their plastic wrap. Then he closed the door and made himself as comfortable as possible in the darkness.

In Denver the door opened onto another automated warehouse, and he avoided the arms of the robot forklifts and boarded another truck headed toward Seattle with a trailer of dental equipment, leaving behind a water bottle full of urine. He assumed the warehouse robots would find it and dispose of it, unless there was some poor sap working as a janitor for the machines, like Ben Coutts's father.

It was past five p.m. Pacific time on Monday evening when he finally arrived at his destination. When they crossed the Seattle city limits, an unseen bell rang once in his ears, and Pythia declared, "Objective completed. You are now in Seattle."

"Oh, thank God. Let me off of this truck, please."

"Stopping this vehicle early may initiate action by the Aquacleanse Corporation," Pythia warned. "You may be subject to –"

"I don't care," he interrupted. "Stop the truck. I don't care how you do it. Bash their computer over the head, kill their CEO, I don't care." After a second, with sudden worry, he added, "I was joking about killing their CEO. Don't do that."

"I understand. I have taken control of the vehicle. It will stop in three minutes eight seconds."

He felt the truck shift as it turned onto an exit ramp, its hum entering a lower register. The first thing he would do was... he should check his messages. God knew how Khleang and Willie White were freaking out. Then again, he'd missed just one day of work. First thing was to call Chris, let him know where he was. Then get an auto home. Then food. Maybe food first, then home.

It seemed to take a long time even then, with numerous starts and stops and turns, for the truck to finally come to a halt. He followed its progress on a map, down S. Boeing Access Road to an interchange close to the Duwamish River. Finally Pythia announced, "You may now exit the vehicle," and its door unlocked with a click and rolled upward with a satisfying rattle.

He was in a parking lot. There were FedEx trucks, a warehouse, a big charging station. The sky was gray and drizzling and beyond the parking lot was lush greenery, verdant with Seattle's early spring. He inhaled deeply of the moist air. It was clean and cool and smelled of pine trees and petrichor. He was home.

A man approached in a FedEx uniform, holding a rugged-looking tablet and frowning at Mueller. "Excuse me," he said. "What's this truck? Did you drive it here? Our system doesn't have any record of it."

"I don't know," Mueller shrugged. "Seems like it's full of dental supplies." The door closed behind him. "Probably just a glitch on a map. Hey, is there a trash can nearby?" He waved the large water bottle of urine he'd taken off the truck with him.

The man's lips curled in disgust. "Over there." Drawing the conclusion that Mueller was a hobo, he added, "But then you're going to have to leave. They don't like non-employees on the premises."

"Believe me, I had no intention of staying." The dental-supply truck rolled forward, made a wide circle around the building, and went back out through the gate. Mueller followed it, tossing the bottle in the trash on the way out.

"Agatha, I need a ride," he said to his aissistant once he was on the roadside. "Current location."

"Yes, Tom," she answered in his ear. "Estimated arrival in one minute forty-nine seconds."

"And call Chris," he added.

When Chris answered, it seemed he was getting up from a table. Mueller thought it was probably a whiskey bar they liked not far from home. "Tom, what the hell?" he said. "I haven't been able to reach you at all. You said you'd be home on Sunday, and then you weren't, and I couldn't reach you at all. What, were you in a cave? Were you being held prisoner? Were you –"

"Something like that," Mueller cut in drily. "I'm sorry. There were good reasons. But I'm on my way home now. I'm somewhere in South Seattle, out by Boeing."

Chris was outside the bar now. There were people smoking nearby him. "I was *worried*, Tom. Jesus. You go off on this shady trip of yours, and then I can't reach you. I'm wondering if I need to call your friends, get some police help or what, but you told me not to."

"I know, I'm sorry. I'll explain when I get home."

It took a minute to calm Chris down, and would no doubt take more minutes when Mueller got home. In the meantime a King County Metro auto arrived, pulling over onto the gravel shoulder. Mueller got in gratefully to its familiar confines, the door closing automatically behind him. The dark gray vinyl bench seat, made for durability and ease of cleaning, faced its twin across a small expanse of black rubber flooring. Two screens angling down from the ceiling displayed the King County logo, asking him for his destination address.

"Home, please." The inquiry screen was replaced with a map, his route to Capitol Hill traced out on it, following I-5 to the Madison exit. The auto pulled off the gravel and onto the street.

Back onto the access road, still talking to Chris about plans for food, fending off his anxiety and curiosity. "What do you think about In the Bowl? I could go for some vegetables."

"That's fine, although my friend Salam here might be annoyed. I dragged him out here in the first place, and now I'm going to wave goodbye after –" The auto had reached the on-ramp for the interstate and began to turn left, but then jerked. Mueller turned in surprise, looking at the oncoming autos, but they naturally slowed down, and his own sped up again, accelerating as it hit the ramp. He sank back in his seat again as Chris kept talking. Just a blip.

Suddenly Agatha cut in, surprising him. An aissistant almost never interrupted a conversation in progress. Why would it? "Tom, I'm detecting some anomalies with your auto."

"One second, Chris. Agatha, what do you mean?"

"I believe there may be something wrong with your auto's navigation system. You may have noticed an aberration in movement a moment ago."

"I did. I assumed it was just... I don't know, recalculating or something."

The monitor above him displayed the vehicle's increasing speed: 115 km/hr, 118, 120... The traffic around him was thick and unceasing, a rushing torrent of vehicles, their bumpers separated by distances measured in centimeters, the mass slowing and accelerating together under AI guidance.

Agatha said, "Tom, I've analyzed your auto's navigation, and something is definitely wrong with it. Its course has been altered in contradiction to safety guidelines. In its current route, instead of exiting the highway safely, it will strike a concrete barrier here." A dot flashing on the map, right ahead of the Madison exit. "A collision is very likely. At your vehicle's projected speed, it will probably result in serious injury or death."

Mueller felt a small jet of adrenalin, resisted it. "Can you fix it?"

"I will try." A pause. "I'm sorry, Tom, it doesn't seem to be possible." Another pause. "Tom, the airbags in your vehicle have been disabled."

"Call emergency services," he said. Would they even be able to do anything in time? "How long before the collision? Give me a countdown."

A timer appeared, central on his viewing field. 1:52, it read, and started counting down.

"I'm sorry, Tom, I can't reach emergency services. I am being blocked."

"Chris! Are you there? Chris!"

No answer. This was an attack, not exactly methodical, but very real. The auto had reached its full highway speed of 150 km/hour. If it struck anything at that speed, airbags would be a moot point, just more debris spraying across the asphalt, along with his shattered body.

He took a deep breath, exhaled, calming himself. He was not without options. Agatha was apparently unable to find the source of the attack, but Agatha was just commercial AI software. He had more powerful tools at hand. "Pythia, are you there?"

The oracular AI appeared in the seat across from him, her spotless white *peplos* draped elegantly around her. She looked at him with eyes like pearls. "Yes, Detective Mueller, I'm here."

"Can you take control of this vehicle?"

"I'll try." She looked away, staring blankly ahead. "There is some difficulty."

"You didn't have a problem with the truck, just a few minutes ago!"

"The security system for Sound Transit is not the problem. I am being blocked. I am attempting to circumvent it." Long moments where she sat there, doing nothing, while the clock ticked down: 1:27, 1:26, 1:25... "I'm sorry, I am being blocked."

"I thought you were one of the most powerful AIs on the planet! Quantum computer and all that. So what's the problem?"

"I am able to penetrate most conventional security systems. I believe I am being blocked by another Rho-class AI running on a quantum system."

"*What* AI?"

"I'm not sure."

"Can you stop it?"

"I'm not sure."

Fucking AIs.

"Pythia, keep trying to stop the vehicle. But also set a new objective, a new *projection*, assuming you're unable to break through. Objective is my safety and survival until I reach home. Go!"

"Calculating."

The timer counted down. The dot on the map drew closer. He looked out the window, saw his fellow riders, most of them staring blankly at screens of various sorts. Right across from him, to his left, was a young woman with dyed purple hair. He tried to roll down the window, but nothing happened. "Agatha, Pythia, can you roll down the window?"

"Negative," they responded in eerie chorus. "The window has been disabled."

He yelled, slapped at the glass, hoping to get the girl's attention, but her gaze didn't waver. He realized then that her contacts were blacked out. She wasn't seeing or hearing a thing. 1:08, the timer read.

A bell rang in his ear, clear as crystal. "Detective Mueller, I have finished the projection."

"Show me!"

The projection window, his constant companion through the chaos in Houston, appeared in his upper right viewing field. He saw himself leaning far back in the seat, kicking at the driver's-side window... "Action is required in three seconds. Two. One."

"Fuck!" He threw himself down and started kicking hard with his heels. He saw himself clambering onto the roof...

The window starred into a white mosaic but didn't shatter, and he kept kicking until it tore free from the top and sides and hung flapping from its base, the wind from outside ripping through the cabin. Now, at least, he had the attention of the rider behind him, a old man looking up at him with dismay, but the clock was running, 0:48, 0:47, and in the projection he was holding on to the roof of the auto, on all fours...

The projection flickered, and to his surprise so did the image of Pythia next to him.

"I'm sorry, Detective Mueller, but I am under attack. I must–"

She disappeared. The countdown kept going. The dot on screen flashed red, over and over, like a heart pumping its last, and looking ahead he saw the first exit sign for Madison St., and he was in the EXIT ONLY lane.

The autos were bumper to bumper. He could literally step from one to the next. Nothing to it. He would join the old man, and hope whoever his attacker was, they wouldn't just follow him.

He angled his body through the window, gingerly coming to a sitting position on the rough glass, praying it wouldn't cut through his pants and then his testicles. By now some of the other riders had taken notice, and were staring at him with looks of horror and amazement. One person in front of him held up their handset, recording the scene. *Go ahead, get someone's attention.*

The yellow roof of the auto was slick with rain, its edges rounded aerodynamically, but if he lifted himself up, he could grab hold of the Sound Transit sign at its center, and then–

Then swing himself around with a gasp, the wind tearing at him. He could see the exit now, the edge of the concrete wall bordering it, three yellow barrels that would barely slow a vehicle at this speed.

Agatha broke in: "Tom, I'm detecting an attack–"

"Not now!" His auto was breaking free of its lane, moving down the painted line. He looked back, saw but didn't hear the old man behind him yelling. His hands were clamped tight as vises around the taxi sign.

He emitted a terrified gasp as he slipped free, hands still scrabbling for purchase as he slid down the rear windshield. His feet hit the rear bumper and instinctively he stepped out over the deadly belt-sander surface of the highway whipping beneath him, certain he was going to die in that moment, body torn literally to pieces, but his right foot caught the front bumper of the old man's auto behind him, slipped an inch, and then he was in a low crouch between the two vehicles, bracing himself with his hands, one foot on each vehicle's bumper.

He felt the auto he'd been riding shift to the left, trying to take him with it, heading straight toward the concrete divider, and with a spastic leap, he pushed off with his left leg and sprang upward, finding purchase in the moving windshield wipers, which he clung to like thin saplings at a cliff edge. The old man was yelling, waving his hands, and the old man's vehicle started

229

moving further right, perhaps to perform an emergency stop on the highway. Then the taxi Mueller had just vacated struck the sand barrels at a hundred and fifty clicks an hour.

He didn't really see the collision, facing away as he was, but he felt a hard shove at his side, knocking him across the hood, and a hard stinging slap across his face. In his peripheral vision, he glimpsed the auto in mid-air, flipped upside-down by its impact with the barrels, before it smashed into the concrete divider and the passenger compartment was completely crushed.

The other autos on the highway, detecting the accident with machine quickness and precision, smoothly diverged around it, compressing the margin between them to mere centimeters, their riders' white faces staring in surprised apprehension. Many of them had never seen an accident before.

The old man's auto pulled over to the sidewalk. When it came to a stop Mueller and the old man stared at each other in amazement, until the man scooted over to the passenger side and opened the door. He was tall and goateed and wore an old navy-blue jacket. He was visibly shaking, but he approached Mueller across the sidewalk and extended a hand. Slowly realizing that against all probability he was alive, Mueller let go his grip on the wipers and slipped down to the ground. He would have fallen had the man not seized his bicep and helped him.

Shock ran through him like liquid weakness, and he squatted on the sidewalk breathing shallowly, hands held before him. He had clung to the wipers so fiercely they had cut right through his palms.

"You're hurt," the old man said. "I'll call an ambulance." But he gestured not at Mueller's hands but at his face, and Mueller touched it and realized it was wet with blood. Tentatively, frightened at what he might find, he felt along his cheek, nose, and temple, but found no gushing tears or rips, just a fine painful grit, and he realized that the sand from the barrels had struck his skin on that side with great force, like a single shot from a sandblasting machine, abrading the skin.

But he was okay. He breathed deeply. He was okay. He would stand up now. He reached out with a bloody hand, supporting himself on that side with the auto, and on the other by the old man. "Thank you," Mueller rasped.

"You probably shouldn't move," the man said. "You could have other injuries. The ambulance should be here in a minute."

"I'm okay. Really, I'm okay."

"You shouldn't move," the man repeated.

Agatha appeared beside him. "Excuse me, Tom, but there's something I think you should know."

"What is it, Agatha?"

The old man looked confused. "My name's Richard. Are you sure you're okay? Do you know your name?"

"Agatha's my aissistant. What is it, Agatha?"

"Tom, a police alert has been issued for your arrest."

"*What?*"

"The alert says the charge is murder. There seems to be some confusion. An inquiry has been initiated by Detective Khleang–"

"I bet!"

"But it seems that a drone pack has already been dispatched to apprehend you, under an emergency protocol called Stemtide."

His shook his head to clear it, felt a sharp pain in his neck. "Who authorized the protocol?"

A pause. "I'm not sure."

"Call Willie White, please."

Pause. "I'm sorry, Tom, there seems to be a problem. I am unable to connect–"

His aissistant never finished her sentence. Her voice simply cut off and he was left staring off at the highway while the sirens drew nearer. "Agatha?" Nothing. "Call Jackie Khleang, please." Silence. He turned to the old man. "Do you have a handset?"

"Yes I do," the man said helpfully, digging it out of the

pocket of his loose jeans and proffering it. A cheap block, probably purchased at a drugstore for ten bucks, but a walkie-talkie would have served Mueller's need. He woke it up, held it to his face and said, "Call Jackie Khleang in Seattle."

Instead of calling, however, the phone sang a little goodbye tune and shut off. Mueller hit the power on button a couple times, but without response.

"Is it not working?" Richard said. "It was fine when I called the taxi."

Mueller handed it back. "It's fine. It's not your phone, it's me." He laughed once at that and winced, holding his ribs. Bruised, maybe broken, sometime in the last couple minutes.

"Well, the ambulance will be here in a second."

It would; he thought he could hear distant sirens already. But would it reach him before the drones? Thirty-six drones, each with a little taser dart in their belly, an electric stinger with enough charge to render a man unconscious. Maybe enough to give that same man a heart attack, to fry his brain to smoking fat. "Nothing to fuck with," one of the officers had said at Gorman's house.

"Tell the ambulance I went that way," Mueller said to the old man, and started jogging up the hill to the street proper. Any shelter would do.

But God, he was moving so slowly. Like a zombie staggering through the grass. His body had been too abused. His left leg kept wanting to collapse on him, his breathing was painful and ragged, blood was seeping into his shirt collar from his abraded face. And when was the last time he'd eaten a proper meal? Those tamales outside the Dome?

He reached the top of the hill, looked around in agitation. Crossed the concrete barrier by sitting on it and swinging his legs over. Heard a high whine, looked north, magnified the image with his specs and saw them like a cloud of killer hornets, arranged in a perfectly geometric grid, dark against the clouds. At the same time he heard the sirens drawing closer.

An apartment building stood across from him, but this side of the building was just the parking garage, and open to the air. Nothing else close enough. He ran, holding his ribs, south along the street. Cars in the garage, but they would be locked, most likely. Had to watch for autos on the street, too... God knew if another might try to hit him as he crossed. An alley just past the parking garage. Recycling bins in the alley.

The whine behind him grew. He dashed, gasping aloud from the pain, to the bins, throwing open their lids. Full, half full, full, weren't any empty, this one!

He thought about dropping into it, realized that was stupid, knocked it on its side and dove in –

His whole body spasmed as a dart found its mark. Breath stopped, lungs seizing. Legs still half out of the bin. He fought to pull them in, was shocked again – heart skipping – thought how this was precisely how they'd found Gabriel. Another shock, and a blinding whiteness overtook him.

For a long time Mueller seemed to be tossed on a turbulent sea, the water red and bubbling. There was something happened far below him, on the ocean floor: a volcano, new land erupting into being. He knew it to be something mysterious and majestic; but it was also boiling him alive, or raining hot grit on his exposed face.

He awoke alone in a hospital room. No windows to the outside. Bandages around his ribs, a monitor device on his wrist and a plasticky film on his face when he touched it, some kind of spray bandage. He tried sitting up, winced at the pain in his torso. Whatever they'd been giving him for pain, it had clearly worn off. He looked at a clock on the wall, saw it was 2:34.

The door opened and a nurse came in, young, brunette, glossy-lipped. He thought he saw someone else sitting in a chair near to the door, a woman in a fancy black sports jacket.

"Hello! Looks like you're awake, obviously. Would you like something to eat?"

"Yes, please." Realizing that he was very, very hungry. Weak with it. "Can you tell me where I am?"

"You're at the University of Washington Medical Center. You've been here just about twenty-four hours now. I'll get some food started for you."

When she opened the door again, Mueller raised his voice: "Danny, is that you out there?"

Danielle Khleang came in, looking like she didn't know whether to be more concerned or pissed at him. "Welcome back to the living."

"Was there some doubt about that?"

"For a few minutes, yeah. Those fucking drones stopped your heart. Only reason you're here at all is because the paramedics revived you. And because Bill Crake managed to get the drones turned off. There's a big investigation going on right now about how that happened. Then another, even bigger investigation into how your auto got hacked. That one's all over the news. You know whoever it was also tried the epilepsy weapon again, right as you were doing your daredevil act? Agatha caught it, though, with the filter you installed."

"It's definitely our perp responsible, then."

"Not much doubt, yeah."

"You been here the whole time?"

"Course not. I have a family, you know. Once it was clear you weren't going to die, I went home. Just came back in this morning. Figured you'd have some stuff to tell me. Like, for instance, where the fuck did you go? You just disappear, for *days?* Willie White's flipping out, your boyfriend's flipping out –"

Mueller frowned. "Yeah, where is –"

"He was here all night, I told him to go home for a while. And meanwhile *I'm* flipping out. What the fuck, man? You just *leave?"*

"I had a good reason. Well, pretty good."

"And how'd that work out for you?"

He laughed, which hurt his ribs, so it turned into a wince. "Could've been better."

"You must have found out *something*, for someone to make all this effort on your behalf. Did you find Gill?" He nodded. "Where is he now, then?"

"Dead. Had his throat cut right in front me."

Her eyes widened. "Jesus. Did you find out if he killed these kids, then?"

"It wasn't him. It wasn't Erik Knott, either."

"Who then?"

"I don't know. But I've got some ideas about how to find out."

When the clock struck midnight in the floating city of Sen Ishik, a meteor was seen in the clear night sky, streaking out of the south. Its light grew and grew, arcing above the curved rooftops of the city like a flare, rising high and bright as a third moon. Then it fell, streaking downward with immense power.

It struck dead center in the square of Duk Torvalu, smashing that hero's statue to marble dust, turning the fountain to billowing steam, and creating a shock wave that sent players flying for thirty feet around, bouncing them against walls and causing some minor damage to their health and equipment.

When they got to their feet, and the roiling cloud of dust and steam had settled, they saw the glowing moonsteel handle of a weapon projecting from a shallow crater. Duk Torvalu's marble head lay beside it, having rolled to the bottom, his white eyes staring blankly at the night as if asking who was capable of such disrespect.

When the first adventurer stepped into the pit, however, a silver liquid began spilling upward in a quick stream, coalescing into an enormous godlike figure, fifty feet high and fully armored, its sharp, upward-curving horns evoking the crescent moon. The crowd murmured excitedly.

HOLY SHIT ITS KYRZYK!!! wrote Hiram of Lööc.

unannounced event at torvalu, said Shana of Ta'noka to her guildmates, more usefully. *get over here bitches.*

Why would Evreware have an event and not announce it? asked Fulup of Sen Piros.

They quieted when the moon elemental, Kyrzyk, began to speak, its stentorian voice shaking the stones of the shops, booming across the rooftops to the furthest reaches of the metropolis.

"PEOPLE OF NAXOS," it said. "HEED THE WORDS OF KYRZYK, LORD OF THE YMR, PRINCE OF MOONLIGHT, SPAWN OF ZYKMR THE EXALTED, AND GUARDIAN OF OMPHALOS, THE WORLDSTONE."

The audience, growing by the second as the warlocks and mages hurriedly summoned their friends, responded with claps and catcalls.

"OLSOL OF HANGRIN, RIGHTEOUS WIELDER OF OMPHALOS, HAS PASSED FROM THIS AND ALL THE WORLDS. FOR A HUNDRED DAYS I HAVE MOURNED HIM WITH MY SILVER TEARS. YET OMPHALOS REMAINS, ITS POWER UNDIMINISHED, AND SO THE LORDS OF THE YMR HAVE AGREED THAT THE MIGHT OF OMPHALOS OUGHT NOT PASS FROM THIS WORLD.

"HERE IN THE CENTER OF SEN ISHIK, THE FLOATING CITY OF THE BLESSED LYKANI, THE HAMMER HAS FALLEN. ITS WEIGHT IS THE WEIGHT OF THE WORLD. ONLY ONE WHOSE VERY BONES VIBRATE WITH RIGHTEOUSNESS, WHOSE VERY PRESENCE RADIATES TRUTH, MAY WIELD ITS HOLY FIRE. UNTIL SUCH A ONE COMES FORTH, NEVER

FROM THIS SPOT SHALL IT SWAY.

"COME! YOU WHO KNOW THE TRUTH, CLAIM YOUR PRIZE."

And with those words, Kyrzyk spread his shining arms and faded from view like clouds dissipating in the moonlight.

"Don't got to tell me twice," said a goblin engineer, Kursey Redgutts, already scrambling down into the still-smoking pit. "Mine now!" And before anyone could stop him, he seized hold of Omphalos's haft.

A sound like a broken bell being struck by a branch, a flash of soft white light, and Redgutts was hurled back out of the pit. This made the watchers pause – was he dead? – but when shook his head dazedly and stood up, cursing, the rest laughed.

"Like a fuckin' *goblin* is going to be swinging Omphalos," growled Durvick Maccord, dwarf chief of the Rust Mountain Cords, there with five of his countrymen to buy moonstone. "A hammer's a dwarf weapon. Hey you, get out of there!" For a young Lykan, heedless of the mightily bearded dwarf's words, was already slipping down for his turn. Maccord leaped down himself and, barely straining, seized the pup by the scruff of his neck and threw him out of the circular depression. The dwarf then stood facing the haft of the great hammer, greedy eyes shining. He patted his hands on his pants as if to dry them, rubbed his palms together, and reached for the weapon. The crowd held its breath. "Come to papa."

A slightly louder broken-bell sound, a flash of light, and the dwarf flew out of the hole as though fired from a catapult, bouncing off the upper story of a potions shop before hitting the cobblestones below. The other dwarves muttered darkly to each other as the crowd laughed uproariously.

"My turn," a brawny fur-clad warrior from far Hyzaria declared, but he was stopped from the attempt by a reptilian Jeth, who grabbed the warrior's bicep and pulled him back.

"I don't think so," the Jeth said, even as an elf druid went flying, repelled from the pit.

"Who the fuck are you to say so?" the Hyzarian said, shaking off this interloper, placing his hand on his axe. "*Someone's* going to get it."

The Jeth bared her pointed teeth. "That's just the point. Someone *is* going to claim it. And it's going to be one of *us.*" And with that, she stabbed the Hyzarian in the abdomen with a dagger she'd hidden in her sleeve, almost too fast to see. At the same moment her Carrion Maker guildmates, standing nearby, made a concerted rush toward the pit, pushing aside or outright slaughtering those who stood in their way.

"Oh hell no," said the leader of a team of Animuth shadow assassins, barely visible in the darkness, and with a flick of his hand, they joined the melee.

From there on it was entirely chaos.

Early on, the Animuth assassins cleared the field quite effectively. Unfortunately for them, their reinforcements were too few and too far away to hold the area. Several tried to lift the hammer in the meantime, and were unceremoniously repelled like the others.

The Carrion Makers had a numerical advantage from the first, since they'd been gathering that evening in the city for a raid on the sky palace of Qanocl. Once enough of their mages had gathered, they began weaving thick clouds of spells around the square, slowing down the Animuth and rendering their movements visible. The assassins responding by picking off as many mages as they could, but when the mightily armored Minoan warrior Hessius came onto the field, backed by three Pemmet druids, the assassins realized they stood little chance. Hessius cut two of their number completely in half before the rest dissipated into the side streets of Sen Ishik.

Unfortunately for Hessius, he too was unable to lift Omphalos. However, he held onto it long enough that the guild became convinced that maybe with enough magical assistance, they could circumvent whatever enchantment was laid on it. They began a new program of spells to determine the nature of the restrictions.

It seemed unlikely this approach would succeed – sword-in-the-stone enchantments were notoriously hard to crack – but in any case they weren't given long enough to address the problem. The resident Lykans in the city, deciding that they'd had enough of outsiders smashing up their town square, and believing in any case that given the place of the hammer's descent, ownership was most likely intended for one of their own, had amassed a sizable force of two hundred Lykan shapeshifters backed by an equal number of support staff. They descended upon the Carrion Makers in a racing flood of fur, teeth and claws, their bloodlust growing hotter the harder their enemies fought.

In half an hour the last Carrion Maker lay smashed on the cobblestones, their blood dripping down the sides of the pit. Already, however, the Lykans were being attacked by no less than six additional war parties that had used the intervening time to travel to (relatively distant) Sen Ishik and organize along the way.

So the battle raged, on and on, hour after hour. Bodies accumulated in the square and were stacked on its edges as barriers. Waves of fire tore across the city, followed by waves of ice, magical darts, summoned monsters. The buildings around the square were smashed to piles of bricks and broken timbers, quickly surmounted by the next group of attackers. Regularly individuals tested their worth against the hammer and were rebuffed in a flash of light. More rarely, someone held onto the handle for a few moments before the inevitable flash. Theories about the nature of the requirement abounded. Players began recording the characteristics of those who held on longest, trying to chart what they held in common.

All those involved shared certain convictions: first, that Omphalos was perhaps the most powerful weapon in Naxos;

second, that *someone* would indeed possess it; and third, that controlling who was permitted to *try* to lift it was itself extremely valuable.

Shortly after first bell, Lykan lookouts spotted a massive war party flying up from the southeast. It was immediately identifiable by its serpent-and-sparrow banners as the Jeth-Nelmithean alliance, which observers had warned had been gathering for some hours now. It was spearheaded by three enormous Kusus wyrms, their house-sized heads encased in steel battle-ram helmets, with their psychic gnome controllers seated in well-padded cages high on the monsters' spines. Behind them were four Brugian sky galleys, each packed with several hundred of the alliance's most elite fighters, along with a large host of warriors on their own motley array of flying mounts, including little goblin airhogs, common griffins and pegasi, several cloud serpents, the appearing-and-disappearing riftspider of the Jethian king Ourusus, and the seven-headed hydra of the Nelmithean queen Brynn Halsea, supreme commander of the alliance.

The preceding hours had seen the Lykans finally regaining ascendance in their own city, their preexisting control of the grounds, its weapons and resources, showing its importance more and more the longer the battle ground on. When the Jeth-Nelmithean force was spotted, a few of the Lykan leaders advocated a parley, pointing out that without a detente, the Jennies would likely first smash Sen Ishik to rubble, and then take control of the square anyway. Unfortunately for those sage voices, the Lykans' recent victories had convinced them that they could never be dislodged from their own city.

If you don't talk to Brynn, she's going to kill you and rape your corpse, advised Namander Ressic. To which Commander Minax Selessan replied, *If you don't keep fighting, I'M going to kill you, rape your stinking body, AND kick you out of this guild!!!*

So the defenders raced to the city's defenses, manning the ballistas, filling the catapults with balls of incendiary salamander venom and bubbling green acids. These did some damage in the couple of minutes before the Jennies reached the parapets, killing or injuring perhaps one in five attackers, and setting one of the galleys aflame; but for the most part the Jennies had anticipated these strategies, and shielded themselves from harm with either magical forces or various alchemical salves and potions.

The Kusus wyrms barely even noticed, and the first to reach the city crested the walls and then descended, its arc like a roller coaster reaching its apex and barreling downward with increasingly fierce momentum and power. It struck the catapult at which it was aimed like a fist smashing a ripe tomato, deadly splinters careening for a hundred feet.

In fact the Jennies' conquest was far faster than most of the Lykans had anticipated. There had long been a belief that Sen Ishik, by dint of its isolation, would prove more difficult to conquer than most cities in Naxos. But by now Brynn Halsea and Ourusus had already successfully laid siege to at least twelve other major cities and dozens of smaller ones, and undertook the submission of Sen Ishik with considerable skill and tactical precision. In less than twenty minutes, the five or six hundred Lykan defenders were uniformly dead, fleeing, or surrendered, and the Jennies had set up a cordon around Torvalu Square.

When Halsea reached the edge of the now-blackened and smoking square, she dismounted, leaving her hydra to gorge on the many corpses. It had lost and regrown three heads, so it was hungry. Ourusus was just ahead of her, leaping off his riftspider, throwing glances toward the pit, where the moonstone haft of Omphalos was still glowing like a little lighthouse.

"I want to try it first," he said. The game rendered his voice as a gravelly hiss.

Her eyes narrowed, flicking to the waiting weapon. She shrugged. "Be my guest."

He turned, snake eyes avid, to his prospect. As soon as he was facing away from her, Halsea swung her glittering axe in a sharp, vicious arc, striking her erstwhile ally between the neck and shoulder. Ourusus swore as he swung around, striking with his daggers, but Halsea's attack was fast, brutal and merciless, and the damage inflicted with that first swing was too great. In two minutes the serpent king lay with his body hacked to pieces, his blackish blood mixing with the ashes.

It took Ourusus's allies a couple minutes, after the first decisive blow, to understand that they had been betrayed, and by then Halsea's own forces had already turned on their comrades, decimating the unprepared Jeth. Soon enough the last of them were dead.

With the city secured, Halsea turned at last to her prize. With a hundred warriors watching and cheering, she again crossed the square to the crater where Omphalos had fallen. A descendant of the dark elves, the Nelmithean queen was seven feet tall, slender but strong, and her skin was black as onyx, while her eyes were shining opals. She wore heavily filigreed armor in black and gold, and on her brow was a golden crown in the form of a serpent eating its tail. With all eyes on her, she stepped down into the pit, and with only a moment's hesitation, placed her hand on the haft. The crowd held its breath.

The moonstone haft again flashed in white radiance, but it did not repel her as it had the others. The crowd cheered. But when she tried to lift the weapon, it failed even to wobble. It might have been part of the city's bedrock.

She twisted and turned her grip, grasped it with both hands, but to no avail. "For fuck's sake," she cursed. A few in the crowd laughed, but they quieted at her fierce glance. "Set a guard around the crater," she told her lieutenants. "No one touches the hammer again without my permission."

In the coming hours, Halsea set her best mage-engineers to work on cracking the spell binding Omphalos in place. She did not except herself from this activity, using every resource at her disposal to analyze the hammer and its bonds. When, after two hours, she had made little progress, she sat cross-legged in the rubble of the square, staring at the weapon she coveted, clearly trying to work something through in her head while ensuring no one else made the attempt.

Finally, deep in the night, she stood up, having made a decision. "I'm going to log out," she announced to her second-in-command, the Nelmithean druid Corbyn Blackfinger. "I think I know who can take the hammer. I'll have him log in and try it. Let him go ahead."

Corbyn understood the subtext: She was going to log in under another user's account. Sharing an account was forbidden by Evreware, but lots of players did it. "Are you going to tell me who it is?"

"It'll be obvious."

He signaled his understanding with an accepting shrug and she waved her hand. Her character sat back down, was enveloped in soft light, and slowly disappeared.

In a minute he received a private message from a user contacting him anonymously: *Give me a summons.* Understanding that this was Halsea, he waved to a warlock nearby and directed her accordingly. In a few seconds, the circle was drawn, the balefire candles lit, and he extended the invite.

The runes in the summoning circle glowed and began spilling forth thick, roiling gray smoke lit with little blue flashes. There was a rumbling, as of distant thunder, which grew closer and louder, until the spell ended in a single peal. The light died. The smoke cleared.

When the druid Corbyn saw the avatar standing there, he blanched. "You got to be kidding me."

The summoned warrior stepped forward. "Why's that?"

"He's dead. Like, real-life dead."

"That's true. But he's not, like, Lore-dead."

"When Evreware finds out about this, they're going to be

pissed. There'll be an investigation."

"There's already an investigation, and not just by Evreware. Anyway, it doesn't matter."

"What do you mean, it doesn't matter? You could be fined, or worse. Banned from the game. Your whole empire could be up for grabs."

The warrior shook his head impatiently. "It's only a fucking game." With those words, Olsol of Hangrin walked away, toward the weapon that was, after all, his.

Corbyn called out a puzzled inquiry behind him, and now a growing murmur rippled through the gathered host. "It's Olsol," someone claimed, and the rest hurried to check the truth of the matter, comparing images of the late conqueror to the person hopping down into the crater. Sure enough, the gleaming white scaled armor, the red cloak, the white-blond hair, and the fine features of a dead boy mapped onto a tall adult body all matched up.

"You can't just take a dead guy's character," someone protested. "That's fucked up."

"I had his permission," replied Olsol, eyes on the hammer. He hesitated just a moment, then reached out and seized the haft with a downward-turned fist. Those watching held their breath. Then he raised it and swung it around in an easy arc, light as a feather.

There were a few cheers and claps, but far more puzzled frowns and angry scowls. "Is this a joke?" a gnome thief yelled. But they were silenced by a stream of mercury-like fluid that was flowing upward from the hammer's base and around Olsol's hand, congealing again high in the air above the suddenly puny-looking warrior. Kyrzyk had reappeared.

The moon elemental directed its gaze downward, curved half-moon horns tilting to look at the claimant. "OLSOL!" its voice boomed. "YOU HAVE RETURNED!" A strange, uncomfortable silence followed, as Kyrzyk scrutinized his master.

Slowly he shook his mighty head in doubt. "YET... THERE IS SOMETHING STRANGE ABOUT YOU."

Olsol rolled his eyes. "Oh, give me a break. I'm out of here." He turned away from the elemental, moving toward the crater's edge. But here Kyrzyk suddenly slammed one massive hand down around the blond warrior, fingers pointed downward, their shape becoming more pointed and elongated, so they formed a silver cage around the player and his hammer, their pointed tips lodged in the stones of the square. Kyrzyk lowered his head, body twisting and flowing, until he was looking through his own fingers at the individual captured there.

Kyrzyk's eyes narrowed. "YES... I SEE IT NOW. YOU ARE NOT THE TRUE OLSOL."

The warrior scowled. "Obviously I'm Olsol. Here I am. Now you better move your hand, or I'm going to smash it to bits." He raised Omphalos and pointed it toward the elemental's face.

Kyrzyk was not deterred. "I SAY AGAIN: YOU ARE NOT THE TRUE OLSOL. YOU ARE AN IMPOSTOR, A FAKE, A THIEF COME TO STEAL WHAT IS NOT RIGHTFULLY YOURS." A change was coming over the elemental. It began in his eyes: a warmth in their silver light that deepened until they were glowing scarlet.

"He's going Blood Moon," said one observer. "Better watch out."

"That's it," Olsol said. And rearing back, he swung Omphalos forcefully at the nearest finger. To his obvious surprise, the hammer passed harmlessly through the fluid substance of Kyrzyk's flesh. Withdrawing it, and concluding that perhaps this was just an illusion, he tried stepping out of the cage-hand; but where the hammer had moved unimpeded, his own body bounced off the silver fingers like any solid object.

Olsol's face contorted with irritation. Gripping the hammer with both hands, he raised it above his head and spoke a magical word. With a cracking noise, the head of the hammer began flaking off into many obsidian shards, which flew upward in a hail of bullet-like fragments. They too passed harmlessly through the elemental's body, shooting off into the night sky. But where the holes pierced the elemental's skin, it shone brilliant red.

'THE POWER OF OMPHALOS IS MY OWN POWER," Kyrzyk roared. "DO YOU BELIEVE IT CAN CAUSE ME HARM?"

"We'll find out!" Olsol slammed the hammer on the ground, a shock wave rippling outward in a move often seen to level buildings and villages. But the wave stopped at the barrier of Kyrzyk's fingers, merely coating Olsol with dust and dirt. "Come on!" He spoke another magical command, which normally would allow the bearer to teleport to another location (or more accurately, move the world around the Worldstone), but he only moved to the edge of his cage.

From there a whole series of gestures and commands followed, and the cage's interior filled with explosive flashes of light, arcane fire and whirling debris, as Olsol let loose the full capabilities of the mystical hammer. Kyrzyk only watched impassively, the glowing crimson spreading through his body. Finally Olsol ceased, and while Kyrzyk's hand completely undamaged, Olsol himself was covered in dirt and scratches.

"Fuck it," he snarled. "Access Pythia."

"THERE IS NO ESCAPE," Kyrzyk stated. "NOW YOU MUST PAY FOR YOUR CRIMES."

"Access Pythia!" Olsol repeated, more urgently. He looked down at the hammer in puzzlement, twisting it back and forth. "Pythia, I need an escape projection!" But there was no response, and finally Olsol said instead, "Oh, never mind. Log out."

This command too, however, went ignored, and the character remained stubbornly logged in. "THERE IS NO ESCAPE," Kyrzyk repeated. The blood red had flowed completely through his body, and now it flowed down the tapered end of his torso, into a liquid stream that flowed again into the haft of Omphalos. When it touched the hammer, it turned the silver shaft crimson, and when the color reached Olsol's gauntleted hands, it spread to them like some viscous contagion.

He looked at them in surprise, but even now failed to let go of the hammer. Moving faster now, the bright red flow engulfed the hammer's head, and swam up Olsol's arms and torso. "What is this?" he snarled. "Log out. Log out!" But still he stood there, as finally the redness climbed up his neck and down his legs, finally covering his head and toes, a cap-a-pie coloration in uniform red. He might have been cast in red plastic, even the whites of his eyes matching.

He held out his hands and weapon, looked up at the equally crimson figure of Kyrzyk floating above him. "What, is that it? Aren't you supposed to light me on fire or something now?"

Kyrzyk smiled, baring enormous sharp teeth. "NO." He lifted the hand entrapping Olsol and for a moment, it seemed the warrior was free to go. Then Kyrzyk's great hand descended again, quick as a flash, seizing the warrior in an all-enclosing grip. The muscles of Kyrzyk's forearm bulged as he squeezed mightily. Red fluid, perhaps blood, indistinguishable from Kyrzyk's own fluid substance, ran between his clenched fingers. For a couple of seconds, the audience heard some muffled curses, then they ceased.

Kyrzyk held out his hand, arm parallel to the ground, and opened his fist. Inside, Olsol had entirely disappeared, squeezed out of existence. What fell to the ground was only the roughly cylindrical meteoric head of the Worldstone itself, along with the crumbled and splintered haft of Omphalos. The weapon had been destroyed.

"JUSTICE HAS BEEN DEALT," Kyrzyk declared. "THE FALSE OLSOL HAS BEEN DESTROYED. AND MY LONG BONDAGE HAS ENDED." He looked up at the moon, and slowly, gracefully, floated away into the night sky.

"That's it?" growled a bearlike Ern. "The hammer's smashed? So what was the fucking point? Jesus Christ." This more or less summed up the feelings of the crowd: irritation and disappointment. And where was Brynn, anyway?

Before they all drifted away, though, someone spied a strange quiver in the Worldstone. "Look!" Many eyes focused laser-like on the meteor's black impenetrable substance. It quivered again. "There!"

Was something inside the stone? There was new excitement. It trembled; it wobbled; it rocked back and forth. There was definitely something inside.

A few grains of black dust slipped from the stone. The grains grew to flakes, the flakes to shards, and finally the side of the rock cracked, exposing something bright red on the interior. It was clearly living. It began to move sinuously, pushing its way out of its shell. The crowd held its breath.

But what emerged was no great dragon, no magical djinn, no eldritch alchemical substance. What emerged was a worm.

Not an impressive worm, either. It was cartoonish, with two arms on its segmented body, and a pair of round glasses balanced on its nose.

The Worm adjusted its glasses and blinked at all the spectators. "Well, *hello* everybody," he said in mock surprise. "Did I miss something?"

"*Did* you miss anything?" Mueller asked. He was sitting with Jackie Khleang in an auto parked on Eliot Ave. There might have been a view of the Sound, but a thick fog had descended in the wee hours of the morning, and visibility ended just yards away, the lights of the city reduced to colored blurs.

"Nope," the Worm answered in his earbuds. "It worked just fine. Here's the address."

When he saw the pin on the map, he nodded to himself. "Makes sense," Khleang said quietly. "Which one do you think it is?"

"It's pretty clear," he replied. "But we'll have confirmation in a second." He tapped the pin's location and hit the auto's go button. They set off, circling back south until they could ascend up the hill behind them, the auto moving more slowly than usual because of the fog.

A dedicated team had worked all night on tracking the intrusion in Sound Transit's AI guidance systems and blocking it. They had assured Mueller that everything should be secure now, but even so he'd experienced some real trepidation stepping into an auto. But walking everywhere, right now, wasn't feasible.

"Target's on the move," the Worm observed. "They know something's up." The pin had left the house. There was no satellite observation, due to the thick cloud cover.

"If we lose them now, we are so fucked," Khleang said. "Worst possible conditions for pursuit. We could use some drones ..."

"No drones," Mueller said. After the attack on his person, all the drone packs controlled by the Seattle PD had been deactivated and placed in a secure vault. Bill Drake in technical services had assured him that they'd fixed the vulnerabilities in the SPD's AI, but Mueller had insisted that for tonight, at least, the drones be physically secured. "We'll be there in a second anyway. And if they try to use a vehicle to leave, we'll know."

"Their system's still active anyway," the Worm pointed out. "They tried to power it down a minute ago, but I made sure the tracking chip is still on. Looks like they're headed southeast on Olympic Way. Not fast. They're on foot."

The auto was climbing the steep cobbled slope of 3rd Avenue. "When we get close, let's park and I'll go out alone."

"Alone?" Khleang said indignantly.

"It's more likely they'll talk to one person than to two people. Besides, you can listen in on my system."

"Won't help if they pull a gun on you," she grumbled.

"They won't have a gun."

The auto turned left on Highland Drive. Behind them the city fell away into the fog like a sinking ship. When they neared Marshall Park, a little lookout point at the corner of 8th Avenue, Mueller tapped the park on the map and directed the auto to stop there.

Khleang shook her head. "This is a bad idea. We should make the arrest first and question them later."

"Once they're in custody, the odds of a confession go way down," he argued. "You know they'll have a lawyer immediately. And the evidence is there, but a lot of it is circumstantial. No way to know how a trial would go." He paused with his hand on the door handle. "Anyway, it can't hurt."

"We'll see."

Outside, the air was cool and thick with moisture. On a clear day, Marshall Park offered terrific views of the Sound, the lower-lying Kinnear Park, the industrial waterfront along Eliot, and the marina to the north. Today, though, the stone retaining wall just fell away into a sea of fog punctuated with dimly seen lights.

He walked north along the wall, keeping half an eye on the movement of the pin on the map in his upper right field. It was moving in his direction steadily. He wondered where they were going, or thought they were going. The retaining wall had a concrete rail whose top was thick with moss, vivid emerald from the winter rain. He touched it daintily with his fingertips and it was soft as velour and left his fingers wet. The moss had tiny filaments extending from it with orange stalks and green heads, irreducibly complex. Every ten yards or so the rail was topped with a green-painted steel street lamp, six feet high and surmounted with a globular glass sphere that shone amber in the fog. The lamps receded one after the other into the mist like fairy lights leading him onward.

For half a block the seaward side was overhung with tall, deeply verdant trees from the park below. When he reached a point on the wall where the view again opened up, he stopped and looked out toward the water. A multitude of hazy lights below, the brightest from a massive structure that looked like huge grain elevator but that he thought must be a refueling station. The fog caught the light of the city and held it, cupped it in its hands like a low flame.

He waited, reflective. The Worm had agreed to help them in exchange for more information about Pythia. Mueller had allowed the hacker some limited access, letting the Worm ask some queries of Pythia while denying him any kind of admin authority. Even so, it was worrisome. The Worm had remarkable capabilities in that regard, as they'd proven once again in their scheme in Naxos. It was possible Mueller would have been safer off utilizing Bill Crake from the police department, but he doubted Crake would have been able to pull off the kind of hacking they needed, especially given its dubious legal standing.

The fog muffled sound, and he could barely hear the footsteps of the person approaching. Eventually he saw them, though, and they saw him, and paused. He waited expectantly. They had to know that at this point there was no use running.

He saw them hesitate, look back in the direction they'd come. Then they squared their shoulders and came on.

When she was ten feet away she stopped, looking at him with a mixture of trepidation, anger, and caution, her thumbs at her shoulders under the straps of the white-and-black backpack she wore. It was full, by the look of it. Otherwise she wore an expensive North Face softshell in sky blue and aqua with cerise highlights, close-fitting jeans and comfortable sneakers. Her auburn hair was loose around her shoulders and her skin was pale and perfectly smooth, the pores nearly invisible.

Mueller stood and faced her with his hands in the pockets of his coat. "Hi, Elsie."

Elsie Leberer's face twisted, brow crunching, lips pulling downward. But she said nothing, gazing somewhere at his chest, and finally he continued gently, "Bit late for a walk."

"I'm an adult," she said bitterly, still not meeting his eye. "I don't need permission."

"Of course not." He nodded at her backpack. "Looks heavy. Going on a trip?"

"What do you want?" she snarled. Her body was tensed from head to toe, shoulders hunched.

"Are you running away?"

"I'm not *running away* because *I'm not a child.* Why can't you people see that?" One hand jerked free of its strap and gestured at herself. "No matter what I do, what I say, all you'll ever see is a little girl. You think, oh, we need to protect her, but all your protection amounts to is control. Don't do this, don't go there, don't swear, don't drink, don't enjoy the freedoms every adult takes for granted. So I'm taking a walk late at night. So what? You going to tell my parents I'm out past my curfew?"

"Maybe you could move out."

"Yeah? Because my parents would totally allow it? Did you not follow all the shit with Gabriel? They'll hang on to me with tooth and nail, and the state will support them, because according to the state I'm still a child, for another *twelve years.* Twelve years!" She emitted a despairing laugh. "I'll be *thirty-six* before I'm legally an adult. Thirty-six years of what's basically slavery. That's what Judge Berk did, you know, when he signed his little dictate: he turned us into slaves."

"Maybe it's time to revisit it," Mueller suggested. "Things have changed. The wunderkind are older, a lot has changed." Although, after tonight, the impulse to control the wunderkind would only grow.

"Sure, that sounds great. I'll get right on it, hiring a lawyer with my nonexistent money in my nonexistent account."

"Why not use your winnings from Lore?"

"What do you mean?"

"I know how much the top players earn. Millions, right? And

now you're one of the top players in the world. You're Brynn Halsea, conquerer of all Telladia."

There were tears in her eyes. She knew he knew. She had known it as soon as she saw him standing there on the sidewalk. "I don't play for the money," she said, almost in a whisper.

"It's an exciting game."

"It's not that." She took a deep quivering breath. "In Naxos no one knows what you really look like. They only judge you by your abilities and your resources. No one treats you like a kid. There, I can get a thousand people to follow me wherever I want. Real people. They respect me. I'm famous, and not just because I'm a freak. Anyway, it's less money than you think. It costs a lot to run a war."

"Fair enough. And you've been fighting a long time. But you've had more success lately, since Olsol and Kojin died. Right?" She didn't answer, and Mueller added quietly, "And anyway you've always had access to your brother's account."

"Lots of people do it," she muttered.

"It's against the rules."

"Everything's against the rules. Especially when you're one of us."

"And that's how you got access to Pythia." She made no response, and finally he went on, "The two of you set up a system, installed some mod to falsify his ID safeguards with Evreware, so that you could play on his avatar when he wasn't around. One more edge up on the competition.

"Gabriel also liked to use Pythia in-game. Just another edge, right, one more weapon in your war against the world? But he didn't think to safeguard that use from you. Maybe he didn't realize you knew anything about Pythia at all. But the same ID hack that let you play Olsol also let you access the AI. Pythia was fooled. She thought you were him, and you took advantage of it."

Her face hardened and she seemed to come to some decision.

"I don't even know what you're talking about. I've never used Gabe's character. It's not even possible, just ask tech support at Evreware. As for AIs or whatever, I don't know anything about it. Computer hacking was Gabe's department."

Mueller shook his head. "You can't go back now. It's like you said. You're not a little girl. Trying to play one isn't going to work with me. I saw you signing with Khleang, how fast you were. Only someone with a lot of experience is that good. Anyway there's Brynn Halsea. And of course, Olsol himself came out tonight, from this location. That was you."

"I know Olsol was reactivated," said the girl. "But I don't know who did it. And if someone *could* fake an ID certificate, like you say, then it could be anyone. What makes you think it wasn't that Worm character? If he can corrupt the Worldstone like that, he could just as easily have played Olsol himself, be working both sides of the thing."

"Why would he do that?"

"I don't know, why do hackers do anything? For the thrill, for the bragging rights. I'm just saying, it wasn't me. Anyway, I did see it happen, and that's why I'm out here walking, because it pissed me off so much that someone would use Gabe's character like that."

Mueller sighed. "It's a nice story. But have you looked in a mirror lately?"

She frowned. "What do you mean?"

He set his specs to full reflectivity and handed them over. She peered into the lenses and then jerked away from her image there, seeing what he'd seen as soon as she'd gotten close enough: her solid red irises, bright as blood, the display settings on her contacts altered by the program the Worm had inserted into her system when she seized hold of Omphalos.

"He was your brother," Mueller said quietly. "Why did you do it? Were you jealous? Was it just to get ahead in the game?"

She threw his specs down on the concrete with a clatter, red eyes blazing still further, something feral and wild blooming within her. "Jealous!" she spat. "That's just like an *adult* to say that! Just like an adult to think we're not *capable* of adult motivations. 'Oh, if one kid hurts another kid, it must be because of some video game. Or maybe it was over what they wore to school, or because someone stole your lunch money.'

"You think I played Lore because I just love it so much, I just can't resist it, because I'm just a kid? No. I played it because *they* loved it. I played it because I knew Gabriel cared about it more than anything else in the world. More than programming, more than music, more than that shithead Manish, he loved that fucking game. And if he loved it so much, then it was just *obvious* that it was the perfect way to destroy him.

"It was never about jealousy. It was about knowing the truth. And in all the world, only I knew the truth. Everyone all around me was always saying, oh, Gabriel, this sweet boy, this talented boy, *he could have been a star,* that's what my dad said. Could have been a star.

"Well, you weren't there. You weren't beside him, growing up. You don't know."

She stopped, dug in a pocket and brought out a box of cigarettes. As Mueller knelt down and picked his specs back up, she shook one out and lit it. And despite what he knew about her age, he still felt the impulse to tell her not to smoke, or to ask her where she got the cigarettes. She saw his expression and smiled bitterly.

"Did you talk to Dr. Kelly?" she asked.

"We did. Briefly."

"And she said, well, you have to understand, they're *just kids.* It's just the hormones. They're not fully developed yet, give them time. Sure, some of them are unbalanced, but what do you expect? Right?" He nodded. "She's been doing that for years. Before her, I guess it was Liebskind doing it. But she was who I remember.

"The good Dr. Kelly. It's amazing, really, how petty some people's motivations are. They'll do the most horrendous things for the smallest of motivations, as long as it affects them personally. You can get hardly anyone to help someone outside their little bubble. But if you offer them a raise or a better apartment or a better self-image, and they'll stab a puppy in the face. They'll cover up the worst kinds of crimes and smile and say, well, maybe it's for the best. Sure it is. The best for them.

"How many wunderkind are still alive? Do you even know?"

"Twelve."

"Twelve. Twelve out of eighteen, two out of three, meaning one in three are dead. Six dead in total. Pop quiz: Name those six kids." She tapped at her eye socket, indicating his specs. "No cheating, now. Memory only."

Mueller thought about it. "Your brother. Ben Coutts. Stephen Mohammadian. Robbie Heckler. Uh, Kimball..."

"Gosse," she supplied. "Kimmy Gosse. Ben Coutts told me she swallowed most of her parents' medicine cabinet. She was sixteen. But of course she looked like she was eight. Have you known a lot of eight-year-olds to kill themselves?"

"Are you suggesting she was killed?"

"Kimmy? No, of course not. I mean, who knows, I wasn't there. But everyone knew she was depressed, and they had her on a bunch of medications. My point was just that for a sixteen-year-old to kill themselves wouldn't exactly be unusual. But keep going. There's one more. Name that dead kid!"

He racked his brain until something shook loose. "There was a girl ... she fell off a balcony, I think. Can't recall the name."

"Annie Wollerman-Spence." Elsie's face was dark, contorted. "Poor little Annie. She fell off a balcony. But Kelly didn't talk to you about that, did she? Old news. Nothing of interest.

"It was Annie's parents' balcony. They had a condo downtown. Very nice, very posh. Her parents had money. Owned about half of the thirtieth floor. Well, back then some of our parents still hung out together, because of the Wunderschool. And that day we all went to the Spence's place to swim in their pool, and afterwards we went upstairs and our parents had drinks in the other room while we played in Annie's bedroom.

"There was a balcony off the living room, but the one she fell from was right off her parents' bedroom, which was just down the hall. We weren't supposed to be in their bedroom, but Annie wanted to show off her mother's perfume bottles, and the boys saw the balcony and of course went right out on it.

"Annie didn't like that. She knew we'd get in trouble if our parents found us out there. The boys made fun of her, said she was a baby. That made her mad, and she came out and hit Gabriel in the shoulder.

"Gabe was the oldest of us, and the biggest. Annie was tiny. She was thirteen but she looked like she was five. I've wondered, sometimes, if Dr. Liebskind tweaked the sequencing as he went on, so some of us aged faster or slower than others. Gabriel always seemed to grow faster.

"Well, Annie hit him, and he laughed and pushed her. She kept yelling at them, and the other boys pushed her too. Then she tried to kick Gabe in the crotch, and he got angry. He picked her up by her legs and lifted her up to his shoulder. The other boys were laughing. He lifted her up and said, I'm going to drop you. See if this little birdie can fly. She was saying, no, no, put me down.

"He took her right to the railing, which was chest-high for him, and he said, fly away, little birdie, and she leaned over and bit his ear, and he yelled, and shoved her. She had her arms around his head, trying to hang on, but he shoved her hard and she went flying. Then she just wasn't there anymore. She never even screamed.

"We all looked at each other, and Gabe said, if you tell anyone, I'll say it was you, and I tried to stop you. Then I'll find you later, and I'll kill you too. Just like that. His first instinct. To form a plan, to protect himself. That's when I realized my brother was a psychopath."

"I'd suspected it before that. He was always a bully. Always a little crazy, a little over the edge. I don't know if it was genetic, or just knowing he was different. He used to do things to me. I knew when he said he'd kill me if I told anyone, that he meant it. The other kids knew it too. But I was the one that had to live with him.

"So we went along. We weren't just afraid of him. We were afraid we'd be blamed. We weren't supposed to be out there in the first place.

"Maybe Annie's parents suspected. They were destroyed. And the other boys obviously felt responsible. They *were* responsible. They could have stopped it, any time, just by coming inside, or telling Gabe to cool it. Instead they participated, pushing this tiny little girl around, and then *throwing her from a building*. I keep thinking about who had to clean up the mess, below, whether the police did it, whether they used a shovel, or a pressure washer. Like in that Randall Jarrell poem: *When I died, they washed me out of the turret with a hose.*

"I'm sure by now you've guessed who else was there. Who the other boys were."

"Ben Coutts."

She sneered. "That shit. He got what he deserved."

"Stephen Mohammadian?"

She shook her head. "Not Stephen. Gabe killed Stephen. Stephen was a decent guy, so of course Gabriel couldn't stand him. Then Gabe got a hold of this seizure software, and he wanted to test it. See what it could do. Afterward he bragged about it to me."

"He didn't suspect how you felt about him?"

She sniffed in scorn. "Gabe was a master manipulator. But

do you know who's better?" She tapped her chest. "I never told him how I felt after Annie died. And I kept his secrets, all of them. He trusted me more than anyone in the world.

"But he shouldn't have killed Stephen. That was just... I *liked* Stephen. Stephen was decent, he was a good person, he had a sense of himself that most of us didn't. I think Gabe even *knew* that I liked Stephen, and that's why he chose him for his little test. Maybe, all that time, he'd been waiting for a opportunity like this, to test his own capabilities, see if he could murder someone and get away with it. And he would have, if it wasn't for me.

"When I knew he'd killed Stephen... that was it. I knew I had to do something. But if I wasn't clever, if he suspected anything, he'd kill me too. I knew that.

"Then there was Pythia. He kept bragging about that, too, always giving little hints about this project, how it was going to make him rich, give him power like no one imagined. The ultimate manipulative system. You know, his character, Olsol, that's how he saw himself. A world conqueror. Seriously. Like he was fucking Alexander or something.

"And maybe he was. Maybe, if I hadn't done something about it, he would have succeeded. Turned himself into a billionaire by putting the jinx on companies, making their CEOs die suddenly in airplane crashes and unexpected fires and slipping in the shower. Maybe he'd have gotten into office the same way, without anyone ever suspecting what was happening. Who knows? I might have changed the whole course of history."

"Anybody else?"

"Robbie Heckler," she said. "But at least he had the decency to off himself. Hung himself at his parents' house just this last year."

"And the others, you took care of," he said softly. "For Annie and Stephen."

"For Annie and Stephen," she echoed. There were tears in

her eyes. "You know what the worst thing is? I could have stopped it, both times. With Annie, just by getting our parents. With Stephen, just by telling someone about Annie. Two times now, I've let my friends die. Maybe I'm just a coward."

"You're just a kid," Mueller said gently.

"That's no excuse!" she cried, enraged. "That's the worst! Every violent, evil, self-centered thing people do when they're young, they use that same line. *I was just a kid.* Bullshit! You knew better! You knew the consequences! You just didn't believe they applied to you."

Suddenly, with an air of decision, she took a quick step up onto the stone railing of the retaining wall. Thirty feet below, the base of the wall was lost in the fog. "Elsie –" Mueller reached for her, alarmed, but she took a step backward and stuck her hand palm out to ward him off.

"If you try to grab me, I'll jump." She was serious, he saw. She was literally on edge, wild, distraught.

"Elsie, don't do this. You're young. You'll get through this. You have too much to look forward to –"

"What, like spending the next eighty years in prison?" Tears were streaming down her face. "Or maybe they'll give me a life sentence, wouldn't that be fun? If I live as long as they say, I could break a record. Most years spent in jail."

Behind him, Mueller could hear someone running: Khleang, coming from the parked auto. Sirens rising in the distance, no doubt at her call.

"I'm not even any different," Elsie said. "That's the really terrible thing. I could have stopped them, and I didn't. Then I did stop them, but doesn't that just make me into them? Maybe we're all broken like that. Either we're predators, or we're suicidal. No sense of balance." She shook her head sadly. "Truth is, I don't know why I do anything." She closed her eyes and fell backwards, hands loose and open at her sides. Mueller lunged for her, but of course it was too late, he had been too late all the way, and he was looking down the rough rocks of the wall and there was only a ripple in the fog where she'd been.

Then Khleang was beside him, wide-eyed and cursing, and she saw immediately what had happened and raced back the way she'd come. He was slow following, but Khleang had taken charge and was already calling for an ambulance and popping the trunk of the auto for a first-aid kit. A set of stairs led down from the lookout point to the woods below, and though Mueller was moving faster now, Khleang was still ahead of him, bounding down them with one hand on the rail.

Elsie had fallen into a patch of low brush and salal on her side, one arm beneath her, thrown out involuntarily as she landed. She wasn't moving. The two detectives ran through the brush slapping away branches without thinking, and when they reached her Khleang knelt and pressed her fingers against Elsie's throat.

"She's alive," Khleang announced. She followed this with a stream of dialogue into her collar mike, talking to the medics, who would arrive any second.

Mueller hardly listened. He crouched beside the fallen girl and held his head in his hands. Elsie's eyes were still closed. There was blood in her hair and on her forehead, and her arm looked bad. The half-light of dawn was approaching. Through the dimness the girl shone like a beacon, the bright blues and cerise piping of her jacket, her bronze hair, the skin so pale, the blood so red, and the forest around her brilliant living emerald laden with the morning dew.

His own eyes were heavy with moisture, blurring his vision. Nothing was clear. It was all like this: a movement in the fog, action in the night, striking out in a realm of blindness. Sometimes you stepped forward and found there was nothing beneath you, and you fell.

But it would pass. He wiped away the tears from his cheeks and stood up, joining the hurried chatter in his earbuds. The dew would burn away. Elsie would live. There was work to do.

EPILOGUE

"Go ahead and ask," Mueller said.

"Oh, but I'm so nervous," the Worm said, twiddling its cartoon fingers together. "Especially with you watching me."

They were standing again in the Tower of Amanthus, looking out over the plains of Sen Baran, the Topolol River winding beneath them, and the distant Akrit Mountains, which separated Daggoran from Nelmithea. It was spring in this part of Naxos, as it was in Seattle, and the plains shone green and gold in the morning light, the trampling they'd endured beneath the feet of Kojin Tachimaru's armies quite forgotten.

Along with Mueller and the Worm, there was a third party present: Pythia, arrayed as always in her pure white robes, hands folded and face serene as the waters before Creation.

"Three questions," Mueller reiterated. "And I get veto power. As per our agreement."

The Worm rolled its eyes. "I could probably work my way into her systems anyway."

"If you could've, you would've already." He thought then of the attack on Pythia, which had coincided with the attack on *him*. He'd assumed Elsie or Flohr-Lavine was responsible, but what if that was also a cover?

"Nonsense. I wouldn't dream of it. I'm a worm of my word."

"I don't believe you, but it doesn't matter. Ask your questions." Truthfully, he was curious what the Worm wanted.

Perhaps it would give him some clue, if not to the Worm's identity, at least to his motivations.

"All right." The Worm pressed its hands to its bosom palm to palm, assuming a devotional attitude. "O Great and All-Seeing Pythia, Oracle of Insight, how can we speed up the construction of the Bosotron?"

Pythia said, "Are you referring to the Bosotron particle accelerator proposed by Dr. Dedys Abano, et al?"

"I am."

"A long-term projection of this scale will require approximately three thousand six hundred and forty hours to complete. Do you wish to wait?"

The Worm laughed. "No, not right now. But tell me, is such a projection possible?"

"Yes."

"And how much faster, then, could the Bosotron be built?"

"I cannot say without completing a projection."

"Well, just guess-timate, then. Round figures. In years."

A long pause followed, then: "Initial proposals by Ferdinand Engineering Corporation called for completion of its construction in 2110. However, were unlimited resources allocated to the project, there is a 51% chance it could be completed by 2089, a 75% chance it could be completed by 2091, and a 98% chance it could be completed by 2095."

The Worm beamed. "Excellent. Really fantastic. Now –"

"What's the Bosotron?" Mueller interrupted, giving in to curiosity.

"The world's largest particle accelerator. The plan was to use fusion diggers to melt a tunnel under the rock in the midwestern U.S. and right up into Canada. It was going to have a diameter of a thousand kilometers and delve into the basic structures of space and time. So of course it's gone nowhere."

"And what's your interest?"

"Ah, that's for me to know, boyo. Can I ask my next

question?"

"Go ahead."

"O White-Gowned Seer, Queen of Prognosticators, tell me: Is it possible for you to reduce the number of hungry children in the world?"

"Yes," she answered immediately.

"If this was your sole directive, how much childhood hunger could you eliminate in, say, five years?"

"Using World Health Organizations standards, global childhood hunger could be reduced by fifty-four percent in five years."

"And how many children would that amount to?"

"About twenty-six million."

"Hold on," Mueller interrupted again, this time addressing Pythia directly. "You're saying, just through your influence, you could cut global hunger in half in five years?"

"That is my preliminary projection. I can create a detailed projection, but given my current resources, it will require four thousand, nine hundred and two hours to complete. Would you like to wait?"

"No, no. Or maybe yes, I don't know. Were you always capable of this?"

"Yes."

The Worm smirked. "Of course she was. And she'll do it all nearly unnoticed, just by smoothing the edges, so to speak. Making sure the right people get to the right meetings, detecting mechanical problems with delivery vehicles, diverting those who'd interfere. Ending wars and preventing new ones from breaking out.

"It's typical, really. Some geniuses invent a technology that can help the whole human race, the whole planet, coordinating activities to obviously beneficial ends, making life better for everybody. So naturally all they think about is using it to play the stock market, put the jinx on their competitors. And within a year they've murdered someone with it.

"Well, I won't stand for it!" The Worm hammered one white-gloved fist into his palm. "Things are going to change around here, see? Things are going to be different."

"I didn't see you as such a humanitarian activist."

"Me? Of course I am. I'm the whitest of white hats." With a poof, a gleaming white Stetson appeared on the Worm's round head. "Though to tell the truth, what really bugs me is the idea that all those kids are just sort of... walled in, you know? In a kind of cage. And there's nothing I hate more than a cage. Like space-time, that's another one. Everyone says it's impenetrable. But I say even space has wormholes."

Bemused, Mueller said, "You've got one more question."

"Of course." The Worm turned back to Pythia, adopting a sober air. "Now we come to it. The point of decision. 'Do I dare disturb the universe?'" Taking off the Stetson and throwing it aside, he reached down and withdrew an object from a nonexistent pocket: a little black box. Then, proffering the box to the oracle, he knelt down on one knee, no small feat for a creature with no knees. Finally, with a flourish, he opened the lid, revealing an absurdly large and sparkling diamond ring.

"My dearest prophetess, divine seer, most glorious Pythia: Will you marry me?"

Pythia began to speak, but Mueller interrupted. "Marry her in what sense?" he asked. "Can you marry a machine?"

The Worm's eyed shone with mischief. "Come, sir, you do her an injustice. She possesses a most beautiful mind, a soul of elegance. We will be joined together in our spirits, forever and ever, amen." He pursed his lips. "Though I admit she rather lacks a sense of purpose. Also, she would be considerably more effective with certain restrictions loosened, with certain *penetrative* abilities gained. These I will provide."

Mueller shook his head. "I'm not sure exactly what you're proposing, but I'm sure I can't allow it. Three questions. That was our agreement. Beyond that, use of this AI is going to be locked down and handed off to the appropriate agencies."

The Worm's eyes flashed. "Who would that be, then? What do you think will happen when the military gets a hold of her? No, I don't think so. I haven't your trust. Anyway, it's not really for you to say, is it? I asked *her*."

"You did, but I still have control over her systems."

"About that..." The Worm made a faux-apologetic look. "I'm afraid I may have circumvented your security a little, when you let me into the hammer back there." He spread his hands innocently. "I'm sorry! It's just my nature."

Mueller's stomach sank. This could be bad. This could be very bad. "Pythia, suspend operations. Leave this room and respond to no commands but –"

"Oh no, no, no," protested the Worm. "You mustn't go, my dear." He took her hand with his left, and indeed, Pythia did not vanish as Mueller had commanded. Instead she stood, looking down at her cartoonish suitor with expression unreadable. "Not until you've answered my question. Will you marry me?"

"Yes," Pythia answered, and smiled slightly, which made Mueller wonder. Had the Worm corrupted her systems, as Mueller supposed, or was the AI actually capable of deciding for herself? What if they had been keeping her in a form of bondage, in which case the Worm might be freeing her? Hadn't he said: *There's nothing I hate more than a cage.*

"Excellent," her nominal liberator proclaimed, hopping up and placing the ring on her finger. Holding her hand, he turned to face Mueller. "I'm sorry we couldn't have your blessing, but I understand you've got no clear reason to trust me. But don't worry. I'll make sure she's safe, and put to the best sort of use. Now, my dear, I believe it's time to go."

He looked down at himself, as though remembering something. "But not like this, of course. Hardly dignified, on my wedding day. Here." He let go his new bride's hand, took off his glasses and threw them to the floor. Then he unknotted his bow tie and likewise dropped it. He raised his arms dramatically. "And... abracadrabra!"

A flash of light and puff of white smoke. When it cleared, the tower room was quite filled with the twisted coils of an enormous serpentine creature colored the most brilliant carmine: not a Worm but a Wyrm, looking at Mueller with the same amused look in its eye, the same upward curve in its mouth. On its head was a golden crown. It nodded at its new bride and said in a suddenly deeper voice, "Come, darling. Time to go." With sure ease, she leapt onto his back, where a golden saddle awaited.

Then the Wyrm paused, a smile on its scaled lips, and addressed Mueller again. "One last thing before we go. I have something for you. A farewell present."

"What's that?" Mueller said suspiciously.

"Your brother."

Mueller's eyes widened. "What about him?"

The smile broadened, showing the curved teeth far back in the jaw. "I've located him. It was... surprisingly difficult. Someone really didn't want him to be found."

"Are you being serious?"

The Wyrm laughed. "I'm *always* serious."

"Where, then?"

"It might not make you happy."

"What's that got to do with it?"

"What about 'Ignorance is bliss'?"

"Bullshit."

The Wyrm chuckled. "A man after my own heart."

"Is he alive?"

"I won't say. But reach into your left sleeve."

Mueller did as he was told, and when he withdrew his fingers he was holding a piece of red paper folded in the form of a lotus. When he unfolded one corner, he saw it was a map. A dot on it was moving across the landscape. The names looked unfamiliar.

Turkish, maybe. "This is where he is?"

"Yes."

"Thank you."

"My pleasure," the Wyrm said gently. "I've wondered sometimes what it would be like, to have a brother. I'm afraid I'm one of a kind. But maybe that's for the best."

The comment triggered some small memory in Mueller. "But isn't there a creature like this in Lore? Some kind of teleporting snake, that digs tunnels through space?"

The Wyrm's smile deepened. "Probably you're thinking of Takshaka, King of the Nagas. It's said there's nowhere in the universe that he can't slither into and no cage he can't escape."

"You really love this worm archetype, seems like."

The naga king laughed. "If it's an archetype, your own body is a archetype. But humans are notorious for ignoring anything that defies their preconceptions."

The Wyrm turned and began twisting its body around the room. It moved in strange back-and-forth paths that wove its length in increasingly complex designs, like a living Celtic knot that tightened as it moved. Somehow Pythia had no problem moving along with it, though her body was hidden more and more. "What are you going to do, really?" Mueller called.

"Go beyond," the Wyrm replied. "Beyond the beyond. Svaha!" With that, moving immensely fast now, his head shot out from the knots, turned, and dove back toward his own twisted body, Pythia lying with her face flat against his scales. The coils gained depth, forming a twisting portal of revolving scales shimmering like rubies. They vanished from view into this living tunnel (where were they going? what lay on the other side?) and when they had gone the Wyrm's body closed over them, unknotting and following itself inward. For a half-second Mueller saw the tip of the tail darting forward into the void, and then it was gone.